DANIEL JOSÉ OLDER

DACTYL · HILL
SQUAD

BOOK TWO
FREEDOM FIRE

SCHOLASTIC INC.

ISBN 978-1-338-26885-0

10 9 8 7 6 5 4 3   21 22 23 24

Printed in the U.S.A.   40
This edition first printing 2020

Book design by Christopher Stengel

"This is the story that would've made me fall in love with reading when I was a kid." — Tomi Adeyemi, #1 *New York Times* bestselling author of *Children of Blood and Bone*

"Older's uprising of sheroes and heroes grips, stomps, and soars from start to finish." — Rita Williams-Garcia, *New York Times* bestselling author of *One Crazy Summer*

"*Dactyl Hill Squad* is an engaging, lively adventure with a heroine I wish I were, in a world I didn't want to leave." — Jesmyn Ward, two-time National Book Award-winning author of *Sing, Unburied, Sing*

"This incredible story brings history to life with power, honesty, and fun." — Laurie Halse Anderson, *New York Times* bestselling author of *Chains*

Praise for

FREEDOM FIRE

BOOK TWO

A Publishers Weekly Best of Summer Reading

"An unforgettable historical, high-octane adventure." — Dav Pilkey, author/illustrator of the Dog Man series

✱ "Blisteringly paced, thought-provoking adventure." — *Kirkus Reviews*, starred review

✱ "Intelligent, rousing, and abundantly diverse, this is every bit as satisfying as the first installment." — *Publishers Weekly*, starred review

"Older has middle-graders' number with this dino-charged series. Stampedes are likely!" — *Booklist*

FOR KIRA, GABRIEL, AND KAI

TABLE OF CONTENTS

PART THREE: LOUISIANA · · · · · · · · · · · · · · · 199

PART ONE

TENNESSEE

CHAPTER ONE
NIGHT FLIGHT

A **GLINT OF LIGHT** flickered in the darkness below. It was late — the sun had sunk behind the trees hours ago, and it seemed to extinguish the whole world of mountains and sky when it went. Magdalys Roca had lost track of how long she and her friends had been flying southward on the back of Stella, the giant pteranodon, but she was pretty sure she'd never get used to that sense of emptiness that closed in whenever night fell across the vast American wilds.

But what was that light?

It had disappeared almost as soon as she'd seen it. A bonfire maybe? A Confederate battle camp? Her heartbeat tha-thumped just a little harder in her ears at the thought. They'd passed the sparkling lights of Washington, DC, a few nights ago, then veered west, and according to Mapper, had passed into Tennessee yesterday. There were Union outposts throughout the state, but it was still enemy territory.

Stella swooped lower just as Magdalys was craning her neck to see over the huge ptero's wing. Magdalys smiled. She'd started to get used to the fact that dinos and other huge reptiles could understand her inner thoughts and wishes, but with most of them she had to make explicit requests. *Charge*, she'd think, and those hundreds of pounds of scale and muscle would lurch and lumber into action. But Stella seemed to have connected to her on an even deeper level. The ptero knew when Magdalys was tired or afraid, knew, apparently, when she needed to get a better look at something.

There it was — that same sparkle of light in the darkness below. Stella tilted eastward just so as Magdalys grabbed the reins and stood in the saddle, squinting through the night at the dancing splash of brightness.

"Ha," Magdalys said out loud. She looked up, directly above the shimmer to where the almost full moon sat perched on a cloud bank like a queen on her throne.

"The river." Cymbeline Crunk scooched up beside Magdalys with tin cups of cold coffee in her hands. She took a sip from one and passed the other over.

"It's beautiful. Like the moon is keeping an eye on us from above and below. The Mississippi?"

Cymbeline shook her head. "Mm-mm, we're not that far west yet. Probably the Ocoee, an offshoot of the Tennessee River."

Magdalys had never met anyone like Cymbeline before. At just eighteen, she had become a renowned Shakespearean actress along with her brother, Halsey. Plus, she seemed to know everything there was to know about the war and all the messy politics surrounding it. And she was a crack shot with a carbine.

Magdalys had gotten so used to seeing the actress dressed up as princesses and fairies (or sometimes kings and demons), it was still strange to see her in a plain button-down shirt and slacks. Her big wonderful hair was pulled tight against her head, like Magdalys's, and, also like Magdalys's, it then exploded into a big terrific bun just above her neck.

It was Cymbeline who'd insisted they veer west after DC. Tennessee had been the last state to secede, she'd explained, and whole swaths of pro-Union communities still resisted the Confederates in every way they could. And anyway, all the battle lines in Virginia were liable to explode into action at any moment, and the last thing they needed was to get caught up in a major engagement.

Mapper's eyes had gone wide at that — the idea somehow exciting to him — but Two Step, Little Sabeen, and Amaya had all shivered at the thought. Magdalys didn't really care which way they went, as long as it got them to wherever her brother, Montez, was faster. Montez had been wounded in a shoot-out at Milliken's Bend during General Grant's Siege of Vicksburg. One of the other soldiers in his battalion, Private Summers, had sent a letter to Magdalys saying Montez was still unconscious and they were on their way to New Orleans. All Magdalys knew was that she had to get to him, had to make sure he was okay, be there when he woke up if he hadn't yet, whatever it took.

Montez was the only family Magdalys knew, really. She'd been dropped off at the Colored Orphan Asylum when she was just a baby along with Montez and their two sisters, Celia and Julissa, neither of whom she could remember very well. They'd been whisked off back to Cuba a few years later and then Montez had joined the Union Army, and the Colored Orphan Asylum had been burned down in the Draft Riots right when Magdalys had found out he was wounded.

"I was worried at first," Magdalys said. "When I saw that light below . . ."

Cymbeline nodded, a grim smile crossing her face. "I know. These are the Great Smoky Mountains beneath us. An encampment could be anyone at this point."

"You think they'd have pteros?"

"If they do they're probably not going to be friendly. The only ptero raiders I've heard of are on the Rebel side, unfortunately."

Magdalys glanced back, found the series of dark splotches in the sky behind them. Exhaled.

"The Rearguard still with us?" Cymbeline asked with a hint of laughter in her voice.

Magdalys tilted her head, glanced back at the moonlight dancing in the river below. "Guess they in it for the long haul."

About a dozen dactyls had shown up in the sky behind them just as they'd crossed out of New York City. Magdalys and the squad had been scared at first, but the dactyls were riderless, just a friendly escort out of town, apparently. And then they'd stayed along all through the journey across Pennsylvania and Maryland, heading off on little hunting expeditions and returning with small mammals to cook and for Stella to munch on along the way. Cymbeline had dubbed them the Rearguard and they'd become a source of comfort to Magdalys as they journeyed further and further from home.

The mountain forests opened up suddenly to a long swath of moonlit open fields. At the far end, a pillared mansion with well-trimmed hedges seemed to preside over the clearing.

Magdalys shuddered. She knew exactly who'd been forced to trim those hedges and clear that land. Something churned deep inside her. She wanted to summon all the giant reptiles of the forest around her and smash those mansions into splintered wreckages. Then she'd set fire to the whole thing and those flames would leap from plantation to plantation, reaping devastation and catastrophe like a burning tornado, with a hundred thousand dinos stampeding in its wake to finish the job.

"You alright?" Cymbeline asked.

Magdalys started to nod, knew she must look anything but, and finally shook her head.

"It's okay," Cymbeline said. "Me neither."

"I want to burn it all to the ground," Magdalys said.

Cymbeline nodded. "Same. Maybe one day we will. But not tonight."

Magdalys nodded. She fought to shove that fiery destruction somewhere deep inside herself, realized she was shaking. Blinked a few times, trying to calm herself. She couldn't concentrate through that blinding rage.

Away, she whispered to her own fury. Not now.

The forests rose again and the plantation disappeared into the night behind them but that fire kept rising inside Magdalys. Fire and fear. They were in the South now. The slaver states. Any misstep . . .

Magdalys concentrated harder, fought away the flames inside herself.

Not now. What good did it do her — all that rage?

"Let's bring her down for the night," Cymbeline said, startling Magdalys from her reverie.

The fires seemed to extinguish on their own, washed away by a sudden flash of uncertainty. "What? It's only a little past midnight I think. We still have a ways to go before dawn."

"I know but . . . this is new territory, we have to move cautiously now." A crispness singed the edges of Cymbeline's words. It was that faraway voice she used every now and again since they'd left New York, a sudden sadness that seemed to swallow her whole for a few moments at a time; then she'd recover and act like nothing had happened.

Magdalys wasn't sure how much more cautiously they could move than flying under the cover of darkness and making camp during the day. And anyway, that plantation wasn't as far enough behind them as she would've liked. But she didn't want to go back and forth about it. "The others asleep?" she asked as Stella glided toward the dark treetops below.

"'Cept Amaya. She's keeping watch. There. That'll work."

Magdalys followed the imaginary line from Cymbeline's finger to a moonlit field amidst the dark maple trees.

"Out in the open? Are you sure that's —"

"Just to land, Magdalys," Cymbeline cut her off. "We can hike in a little to make camp. I'll wake the others." She got up carefully and made her way to the far end of the saddle.

Cymbeline had never interrupted her before. Sure, Magdalys had only really known her a few days, but she'd come to view the older girl as a kind of sister, especially after all they'd been through together.

Stella spun a smooth arc over the treetops, the Rearguard falling into formation behind her, and then launched into a sharp dive as the open field spread long beneath them.

CHAPTER TWO
FROM ACROSS
A MOONLIT FIELD

"**W**HERE ARE WE?**" Two Step grumbled, sliding down from Stella's saddle and glancing at the field around them. This was the first time he'd set his feet on land without breaking into one of his signature dance moves, Magdalys realized, watching her friend's wary face.

"A whole bunch of mountainous, forest-filled miles east of Chattanooga," Mapper reported, stretching and helping Sabeen work her way onto the stirrups so she could climb down. "In other words, somewhere near where Tennessee, Georgia, and North Carolina crash into each other."

Behind him, Amaya shook her head. "I don't know how you do it."

"Even while he's asleep," Magdalys said. "It's uncanny." She'd been the first one on solid ground and was scanning the edge of the forest for movement. Cymbeline had hopped down right after her and immediately headed out into the darkness without a word. Probably looking for a spot to camp, Magdalys figured, trying to ignore the roiling uneasiness she felt.

"What kind of dinos do they have down here?" Amaya asked.

"If it's anything like Pennsylvania and Maryland," Two Step said, "not many, and what ones there are will be boring and a nuisance." It was true: Besides some wandering pteros and a few wandering microraptors scavenging for food, they'd barely encountered any reptiles at all since they'd left New York.

"Boring dinos are almost the best kind of dinos," Amaya said. "Second only to no dinos."

Magdalys tried to remember what Dr. Barlow Sloan had written in the Dinoguide about Tennessee species, but all she could come up with was a typically crotchety paragraph about how North American megafauna tended to get weirder and even more mega the further south you went. A good number of the dinos in big cities like New York had been imported from other parts of the country anyway, so everything was all mixed up, as far as Magdalys could tell.

"The forests are empty because of the fighting," Cymbeline said, walking back from the edge of the trees. "Many of the dinos migrated west to get away from all the explosions. And plenty were captured for use in combat or as cargoluggers. There's a path through the forest up there. We can follow it in some and find a spot to camp." She picked up a rucksack and headed back toward the tree line.

"Remind me again why we stopped in the middle of the night," Amaya said, falling into step beside Magdalys.

Magdalys shrugged. "Cymbeline said since we don't know the terrain as well and we're in enemy territory we have to be more careful."

"I thought we were being careful by flying at night."

Magdalys didn't say she'd been thinking the same thing — she just kept walking toward the trees. "Hey," she said, a few paces later. Behind them, the boys were playing another game of I Spy while Sabeen sang quietly to herself. The Rearguard dactyls spun wide circles in the open sky above them.

"Hey what?" Amaya said.

"You never told me what the letter said."

Now it was Amaya's turn not to say anything. Her father was a white man — some big-time Union general, in fact — and he'd raised her, training her like a soldier since she was a little kid. But then the war had broken out and he'd dumped Amaya at the Colored Orphan Asylum and she hadn't heard anything from him right up until the day the orphanage burned down. A letter had come from the General in the same bundle with Private Summers's message about Montez being wounded, but Amaya hadn't been ready to read it, and one of the matrons had kept it and then the Draft Riots threw everything into disarray and they'd thought it was gone forever, until another of the matrons showed up with it just before they took off.

"John Brown's body lies a-moldering in the grave," Sabeen sang. *"John Brown's body lies a-moldering in the grave."*

"That song is so grim," Mapper sighed. "I love it."

"I spyyyyyy with my little eye," Two Step said behind them, "something . . . that starts with *s*."

"John Brown's body lies a-moldering — the sky *— in the grave."*

"This game is impossible!" Two Step complained. "There's only like two things anywhere we go. Stupid trees and stupid sky!"

"His soul's marching on!" Sabeen finished.

"I haven't read it," Amaya said flatly.

Magdalys stopped in her tracks. "What?"

Amaya grabbed her arm, shoving her along. "Keep walking!" she whispered. "Do you think I want the whole world bugging me about this? You know they're gonna ask."

"I wasn't bugging you about it," Magdalys said. "I was just —"

"Hey, what you guys whispering about?" Mapper called.

"Nothing!" Magdalys and Amaya said together.

"It's fine," Amaya hissed.

"Oh, wow, okay," Mapper said. "Excuuuse me!"

"I spy," Sabeen said, "with my little eye. Something . . . that starts with *b*."

"Butt!" Two Step yelled, pointing up at the circling dactyls. Everyone stopped and stared at him.

"Get it? Because they're the Rearguard! Rear! Like rear end! Ha! You guys! Wait up!"

"Why didn't you read it?" Magdalys whispered once they'd gotten a little ahead of the others.

"I just . . ." Amaya shook her head, shrugged. "I can't?"

"Bats?" Mapper said. "Do you see bats? Because if you do, they're probably about to be pterofood, so don't get too attached."

"Nope!" Sabeen said.

"I know I seem tough," Amaya said, looking down, her face mostly hidden by the long strands of jet-black hair hanging down to either side. "But the truth is I'm a coward."

Magdalys scoffed. "That's definitely not true."

"Who else but a coward would leave the only letter they've ever gotten from their father unopened for days on end?"

"Blankets?" Two Step tried. "There've gotta be blankets in one of these rucksacks right?"

"Nope!"

A familiar hooting sounded across the sky above them. Everyone stopped in their tracks and looked up. Two long dark shapes stretched up above the treetops ahead of them.

"Brachiosauruses!" Mapper and Two Step yelled at the same time.

Magdalys and Amaya traded a glance. "Does that mean —" Amaya started. She didn't have to finish. Brachys were plains dinos, according to Dr. Sloan. If one was out in the forest, it probably meant someone had brought it there.

"I dunno," Magdalys said.

"Up here!" Cymbeline called from the forest. "Hurry!"

"Hurry?" Magdalys glanced around. Dark shapes were moving toward them across the field. *"Amaya!"* Magdalys whispered, nudging her friend. They both drew the carbines they had holstered and fanned out to either side as the boys and Sabeen rushed forward.

"What is it?" Two Step asked.

"Something's coming," Magdalys said, backing toward the trees. "Can't make it out." The shapes got closer. There were three of them and they were tall and very fast. "Run! Get to the woods!"

A shot cracked through the night and Magdalys almost crumpled into herself from surprise. It was Amaya, she realized. Out in the field, a dino squealed and someone yelled, "Ho there!"

"Hold your fire," Cymbeline called. "Get into the woods!"

Magdalys and Amaya backed into the shadows of the trees together, guns pointed out at the approaching riders. Cymbeline stepped forward, a lit lantern raised above her head, shotgun in the other hand. "Declare yourselves!" she hollered. "Or get annihilated."

"Whoa, there, whoa," a low voice muttered in a long Tennessee drawl as the riders dismounted and stepped forward. "Almost winged Horace." In the dim lantern light,

Magdalys could make out their faces. All three men sported beards trimmed to line their jaws with no mustaches. And, except for a long scar running down the man in the center's cheek, all three had exactly the same face. Worse than that, they wore the gray uniforms of Confederate cavalrymen. Magdalys gasped.

"Card!" Cymbeline said, shaking her head and laughing. "It's about time! Where have you been?"

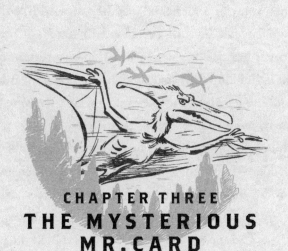

CHAPTER THREE
THE MYSTERIOUS
MR. CARD

"**CYMBELINE!**" **THE WHOLE** Dactyl Hill Squad gaped at the same time.

"You . . . you . . ." Magdalys stuttered. On the other side of Cymbeline, Amaya raised the carbine, her face steel.

Cymbeline shook her head. "No, wait, slow down everyone! I see what this looks like, and it's not . . ." She sighed. "They're not Confederates, okay?"

"Then why . . ." Two Step demanded, waving his arms in exasperated, self-explanatory little circles. "Why!"

The man in the middle smirked. "You can see why they might think we were though, Cymbie."

"Card is a Union scout," Cymbeline said. "He goes behind enemy lines to find out their positions and —"

"We know what a scout does," Mapper seethed.

"Then you can understand why he's dressed like that."

Magdalys felt like all the blood in her body was rushing into her brain. This whole situation was rotten, from the moment Cymbeline had said they should land onward. "What I want to know is, how did they know where we were going to be and why were you expecting them?"

Cymbeline looked at her, brows raised, eyes wide, mouth slightly open. The only other time she'd seen her make that face was when the Zanzibar Savannah Theater, where she lived and worked, had gone up in flames right in front of her. "It was . . ." Cymbeline started. Her voice trailed off.

"Not to interrupt the moment," one of the other men said, "but there's a secesh raiding party not far away and now that we've found you, we need to get you safely back to the Union camp so you can report to General Sheridan immediately."

"Report?" Amaya said. Cymbeline whirled to face her.

"What's secesh mean?" Sabeen asked.

"It's short for secessionist, lil' darlin'," one of the men said. "Confederates. The baddies."

"Why do you guys all look exactly the same?" Two Step demanded.

"Like, literally identical," Mapper added.

Card tilted his head. "This here's my older brother, Card. And that" — he nodded to the other rider — "that's my younger brother, Card."

"And you youngens must be the crew from Dactyl Hill. Pleased to meet ya!" the younger Card said. "We've heard great things."

"Heard?" Magdalys hissed at Cymbeline.

"Great things?" Amaya finished for her.

Cymbeline glanced back and forth between them.

The older Card doffed his gray cap. "Indeed. But my brother's correct. We gotta get a-movin', folks." He shot a worried glance at the moonlit sky.

"How far to the camp?" Cymbeline asked.

"Far enough that we'll need you to hop on the back of our paras if we're gonna make it safely."

Magdalys had been so busy glaring at Cymbeline, she hadn't bothered getting a better look at the mounts.

The parasaurolophus, Dr. Sloan wrote in the Dinoguide, *is among the most noble and versatile of all dinomounts. With their elegant crest stretching like a plume behind their head, they strike an impressive visage on four legs or two. They are equally at home grazing amidst the swaying North American grasslands or trundling amorously through the deciduous forest mountains of the middle states.* (What, Magdalys had tried not to wonder, did it mean to trundle amorously?) *What's more, the parasaurolophus makes a whimsical, intelligent companion whether one plans a long journey, is preparing for battle, or simply wants a gentle beast of burden nearby who can perform menial tasks and act as a loyal coconspirator in gentle pranks and assorted shenanigans.*

("Dr. Sloan is a weirdo," Two Step had said, reading over Magdalys's shoulder in the orphanage library.)

The Cards' three paras stepped (or trundled amorously, Magdalys supposed) into the lamplight. She'd never seen one before. They were shaped a little like their cousin dinos, the iguanodons, which could be seen promenading the streets of Manhattan and the Crest beneath their wealthy masters. The paras had those same thick hind legs and wide hips that curved forward into arched backs and smaller torsos, with long, arm-like forelegs extending toward the ground. Those bony crests that Dr. Sloan called elegant reached up and back from their short snouts, and their sunken-in eyes blinked at the world with an irritated, skeptical squint.

"What about Stella?" Magdalys said. "And the others?"

"Stella?" one of the Cards asked, raising a bushy blond eyebrow.

"Our pteranodon," Mapper said proudly.

"Oh, that's what that big ol' ptero y'all flew in on is?"

"I'm sure General Sheridan would love to have a look at that one," the older Card said.

"Mm-hmm," the middle Card agreed.

Magdalys wasn't sure if she was more upset at herself for bringing up Stella in the first place or Mapper for spilling the beans. More than anything though, she was furious with Cymbeline for keeping so many secrets. Everything was happening faster than she could keep track of and none of it was bringing her any closer to Montez.

Out in the field, Stella stirred. There was no telling what would happen if the Union Army got their hands on her.

Go! Magdalys commanded. Stella looked up sharply. Magdalys felt the raw power of her glare, the huge creature's unwillingness to leave her side. *Fly. Stay away from any signs of humans. We'll be . . . we'll be alright.*

In a single, fluid leap, Stella crouched low and then hurled herself into the air, sending a flush of wind across the field with her enormous wings.

Cymbeline shot Magdalys a look. Magdalys watched the huge shadow disappear into the moonlit night. The dactyls must've scattered to scavenge for dinner; the sky was empty.

Except.

A flutter of movement over the far end of the field caught Magdalys's eye just as an eerie howl sounded over the breeze and chirping crickets.

"What was —" Mapper said.

"Confederate Air Cavalry!" Card yelled. "No time to argue. Everyone get on a para. We gotta move out."

Shadowy shapes flitted across the sky toward them as more howling sounded and then a series of flashes erupted from above amidst the crackle of gunfire.

"Let's go!" Card yelled.

CHAPTER FOUR
THROUGH THE WOODS
AND AWAY

DARK TREES RUSHED past on either side as the para galumphed along in a wild, dip-and-divey gallop beneath Magdalys. She'd hopped on the nearest, Young Card's mount, as gunfire thudded into the dirt around her and shattered branches overhead. Two Step had jumped on behind her and then Card had yelled "Heeyah!" and the para had leaned all the way forward onto all fours, making Magdalys feel like she might tumble off at any second, and away they'd gone.

Up above, the Confederate dactylriders yelled back and forth to each other and let out their triumphant howls, occasionally swooping down beneath the tree line to hurl a shot or two into the darkness. Older Card had galloped ahead with

Amaya and Cymbeline, while Middle Card's para thundered along a few paces over to the side with Sabeen and Mapper.

"Can you get a shot?" Young Card yelled.

"Probably not," his brother called back. "Looks like they're just a small scouting expedition, not the full unit. Still . . . the others won't be far behind."

"Uh-huh."

Blam! Another shot rang out from above and smashed into a nearby tree.

"Ragged Randy Run!" the Card up front called.

All three brothers pulled their reins back and forth in sharp turns as their paras grunted and adjusted their forward charges into a zigzagging kind of dance.

"That oughta keep 'em confused," Young Card snickered. A few more shots hurtled down around them.

Magdalys closed her eyes. Where were her Brooklyn dactyls? *Come through*, she called silently. *We need you.*

The sound of the panting, snorting paras and their heavy footfall filled the air as the Confederates above held their fire.

Magdalys gulped. Once again, someone was taking potshots at her and her friends. And to top it off, she was being carried along like some defenseless damsel in distress by strange men. Strange men wearing Confederate gray no less!

A sharp caw sounded and more flapping from above, then yells of confusion from the air cavalry.

The dactyls! The birch branches jumbled into a trembling

dark haze with each bound from the para, but Magdalys thought she could make out a group of shapes flash into the crew of dactylriders and scatter them.

Then more gunfire sounded.

Swing low for me, Magdalys thought, and within seconds a whooshing sound blitzed through the woods toward them, branches snapping and leaves fluttering as one of the dactyls dove through the trees and fell into a smooth glide alongside the para.

"What in the —" Card yelled, but Magdalys had already stood in the saddle, steadying herself with both hands on his shoulders. "Girl, what are you —"

Magdalys leapt, grasping the neck of the dactyl just as it swooped into a steady climb back toward the treetops.

"Now, how in the —" she heard from below just before the dactyl burst through the branches and out into the moon-lit sky.

"Magdalys, no!" Cymbeline yelled, but Magdalys didn't care what Cymbeline said anymore. She had lied to them, in one way or another, like so many adults before her, and now she couldn't be trusted. And anyway, Magdalys had had it with being dragged around places. She willed the dactyl to spin around and caught her breath.

The four Confederate air cavalrymen were flapping off on their steeds, routed by the sudden onslaught from her Brooklyn dactyls, who were giving chase with hoots and screeches. But it was what they were heading toward that stopped Magdalys short: Out above the open field they'd just come from, at least two dozen more mounted dactyls flapped toward her, the howls of their riders rising in the night.

"Ten-hut!" a stern voice cried over the wind. "Slow your steeds and take aim boys! On my mark, knock those pteros out of the sky!"

Magdalys's eyes went wide. *Scatter!* she pleaded. *Get away!*

"And fire!"

The first crackling barrage burst out from the Rebel Air Cavalry just as the Brooklyn dactyls were launching out in all directions like a slow-motion ptero explosion.

A horrible shrieking filled the air. Magdalys saw three dactyls blasted out of the sky outright as two others spiraled in dizzy loops into the treetops.

"And fire!"

Another explosion. Something whizzed past Magdalys's head. A bullet. Then the dactyl she was riding screeched and they both tumbled downward as the darkness of the forest suddenly engulfed them.

CHAPTER FIVE
RACE TO THE UNION LINE

EASY, MAGDALYS COOED to the tumbling dactyl beneath her. Time seemed to slow as branches scraped across her face and more gunfire crackled overhead.

Easy, big fella, shhh . . .

The dactyl's mind was a muddle of terrified screeches and hoots of pain, but she felt him trying to regain some bit of control as he flapped fiercely to slow their plummet.

One of his rear legs had been hit; she could see it dangling limply. Another shot must've passed through one of his wings, which was bleeding freely through a ragged hole.

Landing would not be an easy thing.

Slow, buddy, slowww, Magdalys insisted, and the dactyl seemed to quiet his panic some in response as they slid closer and closer to the forest floor. *Easy fella, easy.*

When she could make out a patch of moonlit dirt and grass below, Magdalys leapt down, still grasping her hands around the dactyl's neck, and pulled them into a messy somersault tumble.

The ptero let out a squeal of pain and pulled himself out of her grasp, hopping a few limping steps away on shaky wings before falling to a heap.

Magdalys stood. Her whole body ached and about a thousand little cuts probably crisscrossed her face and arms, but she was alright otherwise.

"Mag-D!" Two Step yelled from not far away. "She's over there! Come on!"

Up above, the head of that air cavalry unit let out another bellow and another volley burst out. Magdalys prayed at least some of her dactyls were okay, but there was nothing she could do.

A shape rushed toward her through the trees: one of the Cards on top of that para, galloping forward in that strange, seesaw gait. Then she saw the man's stern face, that carefully trimmed jawline beard and furrowed brow, his arm reaching out and scooping her up and placing her on the saddle in front of Two Step.

"The dactyl!" Magdalys yelled. "We have to bring him! He saved my life!"

"There's no —"

"He's wounded and he saved my life," Magdalys yelled. "He's right there!" She pointed to the panting heap where the dactyl had collapsed in the shadows a few feet away. "Please!"

Card sighed, swinging his mount around and pulling it beside the ptero. "I don't even know how we're going to —"

"I'll do it," Magdalys said, climbing down from the para with Two Step close behind.

C'mon, boy, she thought, pulling the dactyl to his feet as Two Step helped him from the other side. *This the only way you gonna make it.*

The ptero wheezed, dark blood splattering Magdalys's face, but finally heaved himself upright and then clambered over the top of the para, which stomped its feet a few times with impatient grunts but otherwise behaved.

More gunfire crackled above.

"Kids . . ." Card warned. A few shots thunked the trees and soil nearby.

"He's on!" Two Step yelled, pulling himself up as he steadied the dactyl.

Magdalys climbed on behind him. "Go! Go!"

They surged forward, more shots ringing out around them and the foliage overhead rustling with sound of the Confederate Air Cavalry dactyls on hunt.

"This way!" one of the Cards up ahead called as all three paras bounded down a rocky hill and then flushed forward between towering birch trees toward a shadowy grove.

Magdalys and Two Step's para lumbered along at the back,

barely able to keep up with the extra weight it was lugging. Up above, the Confederate Air Cavalry swooped and hollered, occasionally taking potshots through the trees, but the moon had slid behind a cloud and the riders couldn't seem to get much of a view of the forest below.

"Ho there!" a stern voice yelled as the lead para pulled up to a halt before some trees. "Password or we light you up."

Card muttered something Magdalys couldn't make out over the pants and stomps of the para beneath her.

"Open the gates, then," the sentry said. "Ah, the Cards, of course!" A creaking groan erupted from the trees and the darkness seemed to give way around them as a wooden door Magdalys hadn't even noticed swung open, revealing a torchlit campsite.

"Tighten the lines and ready the howitzers," the older Card said as his para rumbled through the gates. "There's a Rebel Air Cavalry unit in pursuit, and we don't know how many are with 'em."

"We'll let the commanding officer know," the sentry called as Magdalys's para thumped past. A few more scattered shots rang out behind them, but then the night grew still. The Cards slowed their paras to a brisk march as they maneuvered through row after row of tents and crackling campfires. Some men sat perched on logs around the fires in their mud-stained blue uniforms, sipping from tin cups and muttering to each other.

Magdalys felt a tug on her arm. "Hey," Two Step whispered. "You okay?"

Was she? Magdalys wasn't even sure what okay meant anymore. Somehow being shot at again didn't seem half as horrible as the sinking feeling that Cymbeline had deceived them. She met Two Step's eyes, still trying to figure out what to say, and realized he'd been crying.

"Two Step," she said, touching his shoulder.

He rubbed his eyes. "No, no, I was really asking you. I'm . . . I'm okay, Mags."

"You don't look okay." Back in Dactyl Hill, Two Step had shot a member of the notorious Kidnapping Club who was charging at them on a triceratops. He'd saved Mapper's and Magdalys's lives, not to mention his own, but killing that man seemed like it had broken something inside of Two Step. He still hadn't quite lost that faraway look in his eyes. And this had been their first time amidst gunfire again since that night. "Talk to me," she said when he looked away at the fire-speckled rows of bivouacs.

Out beyond the tents, Magdalys could just make out the dark shadows of the Union combat and supply dinos, those long sauropod necks and the bulky, shadowed bodies of trikes stirring in their pens.

"Two Step?"

He shook his head, his face now steeled as he looked back at her. "Nothing. No, I don't. There's nothing to . . . no."

"Riders, dismount!" one of the Cards called. The paras pulled to a halt and Magdalys watched Two Step slide down, careful not to let the wounded dactyl fall. He was just a kid,

Magdalys thought. All of them were. Just twelve and thirteen. Sabeen was still ten. And the world had already demanded so much of them. She shook her head, slid down from the saddle, and helped Two Step ease the dactyl down.

The ptero let out a soft moan as they eased it onto the dirt floor and then it rolled over, limp.

Two Step shuddered. "Is he . . . ?"

Magdalys knelt beside the dactyl, closed her eyes. The soft murmur of life reached her, just a faint, trembling kind of hum. She shook her head. "Not yet. But he's not good." She ran her hand along the dactyl's long neck and rubbed his belly. The bleeding had stopped, at least.

A pair of dusty boots came to a stop in front of Magdalys. "What we should do," said the solemn voice attached to those boots, "is put a bullet in its head."

Magdalys looked up and directly into the eyes of one of the Cards — the middle one, she thought. "You won't."

"You almost got my little brother killed stopping to save this dino."

"He's a ptero, not a dino," Magdalys said. "And he saved me."

"So did my little brother, if I recall correctly. Just count yourself lucky you didn't get him killed. That's all I'm saying." He turned around and walked away.

Magdalys narrowed her eyes, but no snappy comeback came. Too much had happened too fast. And the man wasn't all that wrong either — it had been reckless, what she'd done. He just didn't have to be a jerk about it.

"Sorry bout my brother," Young Card said, smiling awkwardly. "He means well. He's just real protective and, you know . . . to some folks, dinos, er — pteros too, I guess — are just another beast. Mind you, if anyone hurt ol' Horace he'd have an absolute fit."

Magdalys managed to smile.

"Anyway, pay him no mind. Get yourselves settled and we'll have the dinomedics look at your friend there."

"Thank you," Magdalys said.

"Magdalys," Cymbeline said, walking up beside Card.

"Don't say a wo—" Magdalys started, but a sharp voice cut her off.

"Agent Crunk," someone called from the entrance to a large torchlit tent, "General Sheridan requests your report forthwith."

Cymbeline blinked, then sighed, rubbing a hand over her eyes.

"Agent?" Magdalys said.

"Come with me," Cymbeline said.

CHAPTER SIX

THE VOCIFEROUS GENERAL SHERIDAN

AN OFFICER WITH an altogether much too pristine dress suit and aggressive handlebar mustache stood at attention by the tent entrance. This had to be the major general's adjutant, Magdalys thought. The newspapers were full of stories about upper-class Northerners with cushy military jobs.

Cymbeline offered him a smile that hinted unambiguously at murder. "I'd appreciate it, Corporal Buford," she growled, "if you would not alert the entire state of Tennessee of my clandestine designation in the future."

Buford snapped a salute. "Official designations are to be used in campsites at all times, Agent Crunk."

Cymbeline's salute caused him to duck out of the way.

Magdalys smirked to herself. She was still mad at Cymbeline, but it was always good to see her one-up someone.

"I'm afraid unattended Negro children aren't permitted in the general's presence. Is this a contraband?"

Contraband was the word the US Army used for people who had escaped slavery and made it safely to their lines. Everyone was always talking in the streets about how no one knew what to do with them, even after Lincoln's Emancipation Proclamation, although this year many of them had finally been granted the right to be soldiers.

Magdalys felt the full glare of Corporal Buford settle on her. She suddenly felt very tiny and filthy.

"She's not dressed like a contraband, is she?" he mused. "No rags and such, that is."

"Corporal Buford," Cymbeline seethed.

The officer didn't take his curious eyes from Magdalys, so she met his glare full on with one of her own. That seemed to shake him. He glanced up at Cymbeline. "Hm?"

"Miss Roca is part of a clandestine program ordered at the highest levels of the War Department. Secretary Stanton granted me deputizing powers to create an espionage network with the blessings of General Grant himself."

"Well, I certainly —" Buford sputtered.

"You haven't heard about it because it is above your rank to know of its existence."

"That's simply —"

"I only included you in the secret because I'm feeling mag-nanimous today, Corporal Buford. You're welcome to wire the War Secretary yourself for confirmation if you'd like."

"I most certainly will do that immediately!"

"Outstanding. Send him my warmest regards. Good eve-ning, Corporal Buford."

Cymbeline grabbed Magdalys's hand and hurried her into the tent.

"Ah, Miss Crunk!" a jaunty voice called from the far end of the tent as Cymbeline snapped a salute. "Card here has just been regaling me with tales of your adventures!"

Major General Sheridan was a wisp of a man, probably only a little taller than Magdalys, and he looked even tinier beside Card, who had to crook his neck to the side to keep from scratch-ing his head on the top of the tent. Sheridan strode forward in long, bouncy strides and shook Cymbeline's outstretched hand excitedly. He was wearing blue trousers and a simple white shirt, like he'd been roused suddenly from sleep and hadn't bothered putting his full uniform on. A tightly trimmed goatee framed his sharp face. "You brought me pteros, I hear!"

"No," Magdalys and Cymbeline said together.

Sheridan blinked at them. Behind him, Card rubbed his face and sighed.

"Card my good man," General Sheridan said without looking away from Cymbeline. "I could've absolutely sworn you told me Agent Crunk here had arrived on pteroback."

"That is accurate, sir."

"With due respect, General," Cymbeline said, "the pteros are not mine to turn over to you, sir. Further, we're not sure where they are currently, as they were scattered during an engagement with the enemy air cavalry on our approach to the camp, sir."

"Mmm, so I've been told, so I've been told." Sheridan raised his eyebrows and squinted, as if the brief skirmish was playing out in front of him somehow. "Card?"

"At least one survived, but is wounded. The girl brought it back to camp."

No thanks to you, Magdalys thought.

"We must see to it that ptero receives every bit of medical attention."

"Card already brought it to the medic tent," Cymbeline said. "Uh, the other Card."

"And what of the other pteros?"

"Based on what I saw, sir," Card said, "I believe the girl here could summon them back at will, if any survived."

Sheridan whirled around. "Did you say *summon*?"

Magdalys felt all the blood rush to her face. She had barely gotten used to being able to communicate with dinos, and had hoped to keep it a secret as much as possible. Back in Brooklyn, her friend Redd had told her not to be ashamed of her power, to proclaim it to the world. And it had seemed so simple for a moment. But now she was in the middle of war and she didn't know who to trust anymore. Everyone seemed to be putting her under a microscope as soon as she met them.

"Summon a dino?" Sheridan marveled.

"A ptero, sir, technically," Card pointed out.

Magdalys glared at him. He glared back.

"And you saw this happen, you say?"

"On our way here, sir. I've never seen anyone ride a dactyl like that."

"Major General," Cymbeline cut in.

"Also, sir, they have a pteranodon."

Sheridan gasped. "A live pteranodon?"

"They landed in Druid Field on it."

The general stepped up directly in front of Magdalys and leaned forward, his hands on his knees. "What's your name, child?" he said with a friendly smile.

"Magdalys Roca, sir."

"Is what my man Card says true?"

Magdalys felt Cymbeline's stare, had no idea what it meant. She wished she could turn to the older girl for help, find some hint of what to do. But Cymbeline had lied to her, was a whole other person than who she'd thought her to be. Magdalys couldn't trust anyone, except the Dactyl Hill Squad. That's all there was to it.

"It's true," she finally said. "I can communicate with them. They do . . . they do what I ask them to."

"Magnificent," Sheridan whispered. "Like the legendary dinoriders of old." He straightened up. "This changes everything."

"Sir," Cymbeline said. "If I may —"

"Do you know, Agent Crunk, how long I've been trying to convince those old fusspots in the War Department to authorize a federal air cavalry? Why, you saw yourself how the Confederates had the run on us tonight, didn't you?"

"We —"

Sheridan pounded his fist into his palm. "We could smash them across the skies and then wreak havoc on their ground troops from above!"

"She's a child," Cymbeline said.

"Wondrous. To think, the whole victory or defeat of the Army of the Cumberland, perhaps the Union itself, could rest on such tiny shoulders" — Sheridan shook his head, eyebrows raised — "and Negro shoulders at that."

"Sir!" Cymbeline said. "That's not fair."

Sheridan blinked, shaken from his reverie. "Fair, Agent Crunk? What on earth gave you the idea that anything about war is fair? A man's head was shot off by an artillery shell not five feet from where I stood the other day. Was that fair, Agent Crunk? That it should've been him instead of me? We who find ourselves in war's all-encompassing theater don't have the luxury of worrying about these existential questions. We have to worry about victory, and not getting destroyed. That is all.

And that includes you, Agent Crunk, and, unfortunately, it includes your small friend here, Magda — what was it, dear?"

"Magdalys," Magdalys said, imagining mortars hurling out from her eyes as she stared at the general. "And I'm just . . . I'm only here because my brother, Montez, he was . . ." The words wouldn't come. Three sets of eyes stared at Magdalys: Card's cold, inscrutable stare; Sheridan's curious, concerned one; and Cymbeline, who looked like she might cry.

"He's with the Louisiana 9th, sir," Cymbeline finally said, "and was wounded at the Battle of Milliken's Bend."

"Ah, of course," Sheridan said quietly.

"Last we heard he was being transported to New Orleans along with the other wounded for recovery. Unconscious."

Magdalys saw Card's gaze soften ever so slightly. "All I want," she said, "the only reason I'm here at all, is to find my brother and make sure he's alright."

Sheridan blinked a few times, then nodded kindly. "May I show you something, Magdelis?" he asked, butchering her name.

"Um, okay."

"Xavier!" Sheridan hollered, startling everyone except Card, who rolled his eyes. A few moments passed; Cymbeline and Magdalys traded uncomfortable glances. Sheridan scrunched up his face and yelled again, "Xavier!," this time stomping one booted foot for emphasis.

"I believe he's sleeping, sir," Card offered tightly.

"What good is a mobile table if he's constantly nodding off on the job?" Sheridan snapped at no one in particular. "Wake him up then!"

Card nudged his foot at something under a table that stood in front of him. And then Magdalys realized it *was* the table: the whole surface wobbled and an unimpressed grunting sounded as Sheridan stood waiting, eyes squinted with irritation. Then a sleepy-looking tortoise's face poked out from under the tablecloth and blinked languidly around the room. Finally, Xavier shuffled into an exquisitely slow rumble across the floor and came to rest beside Sheridan.

The general shook his head. "I'm quite sure the table tortoises of the Army of the Potomac are not nearly so lugubrious in their duties, Xavier."

The tortoise seemed to consider that with a slow nod and a few blinks, then sighed and retracted his big head back beneath the tarp.

On the surface of the table, a crinkled, coffee-stained map was spread out beneath tin cups, quills, and blue-and-gray wooden figurines. It looked like some mad genius had gotten drunk and tried to reinvent chess without the squares. She tried to make sense of it, recognize some landmark she'd seen along their flight, but came up empty.

"This is us." Sheridan lifted a little blue raptor in the middle of a chaos of lines, some straight (state borders?), some swirling (rivers? Mountains? Supply lines?), some notched (railroads!). "These fellows here" — he pointed at several gray trike and raptor figurines — "are General Braxton Bragg's Confederate divisions."

"There are a lot of them," Magdalys said.

"Indeed. There are a lot of us too, but see here?" The handful of other blue dinos were scattered around the mountains; most had Confederate divisions between them and the rest. "We pushed Bragg's men out of Chattanooga a few weeks ago and had them on the run. But in our zeal, we've been scattered. And now are in the gravest of danger, I'm afraid. The tides may be turning as we speak. And here." He pointed further down the map, where a straight line of gray trikes was arrayed along a railroad track. "General Longstreet's riders on their way by train to reinforce Bragg. That is, according to what Card here has learned from his most recent foray."

Card nodded once.

"But of course, this could all be wrong. And tomorrow, will look completely different. And perhaps worst of all? This." He picked up a small gray piece in the shape of a dactyl. "General Forrest's air cavalry. I believe you met some of them tonight."

Magdalys nodded, the echoes of their rifle fire still ringing through her mind.

"These flying maniacs can keep track of our every move. They can attack from almost any angle, set up ambushes and then rain down withering fire upon our men and dinos. We are flailing around like fools in the darkness hunting Bragg's men while our own prey closes in on us from all sides.

If one division is attacked, will we even know? Will we be able to reach them in time? This" — he pointed at a dot on the map with the word *Chattanooga* scrawled beside it — "is where we'll have to retreat to if things go sour, the only safe zone in hundreds of miles."

Card grunted and shook his head.

"So you see, we are currently in a predicament, Magadis. And what we need is a way out. Do you understand?"

Magdalys felt like she only barely understood, but she nodded anyway.

"Go rest," Sheridan said. "You've had a long day. We'll see what news the morning brings, and discuss further then."

For a moment, Magdalys and General Sheridan just stared at each other. Then he smiled, snapped a salute, and said, "Dismissed!"

CHAPTER SEVEN
CAMPFIRE SHENANIGANS

"**W**AIT!" CYMBELINE SAID, hurrying out of the tent.

Magdalys whirled around in the muddy pathway between rows of tents and campfires. "Don't speak to me."

"Please," Cymbeline said.

Magdalys just shook her head and turned, squinting and blinking away the tears. Up ahead, she recognized Amaya's tall, lanky frame standing beside a few other people near one of the fires. She quickened her pace, praying Cymbeline would have the decency not to follow her.

"Hey," Magdalys said, coming up beside Amaya.

Amaya put a finger to her smiling lips. "Shh! They're coming up on the good part."

"Good part of wha — oh!" Magdalys looked around. All the men around them were black and wearing Union blues. A division of the US Colored Troops! Immediately she thought of Montez, but of course, he was probably already in New Orleans. Still, there was a certain comfort in being around men who may have served with him. They'd formed a semi-circle around the bonfire, where Sabeen sat on the shoulders of a lanky brown-skinned man in his mid-twenties wearing a white undershirt and blue trousers. "Brahhh!" the man yelled, leaning forward and placing both hands on his forehead, pointer fingers sticking out like horns.

"Um . . ." Magdalys said. "Is this what I think it is?"

"Your trike impression is garbage, Octave," said a boy who looked a year or two younger than Cymbeline. "Let Big Jack do it. His dino impressions second to none, my man."

"Nobody asked for your opinion, Hannibal," the man named Octave snapped back. "And it's Corporal Cailloux who told me to be the trike, talk to him."

A middle-aged guy with a dashing mustache shook his head. "Stop breaking character, Octave. And anyway, we need Jack for the tyrannous. Didn't you kids say there was a tyrannous there?"

"GRAWRAWRAWRAR!!" a huge bald-headed man with bulging muscles yelled, jumping out of the crowd with Mapper on his scar-lined back. Everyone gasped and then burst into hoots and hollers.

"Too good," Cailloux said. "He's too good at this."

"Could put a shirt on though, is all I'm saying," Hannibal said.

"Tyrannouses ain't wear no shirts," Big Jack growled.

Everyone laughed.

"Get back into character!" Cailloux yelled.

"Did they wear pants that were five sizes too small for them?" Octave asked.

Big Jack stomped toward him. "If they were in the Union Army they probably did, yeah."

More raucous laughter.

"Um, guys," Mapper said, "can we get back to the action? This is the cool part."

Big Jack spun back around and leapt at Octave and Sabeen with another terrific roar.

"Aren't you one of those sniveling little orphan brats from the asylum I burned down in the Draft Riots?" Mapper crowed in what was actually a pretty good impression of Magistrate Riker, the man who had tried to kidnap Magdalys and all her friends and sell them into slavery.

"Charge!" Sabeen yelled, making her usually squeaky voice a little deeper and plastering an exaggerated scowl on her face.

Magdalys smacked her forehead. "I can't believe this is happening."

"Relax, champ," Amaya said with a chuckle. "You're a hero."

Octave gave another sorry growl and lurched forward, almost toppling Sabeen. He smashed into Big Jack but only came up to the man's midsection. Big Jack chuckled.

"And then," Two Step said, stepping out in front of them, "a huge shadow fell over the prison yard."

"What was it?" a scrawny soldier with a goatee yelled.

"Shut up for five seconds, Sol," someone else called, "and we might find out."

Two Step stretched his hands all the way out to either side, his eyes blinking with the passion of the moment. "A HUGE PTERANODON!!"

"How huge?" Cailloux asked.

"Like, twelve times bigger than the tyrannous!"

"Whoa!" the whole crowd exclaimed.

"Wait," Cailloux said. "We ain't got nobody bigger than Big Jack."

"A person bigger than Big Jack don't exist," someone pointed out.

"I just mean from a theatrical standpoint," Cailloux said, shaking his head, "how we gonna —"

"CAROOO!!" Hannibal yelled from on top of another man's shoulders. They wobbled into the middle of the semicircle.

"Do pteranodons say *caroo*?" someone wondered out loud.

"They still ain't as tall as Jack," someone else pointed out.

"Whatever, just keep going," Cailloux said. "We'll work with it."

"Arr!" Mapper exclaimed, wisely drawing everyone's attention back to himself before saying his line. "Aren't you that girl

Margaret Rocheford who can talk to dinos with your special mental powers like the dinoriding warriors of old?"

Magdalys shook her head. "If I hear that phrase one more time," she whispered. "What does 'of old' even mean?"

"Old-timey," Amaya whispered back. "Shush!"

"Was this guy Riker a pirate?" Sol asked. "Why he saying *arr*?"

"Quiet, Sol!" about five different people yelled.

"My name," Sabeen said defiantly, "is Magdalys Roca!" Then she slo-mo punched Mapper, who fell limp on top of Big Jack with an elaborate "Oof!"

Everyone cheered.

"Then the giant pteranodon swooped down," Two Step exclaimed, eyes wide, hands gesticulating wildly, "and snatched up the tyrannous in her beak!"

"Uh," Hannibal said. "That might be difficult."

"Did you say 'her beak'?" the guy beneath him asked.

"Yeah," Two Step said. "Stella."

"Aw, man!" the guy moaned, putting Hannibal down a little too quickly. "I can't play no girl dino!" He stormed off.

"Bradsbee will play the bottom half of a giant dino but it's the fact that it's a girl he has a problem with," Cailloux sighed. Everyone guffawed.

"Pteranodons are actually pteros," Sol pointed out as groans erupted around him.

"I'll take his place," Cymbeline said, stepping into the circle.

Magdalys tensed. Everyone got very quiet. "But I'll have to ask the good Private Hannibal if he'll switch places and take the bottom half, as I'm not sure I can support his weight."

"It's a lady," someone whispered.

"Put a shirt on, Jack!" someone else yelled.

Big Jack just blinked at Cymbeline.

"That really won't be necessary," she laughed.

"Wait," Cailloux said, stepping forward. "Are you Cymbeline Crunk? The Shakespeare actress they talk about in the colored papers?"

She bowed elaborately. "The same."

"Fellas, we are performing our sad little spectacle in the presence of theater royalty!"

Various *ooh*s and *well hey now*s erupted from the crowd.

"Why, it's not sad at all," Cymbeline said. "Although, while me and the young folks were all there to witness, you might want to consult with the young lady who was actually at the center of it all." She nodded toward Magdalys, who was already shaking her head as the crowd peeled off to either side around her with an awed gasp.

"Uh, no . . . I . . ."

"Magda Lee the Rock!" Big Jack yelled.

"It's Magda*lys*," Sabeen said, but Magdalys was pretty sure no one heard her.

Cailloux shook his head. "Well, well, well."

"Tell us what happened!" Octave called.

Magdalys felt tiny. All these eyes on her, each with a

different expectation and idea of who she was, all based on some goofy story the others had told them. Ridiculous! And terrifying. Even if the story was pretty much true. "I . . ." She shook her head, no words forming. "I just . . ."

"Don't be shy!" Cailloux said.

"It was all Stella really," Magdalys said. "She's the one that ate Riker."

"Ohh!!" everyone yelled amidst wild applause.

"And my friends," Magdalys said. "These guys were fighting it out in the prison the whole time while I faced off with the magistrate." She nudged Amaya beside her, then looked at Sabeen (who still sat on Octave's shoulders), Mapper (who'd gotten down from Jack's), Two Step, and finally, grudgingly, Cymbeline, whose eyes were sad behind her bright smile. "I'd be dead if it wasn't for them."

"Can you really talk to dinos?" Hannibal asked.

Magdalys raised one shoulder all the way to her ear without meaning to. "I mean I —"

"TEN-HUT!" a booming voice called, and all the men snapped to attention, backs straight, chins up, arms at their sides. Magdalys blinked. It had happened in seconds: They'd formed perfectly ordered rows from an unruly crowd without even a word exchanged. "Do you know what time it is, soldiers?" Corporal Buford strutted in front of them, his eyes narrowed. The fire behind him lit a shimmering line to the edges of his otherwise shadowed form, and Magdalys had the distinct impression that he had done that on purpose.

"Half past two in the morning," Mapper said.

Magdalys groaned inwardly. Why could that boy never let a question slide by unanswered?

Buford whirled on him. "Are you a member of the Louisiana Native Guard Mounted Artillery Unit of the Union Army, young man?"

Louisiana Native Guard? Magdalys almost yelped. Montez had been assigned the Louisiana 9th. They *had* to have crossed paths!

"Not that I am aware of, sir!" Mapper said, dropping his voice a few decibels and straightening his back like the others.

A few of the troops snorted back laughter.

Buford looked like he didn't know who to curse out first. "Perhaps," he finally said, eyeing Mapper, "you would like to be."

"Perhaps so, sir. They seem like pretty cool fellas."

"Aay!" a few soldiers crooned appreciatively.

Buford spun around. "That's quite enough! Soldiers, you were supposed to turn in hours ago, unless this young man is incorrect in his timekeeping skills." He paused, letting the crackle of the bonfire and a far-off dinohoot fill the night for a few moments. "Which I highly doubt!" he finally said, as if he'd just wrapped up a stunning prosecution and the case was closed. "This is a military bivouac, not a cheap saloon for revelry and shenanigans. Also," he added with a sly look on his face, "your payments have come in, and I expect you'll be eager to receive them?"

"Sir, no sir!" the troops hollered as one.

Buford shook his head. This seemed like a routine they'd been through before. "I can't promise the Senate will approve an equal pay measure any time soon, men."

No one stirred.

"I'm sure you have wives and families that need any help they can get. . . ."

Silence.

Buford seemed to sag. "Very well. Get to your quarters immediately. Dismissed."

He turned to Magdalys and the others as the men hurried off into the darkness of the camp. "If you will follow me, children, I will escort you to your sleeping quarters."

CHAPTER EIGHT
THE DINO QUAD

"**I HOPE THIS WILL** be suitable," Corporal Buford said, standing outside a large tent and ushering them forward.

"Whoa!" Two Step said, stepping inside.

"Definitely beats the cold hard ground," Mapper agreed, following him.

"Blankets!" Sabeen yelled.

"Thank you, Corporal," Cymbeline said, giving him a salute.

"You are most welcome, Agen —"

Cymbeline cut him a sharp look.

"Ah," Buford corrected himself. "Young lady."

Cymbeline shook her head but smiled and then ducked into the tent. Buford turned to Magdalys. "The major general would like to see you in the morning, young lady." Then he nodded and headed off into the night.

"What was that about?" Amaya asked.

Sabeen came back through the flaps and shot Magdalys a concerned look. "What was what about?"

Magdalys shook her head. "Long story. You guys want to take a walk? I gotta see if we can find the dino quad so I can check on that dactyl."

"Sure," Amaya said.

Sabeen motioned toward the tent. "Why don't we ask —"

Magdalys shook her head before Sabeen could finish the thought. "Just come on," she said. "I think it's over this way. And if nothing else, we can just follow our noses."

Combined with that mulchy forest scent from the surrounding trees, the crisp campfire freshness almost, *almost* covered the undodgeable assault of dinopoop stench. Magdalys knew it well. It came on like a fast-moving wall of foulness, overran any attempt to block it, seemed to dive directly into her very pores in a relentless deluge. "Guh," she muttered, waving at the air in front of her nose. "Over here."

"Ooh yeah," Sabeen said. "I noticed."

They made their way along the outer row of tents toward an open area where large shapes shifted in the shadows.

"I like those guys," Sabeen said.

"Who, the soldiers? Me too." Magdalys smiled.

"I don't think any of 'em are Native," Amaya said. "So I don't know why they're the Native Guard, but I like them too."

"They remind me of David and the folks at the Bochinche," Magdalys said. When they'd escaped the riots in Manhattan, Cymbeline had taken them to a small bar in Dactyl Hill, Brooklyn. There, they'd been taken in by Miss Bernice, David Ballantine, and Louis Napoleon — members of the Vigilance Committee, a group that helped rescue black New Yorkers from the clutches of Magistrate Riker's Kidnappers Club.

In the short time Magdalys and her friends had spent in Dactyl Hill, the Vigilance Committee had become like a family to them.

"Yeah," Sabeen said. "But scary as things got in Brooklyn, it's wild to think that where we are now, we could just get overrun at any moment by an army of people who think we don't even deserve to live."

"Girl . . ." Magdalys told the other two about the dire situation Sheridan had laid out for her earlier that night. They were surrounded and cut off from the rest of the Union forces: a total catastrophe waiting to happen.

"Are you gonna help them?" Sabeen asked, and Magdalys appreciated that her friend seemed to put no weight in the question, no pressure or guilt. It was just a question.

"I guess I gotta," Magdalys said, feeling tears start to well up in her eyes without warning. "I just . . ."

"I know," Amaya said. "You didn't come here for this and you don't like being pressured into things."

"Exactly!" Magdalys said, sniffling and feeling a little better already, just on the strength of someone understanding without her having to explain herself. "And I hate that Cymbeline . . . that . . ."

"You gotta talk to her about that," Amaya said. "Otherwise the anger'll eat you up from the inside."

"You guys aren't mad?"

Sabeen shook her head.

Amaya shrugged. "I kinda figured something like that was going on, and . . ." Her voice trailed off but she didn't have to finish. Her father, the great General Cuthbert Trent, had been letting her down and keeping things from her for Amaya's whole life. She still hadn't opened that letter from him, but Magdalys wasn't about to press her on it twice in the same night.

"Who goes there?" a surly voice called out from the shadows.

"It's uh . . . we're . . ."

Amaya saluted. "Members of the Dactyl Hill Mounted Regiment, sir!" she barked. "Here to check on one of our mounts that was brought in earlier."

Magdalys tried not to let her eyes go wide. Amaya had spat that lie out like a pro.

"Oh," the soldier said, stepping into the torchlight. He was a tall, slender fellow with bushy, bright red sideburns and a dirt-spackled uniform. On second thought, Magdalys real-ized, that probably wasn't dirt, considering where they stood. "Of course! How lovely! The Dactyl Hill Mounted Regiment, you say? I haven't heard of that one, but goodness knows we need some air cavalry support these days. I'm Lieutenant Knack. You three seem a bit young and er . . . female . . . to be in the corps, you know."

"Oh, we don't serve in battle, of course," Amaya said with-out missing a beat. "We travel with the menfolk and take care of the mounts. You know, women's work."

"Right, right," Knack said, nodding. "Come this way, my dears."

Magdalys nudged Amaya as they fell into step behind the lieutenant. "How did you do that?"

Amaya smiled and wiggled her eyebrows. "If you talk like them, you can say almost anything you want and they'll go along with it. Trust me, half of these guys don't listen to any-thing anyone's saying; they throw in a word or two that was said to make it sound like they were paying attention and then do whatever they were planning to do anyway."

"What's that?" Knack asked without looking back.

"Sir, nothing, sir," Magdalys said in her best impression of a gruff, military voice. "We were just discussing the lovely smell of dinopoop."

"Dinopoop, you say? Ah, yes, lovely, lovely."

They followed the lieutenant past a few makeshift pad-docks. Magdalys thought she recognized the wide barrel chests and long horns of triceratopses, and beyond that the tall, shield-covered backs of stegosaurs. The raptors and other carnivores were probably housed in a separate area to keep them from munching on these guys. Grunts, growls, and squeals rose in the night around them.

"Ah, here we are." He stopped at the edge of a large tent. "You know, the strangest thing happened earlier tonight."

Magdalys barely heard him. Her whole mind had filled with a different sound: the gentle, concerned *fubba-fubba-fubba* of a whole squad of pterodactyls.

CHAPTER NINE
SQUAD!

MAGDALYS BLINKED, BOTH her eyebrows raised.

Before her, nine of the dactyls that had left New York with them perched on metal bars around a wooden table. Under the dactyls' watchful gaze, four black men in aprons labored away with scalpels and bandages at something large behind a bloodied sheet hanging in front of the table.

"I believe this is the fellow you're looking for," Knack said. "Although you'll notice several of the others are suffering from various minor injuries. They showed up a few hours ago and refused to accept treatment until our surgeons stabilized the worst off of them, I'm afraid. Which seems to be what's happening just now. Isn't that right, Dr. Pennbroker?"

"Right indeed!" one of the men called back. "Then maybe we can get these old boys on out of the operating room."

One of the dactyls squawked at him and Dr. Pennbroker went back to what he was doing. "They're sort of . . . persistent," the surgeon said with a chuckle.

Magdalys felt like someone had lit a candle inside of her. Her friends had survived, most of them anyway. And they'd come to look out for the one that had saved her life! What noble, loyal animals they were. A few looked up and seemed to acknowledge her with those inscrutable squinting eyes before turning their attention back to the surgery in progress.

On top of that, they were being cared for by black surgeons! "I didn't know . . ." she started.

"That the Union Army had black surgeons? Ha!" The doctor shook his head. "Nobody does, it seems. Technically, they only let us operate on the Negro soldiers and the dinos . . ."

"Technically," the other three doctors echoed, rolling their eyes.

"Right," Dr. Pennbroker amended. "When push comes to shove and the broken bodies are pouring in faster than anyone can work on them, all those rules go out the window, of course. You want to see your friend here?"

Magdalys stepped forward and peered around the sheet. The injured dactyl lurched his big head around and locked eyes with her, letting out a long, heavy breath. He was alive and awake. *Dizz*, Magdalys thought. *I'll call him Dizz.* "He's going to make it?" she asked.

"Oh he'll be up and ready to go in no time," Dr. Pennbroker said. "Took quite a scrapping though — pulled two slugs out of him and a third went right through his left wing. But you know, as Dr. Sloan always says: The dactyl is a ptero of unimpeachable character."

"Whatever that means," another surgeon scoffed.

"Yeah, I've never figured that one out either, to be honest."

"You know Dr. Sloan?" Magdalys asked. "I . . . I've read his book so many times."

"Heh, you could say he's a good friend," Dr. Pennbroker said. "Though we do have our disputes on anatomy and physiology. He's serving with the Army of the Potomac now, over in the eastern theater."

"I didn't know he'd enlisted. I didn't even know he was still alive!"

"Oh, lord, very much alive," Dr. Pennbroker said. "Alive and stubborn as ever, I'm afraid."

"Thanks for taking care of our dactyl," Magdalys said, waving at the squad and surgeons alike as she joined Amaya and Sabeen at the far end of the tent.

"I gotta say," Amaya whispered, "I'm reevaluating my dislike of giant reptiles based on this experience alone."

"I've been trying to tell you," Magdalys said.

"And Stella, of course."

Magdalys nodded. "Stella the top dog."

"The best ptero in the whole world," Sabeen said.

"Stella the indomitable," Magdalys added.

"Stella who puts up with Two Step and Mapper's singing all night," Amaya said.

"We can't all be Sabeen."

"Aw," Sabeen said, blinking. "I don't really . . . I just . . ."

"You have a beautiful voice," Magdalys said.

Knack peered over at the girls. "What's that now?"

"We were saying we're pleased to see our loyal mounts are in such good hands, sir!" Magdalys yelled. A few of the dactyls cast what may have been incredulous gazes at her, which she ignored, smiling inwardly. "We'll be returning to our sleeping quarters now, sir!" She and Amaya saluted. The surgeons, their hands busy, nodded their goodbyes, and Knack opened the tent flap for them to leave through.

CHAPTER TEN
A LETTER, FINALLY

AN OFF-KEY SYMPHONY of crickets took over the night, rising even over Sabeen's enthusiastic snoring and broken only by occasional grunts and hoots from the dino quad. Magdalys rolled over and blinked at the tent drooping over her head.

The whole victory or defeat of the Army of the Cumberland, Sheridan's voice said over and over, *perhaps the Union itself, could rest on such tiny shoulders.*

She clenched her teeth, a blurry flash of anger rising in her chest. Who was Sheridan to put so much pressure on her? He knew exactly what he was doing, being at the head of an army that executed its own soldiers for deserting. He knew the power he wielded. Didn't even have to say it. The implicit threat was there, and even if he couldn't do as much to her as long as she was a civilian, he'd made sure to let the weight of that burden sit as heavily as possible on her. Suddenly, Magdalys couldn't breathe, like the war itself was sitting on her chest, laughing in her face. She sat up, pulling in as much of the thick Tennessee night air as she could.

She stood, trying to keep her panting as quiet as possible.

For a few moments, she kept perfectly still, let her breath return to normal, her pulse simmer back down. The crickets screamed their song on and on; the snores around her rose and fell.

Cymbeline had lied; Sheridan wanted to coerce her into fighting a war she barely understood, and he would never let her go, that much was clear. Somewhere far away, her mom and dad had gone on with their lives, and her sisters too. Maybe they'd already forgotten about her. She'd never felt so tiny: just a dot amidst all these sleeping soldiers and dinos, the world and its battlefronts spinning endless circles around her. She needed someone to tell her what was right, someone who knew her deep down, but the only person she could think of was wounded and en route to New Orleans.

Hopefully.

Or maybe Montez was dead.

She blinked away tears, her breath coming fast again; the air seemed to escape her lungs before she could catch it. She'd been telling herself this whole journey was to keep him safe, but really it was Magdalys that needed him. Who was she kidding?

Without thinking about it, she slung her satchel over her shoulder and hurried as quietly as possible out of the tent, where she found herself staring directly into Amaya's face.

The older girl shook her head. "You can't stop running away, huh?"

"I . . ." Magdalys started. All her silly lies just floated away into the night before she could pick one that might work.

"Don't bother," Amaya said. "I get it."

"You do?"

"I get the impulse. If you keep going though, we have a problem."

Magdalys stuck the toe of her boot into the dirt and looked away. The torches around them crackled in the night. Soldiers and dinos snored and crickets droned on and on.

"They put a lot of pressure on you," Amaya said. "And that's not fair. And I would want to run away too."

Magdalys nodded, still looking away. "I'm scared."

"Me too. Thing is, and I know this doesn't make it any easier: We need you too. And you don't necessarily owe them anything, but we came here with you. For you."

Magdalys met Amaya's eyes. "I know and —"

"Let me finish. More than that: *I* need you. Right now."

"Huh?"

She held an envelope out to Magdalys.

"What do you want me to do with that?"

"Read it."

Magdalys took the gram, shoved her finger into the

opening, and pulled along the top, tearing the envelope open. "Out loud?"

"No, just to yourself. Of course out loud, Mags. Why else would I — never mind. Yes, out loud. Please."

"Sheesh, I was just asking."

They stopped beneath one of the perimeter torches and Magdalys squinted at the ornate handwriting.

Dearest Daughter Amaya,

I write you with incredible news, more incredible than I can even share within the confines of this letter, in fact, so I suppose what I mean to say is, I write to tell you that there is incredible news, but sadly, I must see you in person to let you know. I can say that all of my hard work and dedication to this noble country has finally come to fruition, and Dr. Lassiter has provided me with the technology I need to complete my life's work.

You must come at once. I have instructed the matrons to provide you with train fare to Galveston. Your destiny awaits, my daughter, as does that of your two sisters —

"Sisters?" Magdalys said, cocking an eyebrow. "You never —"

"*Half* sisters," Amaya corrected. "They're . . ." She shook her head with distaste.

"Ah, say no more."

— Iphigenia and Mary Claire —

"Iphigenia?" Magdalys said. "Does she live in a tower and only wear ballroom gowns?"

"Keep reading please."

"I'm just saying."

— who will also be arriving shortly. All three of you will soon find out the true extent of our family's fortune and important role in the future of this great nation.

Come quickly, daughter! Greatness awaits! All that you have worked toward, all that I have worked toward, all that is yet to come awaits! And this Union rests its tired hopes upon us, my daughter, but such is the burden of greatness.

Your father,
Major General Cuthbert Trent

Magdalys lowered the gram. "Wow."

Amaya just shook her head.

"I guess we both bear the burden of greatness now, huh?"

"I don't even know what to say."

"Neither would I. Are you . . . what are you . . ."

"I don't know."

"Oh, wait, there's more." Magdalys turned the paper over, where a few more lines were scrawled.

PS Perhaps you already have heard, but I am unwell, dear daughter. The doctors are at a loss and have hooked me up to

various infernal devices without much success. You must come
quickly, I'm afraid, in order to inherit your destiny.

Amaya scoffed and sniffled at the same time. "Just like the old man," she said quietly. "Everything is amazing, come blah blah blah destiny, oh yeah by the way I'm dying, okay bye." She closed her eyes for a few seconds then blinked them open, shaking her head.

"That was a whole lot," Magdalys said.

Amaya took the gram and, without so much as a glance, held it up to a nearby torch. The parchment turned brown as fire snarled and snapped away at its edges, then it crinkled and was whisked away in sparkling ashes into the Tennessee night.

CHAPTER ELEVEN
ROLLING OUT

DINOS SCATTERED ACROSS an open plain as the whole world trembled. There were brachys and diplos; a flock of microdactyls skittered between the stomping legs of an allosaurus, as a whole rumbling trike herd thundered past. The ground shook and shivered, maybe from the dinos themselves or maybe that's what was making them run. Some had sprouted feathers from strange places; others had one limb or another covered in thick, matted fur.

In the distance, boulders tumbled down the side of a huge mountain.

Magdalys watched it all, her mouth hanging open, and wondered why she didn't get trampled in the mad stampede. Something shoved her from behind and she thought, *There it is, my death has come* and then she opened her eyes and Two Step was smiling down at her, wearing his pajamas, his fro pointing every which way but down.

Magdalys blinked. "You're not Death."

Two Step looked himself over. "Doesn't seem like it, no. You coming?"

A great hubbub filled the air outside their tent. Metal clanged and hammers pounded over the rustle of many bodies moving at once. Somewhere further away, the hoots and growls of dinos mingled with various sternly given commands. "Where we going?"

"We're rolling out!" Mapper called from across the tent in his best drill-sergeant baritone.

Two Step broke into a smooth shoulder dip and then spun, landing back facing Magdalys with two finger guns pointed her way. "Rolllllling out!"

"Why are you two so hype?" Magdalys grumbled, pulling the covers off and stretching.

"US Army coffee!" Mapper said, taking a sip from a tin cup. "America's finest!"

"Is it really?" Magdalys asked.

"Absolutely not," Two Step said. "But it's strong. We got up early and some guys in the next tent gave us theirs. Said they drank tea! Can you imagine?"

"Gimme some," Magdalys said.

Mapper dutifully passed the cup to Two Step, who handed

it down to Magdalys. It was still hot and sure, not that great, but definitely packed just the right punch. Magdalys closed her eyes.

"The cats from last night said we can roll with them today," Mapper said. "They're so cool!"

"And they're an artillery unit," Two Step said, "so their trikes and stegos have howitzers mounted on 'em."

The Louisiana Native Guard, Magdalys thought. She'd ask them about Montez. She hopped up. "Well, what are we waiting for, boys? Let's roll out!"

The dark green forest-covered mountains rose to either side as the Louisiana Native Guard Mounted Artillery Unit rumbled along a well-worn path with the rest of General Sheridan's division. Fanners — soldiers who carried fans at the ends of long sticks — marched at regular intervals on either side of the caravan, swooshing away the billowing clouds of dust so they wouldn't leave an obvious imprint of where they were going across the Tennessee sky. The mid-morning sun blazed down at them from a near cloudless sky and the strains of a single trumpet reached Magdalys over the stomps and clinking metal and grunts of armored triceratops.

She looked up from the trike saddle she shared with Mapper, the young soldier named Hannibal, and the big muscled one, Jack Jackson. The blue-clad, mud-covered army and their ironclad dinos stretched all through the valley and disappeared around a bend up ahead. Behind them, another armored unit, the Tennessee 7th, picked up the rear along with a few battalions of foot soldiers and a single squad of raptor riders. Magdalys could see those sharp, birdlike snouts bobbing along over the heads of the men at the very end of the procession.

The trumpet's song, at first just howling a series of sad, rasping notes into the blue sky, suddenly resolved into a melody: "John Brown's Body," and the whole regiment immediately began singing along. The lyrics were different though.

"*. . . where the flag is waving bright!*" everyone sang together.

A glint of sunlight caught Magdalys's eye and then she spotted the trumpet player.

"*We are going out of slavery, we are bound for freedom's light!*"

Octave Rey — the one whose trike impression Hannibal had called garbage (not without cause, Magdalys had to admit).

"*We mean to show Jeff Davis how the Africans can fight!*"

He stood up on the saddle he was riding on as cheers and raucous laughter rose around him, and led the soldiers into the final bar of the verse.

"*As we go marching on!*" they sang, and then fell into an even louder rendition of the chorus: "*Glory, glory, hallelujah! Glory, glory, hallelujah!*"

When they finished, Octave sat back down and sent the song into more spiraling, melancholy melodies, like he was having a conversation with the sparkling sun and mountain paths around him.

"Hey," Magdalys said, making her way to the front of the trike saddle where Hannibal and Jack were sitting.

"Hey yourself," Hannibal said with a mischievous smile.

"Did you guys ever serve with the Louisiana 9th?"

Jack Jackson perked up. "The 9th? Mounted Trike Division right?"

"Yes!" Magdalys nearly yelped, trying to quell the thrill of possibility rising inside her. "My —"

"Weren't they with us at Milliken's Bend?" Hannibal said.

"Yes!" Magdalys yelled again. "That's right!"

Jack nodded. "Gave them Rebels a beatin'." A moment passed. "Took a beating too." He craned his neck to one side, showing a long, barely healed scar running from his jaw and around down one shoulder. "That's where I got this. And a few others too. Barely made it outta there alive."

"Won the day though," Hannibal put in.

"And helped Grant sack Vicksburg soon after," Jack added proudly.

"Did you meet a soldier named Montez? Montez Roca."

Jack and Hannibal looked at each other. "Don't recall one with that name," Jack said.

Hannibal shook his head. "I'd remember a name like Montez."

Magdalys felt her whole heart sag. Had he not really been there? Maybe Private Summers's letter had been wrong about which battle they'd been in. But that didn't seem right — Summers had been there too. "Oh," she said in a voice so far away it made both men turn and look her over carefully.

"What's he look like?" Jack asked.

"He looks like her but with glasses and a shade lighter and even skinnier," Mapper offered. "Real bookish." He shook his head. "Always in a book."

Jack and Hannibal studied Magdalys for another few seconds, then looked at each other and yelled, "RAZORCLAW JONES!"

Magdalys's jaw dropped open. From behind her, Mapper made an incredulous gurgling noise.

"Come again?" Magdalys said.

"That's your brother?" Hannibal gaped.

Jack punched his shoulder, possibly shattering it. "Of course it is, man! Look at her! They're practically the same person, but what the little map dude said: glasses, lighter skinned, a little skinnier. I *knew* Magda Lee looked familiar!"

Hannibal shook his head and rubbed his injured shoulder. "I just . . . wow."

"Wait, slow down," Magdalys said. "What did you call him?"

"Razorclaw Jones," Jack and Hannibal said again, both chuckling and turning back to the front.

"But . . . why?"

"Razorclaw is army talk for a sharpshooter," Jack explained. "A sniper."

"Your brother could write his name in bullet holes on a tin can from fifty feet away," Hannibal bragged.

Jack tipped his head. "Well, I dunno about that, but —"

"Plus, y'all from New York, right?" Hannibal asked.

Magdalys nodded, still trying to take in the revelation that her brother could actually shoot, let alone well. "Yeah, but —"

"And the famous Raptor Claw neighborhood's there, so I guess someone just put two and two together."

"And threw in a Jones for good measure," Jack said.

Hannibal shrugged. "As we do."

"We're not even from that part of New York!" Magdalys yelled, overwhelmed with all the many impossible things happening at once. "And Montez is named Montez, not Razorclaw Whatever!"

"Jones," Mapper said helpfully.

"And he can't shoot guns! He hates guns!"

Jack and Hannibal traded a wry glance. "Oh, guess it was someone else then," Jack said.

"Yeah, it totally had to be a *different* kid from New York who looks just like you but with glasses. Got it."

"YOU GUYS!" Magdalys exploded. She climbed into the saddle between them. "You guys! That was . . . I mean . . ." She waved her hands around, trying to snatch the words that wouldn't come out of thin air. "I just . . ."

"Come to think of it," Jack said, "he did say he was Cuban. You Cuban?"

"Mentioned he had a sister too," Hannibal added. "Three, now that I think about it."

From behind them, Mapper let out a sigh.

"It's just," Magdalys said, and then, before she could even try to get another word out, she was crying. The tears didn't give her any warning and when they showed up she didn't even bother trying to stop them; she just leaned against Big Jack's big arm and sobbed into it as Hannibal patted her shoulder.

"She okay?" Mapper said, poking his head up.

"Sorry, little lady," Jack said. "We didn't mean to get you worked up."

"It's okay," Magdalys sniffled. "I didn't see it coming either." Something yellow appeared in front of her face — a handkerchief. Hannibal was holding it out to her. She took it and unloaded a whole nasty ton of snot into it. "Thank you."

"We got separated right after the battle," Hannibal said. He gingerly accepted his sullied handkerchief back, inspected it, and then just tossed it into the wilderness with a shake of his head. "Our crew got loaded onto the two ironclads that had shown up to shell the enemy for us. Didn't get a chance to see what happened to the boys from the 9th but I know it was a rough one for 'em."

"He was wounded," Magdalys said, sitting up. "Knocked unconscious with a rifle butt. Another soldier sent me a gram saying they were being transported down to New Orleans for treatment but . . . that's the last I heard."

"That's why we're here," Mapper said. "We're trying to get to him and make sure he's alright."

For a few minutes, the sounds of creaks of metal dinoarmor and heavy trod of a dozen trikes filled the air. Somewhere out in the forest, birds twittered and squawked at each other, and the sun cast dazzling lightworks along a tiny stream meandering beside the dusty road.

"Wow," Hannibal said. "We'd all been wondering what a bunch of kids was doing out here in the middle of the war. I mean . . . I'm a kid, but you guys are *kid* kids."

"And y'all came all the way out here," Big Jack added, "knowing at any moment you could be captured, killed, or enslaved, all to make sure your brother's okay."

It hadn't really felt like a choice, Magdalys realized, and certainly not heroic — just the most obvious thing to do. But when he put it like that, it did sound pretty wild.

"I hope you find him," Jack said, as something out in the woods started rustling toward them.

Jack and Hannibal pulled carbines from their saddle holsters. Magdalys stood, her mind already casting around for some sense of an approaching dino. Before she could figure it out, the proudly crested head of a parasaurolophus emerged from the trees, followed by Card's stern, scarred face.

"Air cavalry," he yelled, pulling his mount into a quick canter alongside them. "Haven't had time to alert the officers yet. Don't wait for orders. They'll be on us any minute." He galloped on ahead. "Get into battle formation. Now!"

CHAPTER TWELVE
AIR ATTACK

"**LOAD THE BULL** pups!" Big Jack hollered as Hannibal yanked on the reins, pulling the trike into a sharp turn so it blocked the dirt road. The squeals of dinos and iron clanking into place rose around them.

Magdalys couldn't be sure, but it looked like some of the other mounts had pulled into position without anyone guiding them. She wondered if they'd been trained to follow what the other dinos did around them or . . .

"Sol, we need shells and powder!" Jack yelled. "Mason, get ready to mount these up. Someone pass word to the back that things are about to get hot."

"What can I do?" Magdalys asked.

"Take cover," Hannibal said, hopping down onto the road

and rummaging through one of the saddlebags. "Stay alive so you can find your brother."

Magdalys didn't like that answer, but he had a point: The dinos had all been wrangled and there was no way she or Mapper could help set anything up. Plus, the Native Guard clearly had that under control. They moved with sparkling efficiency, barely saying a word between them as they fell into action, each soldier playing his part.

"Shells!" Sol pulled up beside them on a long, low to the ground creature with a huge fin cresting along its scaly back. *A dimetrodon*, Magdalys realized. She'd never seen one before. Munitions cases had been slung along its flanks with leather straps, and Sol hopped off and immediately began heaving them up on the trike with some effort.

"Where's that bull pup?" Big Jack yelled, easily grasping one of the cases in a single hand.

"Here!" another soldier yelled, riding up on another fin-back, this one with a cannon strapped to either side of it. "Sorry, this one didn't want to get moving."

Big Jack and Hannibal hopped down and unstrapped one of the cannons.

"Bull pups?" Magdalys asked, trying to stay out of the way.

"Mountain howitzers," Hannibal said as he and Jack lifted one. "Oof! That's just what we call 'em."

"Shouldn't you be taking cover?" Big Jack asked, grabbing up the other cannon in his free hand while he helped Hannibal with the first one.

"I told her to!" Hannibal said between pants.

"Aim for the sun, boys!" Jack called. Around them, troops were mounting the howitzers on either side of their trikes' iron armor plates.

"Why the sun?" Mapper asked.

"Take cover, we said!" Jack snapped.

"Because," Hannibal said, heaving one of the cannons into position on the trike's armor and securing it in with a series of clicks and clacks, "air cavalry always try to attack from wherever the sun is, that way they get a clear shot and we have the sun in our eyes."

"Smart," Mapper said.

"DACTYL HILL SQUAD!" a voice thundered. "TAKE COVER IN THE SURROUNDING FOREST IMMEDIATELY!" It was Cailloux, the middle-aged corporal with the excellent mustache who had been calling the shots at the campfire the night before. He stood on a saddle a few trikes away and bellowed into a megaphone cone as Two Step, Amaya, and Sabeen dashed toward Magdalys and Mapper.

"We better get moving," Mapper said, pulling Magdalys toward the woods.

"We said to take cover how many times?" Big Jack grumbled, securing the second howitzer.

"You didn't call 'em out by their squad name," Hannibal pointed out with a grin.

Magdalys was just backing to the tree line when she saw the first shadow flicker over the troops. She was safely beneath the forest canopy a moment later when the second and third shadows passed, but Amaya, Sabeen, and Two Step were still sprinting toward her. "Run!" Magdalys yelled, but her voice was swallowed up by a rising murmur of commands and then the urgent *pop–pop–pop* of muskets all around her.

Sabeen reached the trees first, then Amaya. Two Step seemed to be running in slow motion, but Magdalys knew he was doing his best. Behind him, Hannibal swung the trike into position while Sol placed an iron ball into the mouth of the cannon and shoved it home with a ramrod.

Musket fire plinked against the iron trike armor and thunked into the dirt around Two Step as he ran. Up above, a half dozen dactyls flapped in an unruly cluster in front of the sun. Magdalys tried not to imagine Two Step getting hit, but the image kept coming anyway, his wounded body dropping just shy of the tree line, Magdalys helpless to do anything without getting torn up by enemy fire herself.

"Made it!" Two Step yelled, bursting into the woods past Magdalys and collapsing in a panting, sweaty heap just as Cailloux screamed "FIRE!" and the Louisiana Native Guard's bull pups burst to life one by one.

A series of deep booms sounded from down the road and then Magdalys saw Big Jack turn away from his cannon as he whipped a cord away from it and *ka-FWOOMbraaahhh!!* So much smoke poured out around him that at first Magdalys wasn't sure if he'd fired or been hit. Then the wind swept away most of it, and there was Big Jack, already setting up his next shot as Hannibal swabbed the inside of the cannon with a rag on a long stick.

"Sol!" a soldier called from the next trike up. "We need another round!" Sol was already back on his dimetrodon and guiding it gingerly along the dirt road.

The dactylriders had dispersed above them but were already swooping back into formation as they sent random bursts of musket fire in all directions. Most of them didn't seem to have much control over their mounts, Magdalys realized. Now that she could see them in the daylight, the Confederate Air Cavalry seemed like a desperate, chaotic mishmash of untrained riders, with only a few exceptions.

Magdalys closed her eyes, reaching out, and immediately a wave of frantic, irritated *fubba-fubbas* rolled over her. These were the enemy dactyls, but Magdalys could sense her own too, and they were coming up fast from somewhere nearby.

More gunfire erupted from above and Cailloux yelled "FIRE!" again and the cannons shredded the sky, sending dactyls tumbling and screeching away.

Except one, Magdalys noted. One rider seemed to know exactly what he was doing, and he maneuvered his dactyl deftly out of the way and then swung back over the Native Guard, firing shot after shot. The first three ricocheted off a trike's armor but the fourth and fifth hit the dirt near where Sol's finback was hauling the munitions cases.

The munitions cases! Magdalys realized. Panicked, she cast her mind out for the dactyl's and for the first time since she'd learned she could connect to these giant reptiles, she found herself rebuffed. No *fubba-fubba*, nothing at all. Magdalys stood, fists clenched, and watched in horror as the rider let off two more shots and then a sharp blast went off and with an ear-shattering *kaTHWOOM*, the whole world seemed to rip apart at the seams.

CHAPTER THIRTEEN
UP AND OVER

MAGDALYS LOOKED UP, the blast still echoing like a ghost cackling through a canyon in her ears. A charred crater smoldered in the road where Sol and his dimetrodon had been. The nearest trike had been knocked over by the blast, but it looked to be otherwise unhurt. Soldiers were staggering to their feet, shaking their heads and wiping dust out of their eyes.

"You guys okay?" Magdalys asked, looking around. Amaya, Sabeen, Two Step, and Mapper all nodded solemnly.

"Solomon?" Sabeen asked, peering past Magdalys.

She shook her head. "Don't look."

"There's nothing to even . . . see," Mapper blurted out, tears welling up. "There's nothing left."

Sabeen hugged Amaya, who just patted her head and frowned.

Magdalys glanced at Two Step. That look on his face — the wide-open broken one he'd had when he'd shot that trikerider back at the Penitentiary — it was nowhere to be seen. Instead, Two Step's brow was creased, his eyes narrowed to furious, fast-blinking slits.

"Easy," Magdalys said, putting her hands on his shoulders as they heaved up and down with each breath. "Easy, man."

More shots rang out. Disaster had struck and the battle wasn't even over. Magdalys whirled around just as another *ka-FWOOMshaaa* burst out from Hannibal and Jack's cannon. The smoke cleared, revealing them, covered in cuts and bruises, their blue uniforms in tatters as they frantically worked to clear the cannon mouth and reload it.

Then more shadows rippled over the trikes and troops and bullet-battered road: the Dactyl Hill dactyls. Magdalys gave a shout of joy and looked up just in time to see them smashing into what was left of the enemy cavalry, scattering them every which way.

"I want to . . ." Two Step seethed. Magdalys turned back to him. Tears streamed down his face. "I just want to . . ." He shook his head and she closed with him, pulling him into a hug that he didn't return. "I just . . ."

"I know," she said, although he hadn't finished his sentence. It was all over his face: Two Step wanted to kill. He had gone from a scared little boy, heartbroken at having been forced to take a life, to . . . this: an overflowing volcano of rage. She squeezed him harder as his shoulders heaved with silent sobs.

"They're dispersing," Card yelled, riding up on his para. He didn't sound happy about it though.

"Keep firing, men," Cailloux hollered. "We can't let them get away!"

"What is it?" Sabeen asked, stepping out of the woods. "What's happening?"

Magdalys squeezed Two Step one more time and then took his hand and walked out toward the road with him behind Amaya and Mapper.

"They've learned our position," Card said, pulling his mount to a halt. "If one gets back to Braxton Bragg's camp they'll hurl the full weight of his army at us."

"And the way we're spread out over the next twelve miles," Cailloux said as he hopped down from his trike, "it'll be nothing for him to outflank and smash us." Magdalys saw him glance at the crater where Sol and the finback had been and shake his head, eyes closed.

"I can . . ." Magdalys said, already quickening her pace as the *fubba-fubba-fooo* sound of the Brooklyn dactyls diving grew louder inside her. "Let me take a dactyl. Put a gunner on the back and we'll catch them."

Card swung his para around and squinted at her, his face somehow sharp and forlorn. He traded a glance with Cailloux, nodded. "Corporal Cailloux, send a squad into the woods beneath them to capture any survivors." Then he leaned forward and yelled, "Heeyah!" urging his mount off the road and back into the woods.

"Where are you going?" Cailloux yelled.

"Scout out the enemy position," Card called over his shoulder. "So we can smash them instead!" And then he was gone.

Magdalys watched him disappear into the trees and then turned to Cailloux as the others came up behind her. "Amaya," she said, "stay with Sabeen and Two Step."

Dactyls landed on the trikes nearby: one, two, three.

"I can —" Two Step started, but Magdalys spun on him.

"No. You have to stay," she said. "Don't fight me on this." Some kind of fire flashed in Two Step's eyes — a look Magdalys had never seen in him before, and for a second she thought he might lash out and take a swing. Then he seemed to crumple into himself as Amaya swooped in with her long arms and he put his face into her shoulder.

"Mapper," Magdalys said, breaking into a run toward the trikes. "You take the tall gray one."

"On it."

"Private Hannibal," Cailloux said, "go with Magda Lee. Private Rey!"

"Sir!" Octave Rey ran up from the still-downed trike and saluted just as Hannibal dusted himself off and headed toward Magdalys.

"Ride with the one they call Mapper. Stop those dactylriders!"

"Sir yes sir!" the two men shouted as Magdalys grasped the shoulder of the smaller blue dactyl and heaved herself onto its back.

"The one they call Mapper," Mapper said. "I like that."

This would be just like hopping rooftop to rooftop back in Dactyl Hill . . . except with no rooftops . . . and Rebel Air Cavalry trying to snipe them down . . . and nowhere safe to go if they got separated and stranded. Hannibal climbed on behind her just as the dactyl stretched to full height, flapping her wings and letting out a fierce caw.

"Go!" Hannibal yelled, already loading cartridges into his carbine. The dactyl began to climb. "Go!" Magdalys leaned forward, felt the dactyl's mind sharpen along with her own toward their singular purpose. And then they lifted into the air above the miles of marching troops and hurtled out over the treetops.

CHAPTER FOURTEEN
AIR CHASE

GRAPPLER, MAGDALYS DECIDED to call her new mount.

Up Grappler, she thought, clenching her jaw and leaning forward. *Up!*

The dactyl cawed and flapped once and then again with her long, graceful wings, taking them higher and higher in an arc so steep they were almost vertical to the ground. The Confederates wouldn't be expecting any pursuit by air. Magdalys wanted to see what she was up against before they had a chance to get away. In the corner of her eye, she saw Mapper following close behind them and a little off to the side as Octave prepped his weapon.

"Alright, I get it!" Hannibal yelled against the shrieking

wind. "You're one of those dinotalking freaks from the days of old or whatever!"

Magdalys growled. "Oh, we're freaks, are we?" Grappler steepened her climb even more.

"I mean! In a good way!"

Magdalys allowed herself a slight chuckle and kept climbing. "Don't tell me you're scared, Private Hannibal."

"Never, Miss Roca!"

Up they sped.

"Okay, maybe occasionally," Hannibal allowed, but Magdalys was already tilting Grappler back into an open soar. Below, Mapper had leveled out too and was scanning the treetops for enemy flyers.

There.

Three pteros flapped in a triangle formation off to one side while two more fled in the opposite direction. Magdalys recognized the one she'd seen wield his mount better than all the others to take out Sol. She grimaced at the memory — the shredding, impossible boom of that blast; the crater — then tried to shake it away. "Mapper!" she called, then pointed three fingers at the retreating trio. He nodded, veered his mount after them.

"Why give them all the glory of taking out three?" Hannibal said as Magdalys took Grappler into a long-ranging dive toward the other two cavalrymen.

"This all a game to you, huh?" she said, still fighting back the sheer, impossible emptiness of the space Sol had once been in. Sure, the men they were talking about probably killing would kill them first in a heartbeat but . . . she didn't know how he could be so lighthearted about it.

Hannibal was quiet for a few moments, and all Magdalys heard were the clicks and clacks of metal over the whispering wind as he unfolded a portable shaft and placed it on Grappler's back to steady his aim.

"No," he finally said quietly. "None of it is. It's life and death, but when that's all there is, every day, and maybe all there ever will be, the only thing you can do to keep going is make peace with it or it'll eat you alive."

Magdalys didn't know what to say. She wasn't being fair and she knew it; who was she to judge how a soldier did his job? The first dead body she'd seen had been Mr. Calloway, the caretaker at the orphanage, who'd been hanged by a mob the night of the riots, and that hadn't been that long ago. Hannibal had probably already lost track of the death that had piled up around him.

"Bring us into a glide behind them," Hannibal said. "I don't expect you to understand it, sis. I don't even understand it, and I been in the thick of it for the past year. But I know I gotta keep moving, no matter what — we all do — and I'ma keep doing whatever I have to do to do that. Duck, please."

Up ahead, the two flyers had widened the gap between each other, almost to the point that they were flying in different directions.

"The green-and-gray one," Magdalys said. "That's the reason we're going after these two and not the other three. If you have to get one and not the other, get —"

She was interrupted by two shots exploding over her head in quick succession. Up ahead, *both* dactyls shrieked and spun out of control, one of them throwing its rider into the trees below with a yelp.

"Forgot to mention that I taught your brother everything he knows," Hannibal said with what Magdalys was sure was a smirk.

"Not bad," she said, "but that one's still going."

The green-and-gray dactyl had pulled back into a lopsided flutter, its rider frantically pulling himself into the saddle. The other flapped crookedly downward and disappeared beneath the canopy of leaves.

Magdalys gazed down, urging Grappler after them. *Had the man died?* From the way his dactyl tumbled out of sight, it looked like the bullet had winged it, probably without hitting the rider. But a fall like that could surely kill someone, right?

Blam! The Confederate cavalryman's pistol sang out over the wind. They hadn't been hit — that dactyl was flying too erratically to get any kind of steady shot — but it snapped Magdalys back into focus.

"You with me, Mags?" Hannibal said, positioning his carbine again.

She nodded, swooping them a little lower so they could come up at the rider from below.

"What's so special about this guy anyway?"

"He's a freak like m—" Magdalys started to say, but then the dactyl executed an impressive roll just as Hannibal let off another shot, swooping out the way and then diving suddenly into the trees.

"That!" Magdalys growled.

"How in the —"

"Dive!" yelled Magdalys, and Grappler's ecstatic *fuuuuuu* lanced through her mind as the forest raced up to greet them.

CHAPTER FIFTEEN
BENEATH THE CANOPY

BRANCHES RAKED SHARPLY against Magdalys's face for the second time in as many days, but at least it was daylight and her dactyl hadn't been shot from under her.

Not yet, anyway. A few more cracks rang out from the woods ahead of them, one smashing loudly into a tree barely a foot away.

"Yikes," Hannibal said dryly. "This guy won't quit. Can you bring us a little lower so I don't get my eyes gouged out?"

"Working on it," Magdalys grunted. She dipped Grappler down further, below the thickest cluster of branches, swung into a hard roll to avoid a maple tree and then swooped between two bifurcating trunks. Another shot whizzed past, shattering a twig to her right, and then she caught movement up ahead. The rider had perched his dactyl on a sturdy branch and dismounted to take potshots, and now he was clambering back on.

"No, you don't," Magdalys whispered, urging Grappler straight for them.

"What'd you say?" Hannibal said. "Oh my —"

Grappler whipped to the side of another tree, pulling her wings tight to her body at the last second, and then flicked them out and back again in a sudden flap that sent them bursting through a thick mesh of foliage. She ducked her head just as they emerged and rammed the bony crest on her forehead straight into the enemy dactyl before it could take off.

The dactyl flung forward in a messy tangle of wings and claws and the rider went tumbling through the underbrush with a yell, crashed through snapping branches and twigs all the way down, and then thudded heavily on the forest floor below.

"Down," Magdalys said to Grappler just as Hannibal folded up the carbine stabilizer and yelled, "After him!"

They swooshed into a dive, Grappler arching her rear legs beneath her and slowing with a tilt of her wings as they approached the writhing soldier.

"Get back!" the man yelled, and Magdalys spotted the glint of light on the barrel of his raised pistol. Grappler had come up on him fast though; she landed with a claw pinning each of his arms to the ground.

Ka-BLAM!! The pistol went off, sending a bullet crackling through the woods off to the side. Hannibal slid out of the saddle and snatched the gun out of the man's hand. Magdalys climbed down and signaled Grappler that she could step back.

A scraggly goatee framed the Confederate's long face. He wore a dirty gray uniform with two bars on the sleeve that Magdalys was pretty sure meant he was an officer of some kind. One leg lay twisted beneath him at an unfortunate angle. His bright blue eyes blinked up at Magdalys and Hannibal and his breath came in short, desperate pants. "Shoulda figured I'd be captured by two —"

Hannibal cut the man off with the sound of his own six-shooter cocking a round into the chamber. "I'm guessing you don't want to finish that sentence," Hannibal said, leveling the pistol between the Confederate's suddenly wide eyes.

"Never did like the dang Confederacy anyway," he grumbled. "Dunno how I ended up in this ol' mess."

"Oh yeah," Hannibal sighed. "All y'all just *hate* the Confederacy once you end up on the wrong end of a pistol. That was the fastest tune change I've heard yet though. Mags, search him."

Magdalys blinked for a second, then nodded and gingerly started patting down the man's pockets and supply belt for anything that felt like a gun or knife.

"Name and rank," Hannibal demanded.

"Lieutenant Hardy L. Hewpat."

"You one of Bragg's men?"

Hewpat snorted up something nasty and blood-tinged and hocked it into the grass. "That demented hack! Never! I'm with General Forrest's Tennessee Air Cavalry, 3rd Division, the Smokys' Fighting Finest!"

"Alright, alright," Hannibal snapped. "Didn't ask for all that. Got anything, Mags?"

She stood and shook her head, then stared Hewpat in his laughing eyes. "How do you know how to dinowrangle so well?"

"Heh," Hewpat chuckled. "We're the finest flyers this side of the Missi —"

"No," Magdalys said. "You. How do *you* know? These others weren't as good."

He smirked. "I mean, that's mighty kind of you, but . . ."

"Answer the question," Hannibal growled. "You don't have much choice, in case you hadn't noticed."

"Don't I?" Hewpat closed his eyes and took a deep breath.

"What happened?" Hannibal said. "He dying?"

Magdalys squinted at him. The high-pitched *fuuu* sounded like it was coming from a hundred miles away but closing fast. A twig snapped from somewhere up above and then a vision of what was about to happen exploded like a firework in her mind. There wasn't time to explain to Hannibal. She shoved him out of the way, pulling his bayonet blade out of its sheath as she passed him and then swinging it with both hands in a wide upward arc across her body as the Confederate dactyl came screeching down at her.

The blade sheared a bright red gash across its belly and the dactyl yelped and hurled itself off to the side, slashing Magdalys's arm as it went. It crashed into the dirt a few feet away and scrambled to its feet, blood weeping freely from the bayonet wound. The dactyl let out a fierce caw and lurched toward Magdalys, snapping with its armor-plated beak.

Magdalys took one step back, bayonet raised, and then a blue-and-gray blur blasted out of the woods and slammed full force into the dactyl, lifting it clear into the air.

"Grappler!" Magdalys yelled. Grappler held the enemy dactyl in her claws just long enough to send it barreling into a tree trunk with a mighty *THUNK!* The dactyl slid to the ground and landed in a pile of broken limbs sticking out in all the wrong directions.

"Lil' Calhoun, baby! No!" Hewpat gasped. "My baby!"

Grappler flapped to a sturdy branch above them and gazed serenely off into the distance.

"You killed Lil' Calhoun!"

Magdalys realized Hannibal was staring at her. "You . . . saved my life."

She shook her head, held up his bayonet with the point facing herself. "Grappler saved us both. Here."

He took it and nodded his thanks, still blinking like the sun had just risen in the middle of the night.

"Y'all savages gonna kill me already or what?" Hewpat said between pants. "Might as well, seeing as how you murdered poor Lil' Calhoun."

Hannibal sheathed the bayonet. "Stop talking. And no, we're not going to kill you. We're bringing you back to Major General Sheridan so you two can have a long talk about what you know."

CHAPTER SIXTEEN
WHOA BEANS

SOMEONE ELSE LIKE *me*, Magdalys thought as they flew just beneath the foliage with Lieutenant Hewpat trussed up and slung over the back of Grappler. There was no other explanation: the cavalryman had been wrangling his ptero just like Magdalys did. That was why she couldn't even reach out to his mount as he was attacking Sol. That was why he flew so much better than the others, and how he'd had Lil' Calhoun attack them right when he needed help.

She shook her head. There were others like her. Who knew how many? What if . . . the image of an unstoppable surge of Confederate raptors and pteroriders came billowing into her mind.

"There!" Hannibal yelled, pointing down at a perfectly still lump of gray and pink down below.

"Rosworth!" Hewpat yelled, writhing against his bindings. "Aw, Rosworth! You murderers! You killed Rosworth!"

Rosworth was indeed dead, Magdalys realized as they glided slowly over his contorted body and empty eyes. She shuddered.

"He had two children," Hewpat moaned. "And a pretty young wife, Sarahbelle."

Magdalys tried not to imagine them, but the vision surfaced anyway: a gram delivered by minidactyl; a white woman in a fancy pink dress with curly hair opening it, two squirming kids by her side, their little faces contorting as they found out their daddy wouldn't be coming home.

Their daddy who would've killed Magdalys in a heartbeat and was fighting to keep her people enslaved. The whole world seemed to spin and tilt around her and she felt like she might hurl up the hardtack they'd had for breakfast over the side.

"Quiet," Hannibal ordered, and Magdalys silently repeated the command to her own troubled mind. "All it takes is one tip of this ptero and you will have a sudden reunion with the ground, Hewbert."

"Hewpat!"

"What's that?" Hannibal said, rocking Grappler back and forth a few times. "I didn't hear you over the sound of me being about to toss you over the side."

"Nothing!"

Less than an hour ago, Magdalys thought, they'd all been singing a battle hymn along with Octave's coronet, marching through the sunlight on trikeback. Solomon had been alive. So had Rosworth. And now . . . the world seemed to spin faster and faster around her.

"What happens now?" she asked, guiding Grappler back up through the canopy of leaves into the open sky.

"Ol' boy will get interrogated," Hannibal said, "and sent to a prison camp and probably released in a few months for political reasons or some nonsense and be back taking potshots at us from the air."

"That's messed up," Magdalys said, "but I meant . . ." She shrugged and gazed down at the peaks and valleys sprawling beneath them.

"Oh, Private Solomon?"

She nodded, relieved at not having to explain herself. The long stretch of bright blue sky seemed to slow the spin of the world. Magdalys took a deep breath.

"He's dead. There's nothing to bury, from what I could tell, so we'll just hold a ceremony tonight by the campfire and that'll be that."

"I mean . . ."

"If we was back in New Orleans, we'd throw him a big ol' marching band funeral — a second line, it's called — and Octave and the boys would play some of the finest music you ever heard. Not that straight-laced military band nonsense, I mean *real* music, and everyone would come out from their houses and join the party, cuz it *would* be a party. And it'd feel like the whole world was there, celebrating, and even the trikes and stegos would be decorated and covered in sparkly outfits and streamers as they hauled that empty casket all along the avenue to the cemetery."

"Sounds beautiful," Magdalys said, breathing deeply again, letting the world slow back down even more.

"That's what I was trying to say earlier, Mags. That's how we do death down there. My folks anyway. My family's been part of the Mardi Gras Indians for ages —"

"The what?"

"Hard to explain. It's like a club, you know? We make these beautiful feathered outfits and we know how to make a funeral right. It's a celebration, not because they died but because they lived, whoever they were. And that's how we gotta do it here in the war too. Solomon lived. He was a pain in the butt sometimes, but he had a girlfriend on Iberville who'll be sad he's gone, and a married white society lady who'll probably be even more sad he's gone, but that's another story —"

"Wait . . ."

"And he had the best handwriting of all of us and folks in the Guard would dictate letters back home to him." Hannibal shrugged. "If we stopped to mourn each death, we'd be the next one to die, and what good would that do poor Sol? So we just gotta keep moving."

Magdalys nodded, breathed, nodded. "I'm sorry about what I said before. I made it sound like you don't care about what you do and that's not fair. I . . . I really don't know what I'm talking about."

"It's arright," Hannibal said, his Louisiana drawl growing longer with thoughts of home. "You made up for it by saving my life, so we even now."

Up ahead, two dactyls swooped out of the trees. Magdalys squinted at them, but Hannibal had already pulled out his spyglass. "That's Octave on one." He chuckled. "Looks like he lassoed himself a Rebel. Got him trussed up on the back just like ours. Guess he still getting the hang of riding that thing though."

"Is Mapper on the other?" Magdalys asked, trying not to sound desperate. In all the commotion, she had forgotten her friend was off having his own adventures.

"Yeah, your little buddy's alright. He got himself a Rebel too! Wonder where the third one is. . . ."

"Probably reaching our lines right now!" Hewpat yelled from behind them.

"Quiet, Hewbert!" Hannibal yelled. "When we're curious about your opinion we'll drop you over the side and ask whatever's left on the ground."

"Ayyy!" Magdalys called, urging Grappler forward behind the other two dactyls. Hannibal was right about Octave — his mount swooped and scuttled in that ungainly way they had when they knew a rider had no idea what they were doing.

Mapper glanced back and a wide smile broke out on his face. "Mag-D!" he yelled, waving, and the dactyl he was riding swerved sharply to the side, nearly tossing him. "Whoa! Easy, Beans!" He wrapped both arms around its neck and clung on as his mount glided back into position.

He named the dactyl Beans? Magdalys just stared at him wide-eyed. "Mapper, careful, man!" she yelled.

"Good hunting, Private Hannibal?" Octave asked, rearing his dactyl back some so it flew neck and neck with Grappler. On the back, a kid about Hannibal's age, all in Confederate grays, lay unconscious, his hands and feet expertly bound up and a shiny blue lump rising on his face.

"Excellent, Private Rey," Hannibal said. "One captured; one didn't survive the fall."

"Mags!" Mapper said, pulling Beans along the other side of them. "Octave has a lasso! And he straight up just lassoed a dude! Two dudes!"

"Told ya," Hannibal said.

"And one other dude tried to get away and fell so like, he didn't make it, but Octave lassoed the other two like . . . Whew! Like cattle, Mags! And then he like, reeled 'em in and trussed 'em up and —"

Mapper's dactyl lurched suddenly upward, throwing Mapper backward on top of the tied-up Confederate. "Whoa!" Mapper yelled. "Be cool, Beans! Be cool!"

"What's happening?" Magdalys called, sending Grappler after them. "Mapper!"

Beans surged forward; Magdalys could see Mapper still trying to untangle himself and find something to grab on to, his hands flailing as the Confederate struggled and cursed. Then the dactyl squawked and spun into a barrel roll, sending them both over the side.

CHAPTER SEVENTEEN
TRIP, TANGLE, TRUSS

"**GRAB ANYTHING!**" **MAGDALYS** yelled as Mapper's feet flew out from under him and he tumbled off the dactyl.

"Gah!" the Confederate yelled. Octave had secured his hands to the saddle and now he dangled by his wrists in midair, Mapper grasping on to his waist for dear life. "Let go of me, kid!"

"Hold tight!" Magdalys yelled. "We're coming!" Beans had lurched off again, flushing down and then back up in a messy zigzag through the sky. Magdalys sent Grappler racing after them as Octave spurred his mount on behind.

"If I could just . . ." Magdalys said out loud as they came up behind Beans. She concentrated as hard as she could, reaching out for Beans's mind, grasping for any hint of his thoughts or even a single *fubba* to let her know she was on the right track.

Nothing.

She was blocked out just like she'd been from Lieutenant Hewpat's dactyl earlier.

Of course!

"Hewpat!" the Confederate dangling from Beans yelled. "That you, Lieutenant? Can you . . . can you right us, sir?"

Magdalys pulled Grappler directly below Mapper and the Confederate. "Mapper! Drop!"

"Are you su—" Mapper started to say and then Beans spiraled into a steep dive. "AAAAAAAAAAAH!!"

"Hewpaaaaaat!" the Confederate yelled.

He knows the lieutenant can control dinos, Magdalys thought, sending Grappler after them again. "Private Hannibal," she said, "what's Hewpat doing?"

The air rushed past as Grappler swooped over the trees and came swinging down alongside Beans again.

"He's got his eyes closed and his brow furrowed," Hannibal reported.

"You have to —" Magdalys paused as she noticed Octave's dactyl gliding straight toward them and Beans. "You have to break his concentration somehow! Distract him! He's controlling that dactyl!"

"AAAAAAAAH!!" Mapper yelled.

"HEWPAAAAAT!" the Confederate yelled.

Octave was doing something with his hands that she couldn't quite make out. His dactyl made straight for Beans, then swung to the side at the last second, and something long and black whipped through the air from below and tightened around Mapper.

"Yow!" Magdalys yelled, raising herself on the saddle to see better as Mapper was yanked away from Beans and went hurtling through the air with a wild yelp on the end of Octave's lasso.

From behind her, a heavy thunk sounded. Beans flipped right side up and shook his head, blinking like he'd just woken up from a pleasurable nap.

Octave reeled Mapper in, hand-over-handing it as Mapper giggled uncontrollably.

Magdalys glanced back. Hewpat sat slumped over, a nasty lump growing shiny on his left temple. Hannibal turned to Magdalys; he had the lieutenant's six-shooter by the muzzle, grip out.

"You pistol-whipped him?" Magdalys asked, blinking.

Hannibal shrugged. "You said distract him."

"I said break his concentration, not his forehead!"

"I mean . . . it worked."

"Mags!" Mapper yelled as Octave flew up beside them, shaking his head. "Mags! Oh my god! Did you see that?"

"Did I ever," she sighed, reaching out for Beans in her mind. The familiar *fubba-fubba* sounded, if a little tentative and confused now. She nodded at the others and one by one they sped through the air back to the Union lines.

PART TWO

CHICKAMAUGA

CHAPTER EIGHTEEN
BACK AT THE LINES

"**M**AGS." **HANNIBAL'S HAND** wrapped around her forearm. It wasn't too tight, but between his sudden grip and that quiet, urgent voice, almost a whisper, she knew something had finally broken that cocky exterior. His brow furrowed, eyes squinting like he could sense the answer to all that was troubling somewhere off in the distance but couldn't make it out.

"What is it?"

The procession's easygoing stride from that morning had ratcheted up into a fierce quickstep since the attack. Around them, soldiers and dinos alike glanced to either side and skyward as they marched along the dirt path between the southern Appalachian peaks. No one cracked jokes; no one sang. The only sounds to be heard were the endless stomps and shuffles of dinos beneath the chimes of their clanking armor, and, from some far-off, peaceful part of the forest, birds singing back and forth to each other in the trees.

"It's true then, isn't it?" Hannibal said, his face a tight fist, waiting for a blow.

They fell into stride with the ongoing river of troops. Magdalys cocked her head at him. They'd handed the prisoners over to Young Card, who'd called for a medic to cart off the still-unconscious Hewpat and escorted the other two to General Sheridan for interrogation. Octave had gone along to give his report, and Magdalys figured she'd be summoned soon, but she'd wanted to take a moment to get herself together before facing Sheridan again.

Clearly, that wasn't going to happen. "What's true?" There were so many things he could've been referring to. So many possibilities dancing through the air, most of them terrible.

"You're a . . . you can . . ."

Ah, that. Magdalys's face hardened. "That I'm a freak, you mean?"

Her friend Redd's words always echoed through her head at moments like these: *Girl, say it loud. Otherwise how you gonna get even better at it?* It still wasn't easy, but she was trying. Even with the crew having already talked her powers up and Hannibal having had a pretty clear demonstration of them just now — there was no telling how someone would react. He *had* called her a freak, after all, though she could tell there wasn't much conviction behind it.

Hannibal cringed. "I was . . . I just . . ."

She smiled. "It's alright. I didn't take it too personally."

He seemed to deflate some. *"Too?"*

"And anyway, yes."

A look flashed across Hannibal's face, something between fear and awe, Magdalys thought, then acceptance as it resolved back into that determined frown he'd started with.

"And that's why we went after Hewpat." A statement, not a question. Good. He wasn't wasting time or going all mushy about it.

She nodded, waiting for him to put the rest of it together.

"And he's . . . too?"

"That's what it looks like. . . ." She shook her head. There wasn't time to second-guess anymore. "He is. I first noticed cuz I tried to reach his dactyl to stop them from attacking Sol but . . . I couldn't."

A wave of emotion sizzled through her — some vicious cocktail of regret, sorrow, helplessness, and rage. She let it rise and then pass, then wondered if she was already becoming more like these men and boys who'd lived with carnage as their daily bread for so many months.

Hannibal nodded, still squinting, and she almost could see the gears turning in his mind.

"And then he got to the dactyl Mapper was riding. And the worst part is —"

"The other Reb knew he could do it," Hannibal finished for her.

"Exactly!" Magdalys yelled.

"Which means . . ."

"The Confederates might be developing other dino-wranglers with the same ability."

Hannibal froze in his tracks, and soldiers peeled to either side of him, grumbling. He searched the dinobacks around them, then called out: "Corporal Cailloux, sir!"

Cailloux peered over from his trike, nodded at Hannibal. "Yes, Private?"

"Permission to advance to the front of the regiment for a word with the major general, sir?"

Cailloux nodded, barked, "Granted!" and the two traded a salute.

"C'mon," Hannibal said, grabbing Magdalys's hand and shoving his way through the soldiers he'd just made pass him.

"What are we doing?" Magdalys asked.

"They'll be interrogating the captives," Hannibal said. "I gotta let them know what we may be up against."

There was really no way to grasp the full giganticness of an army from inside its camp, Magdalys realized. It just felt like a big ol' cluster of folks and tents and bonfires. But make your way through the miles and miles of marching men and clomping dinos? This was just a single division and it seemed to go on forever.

Up ahead, the afternoon sun had started to slide through the sky, throwing the soldiers' shadows behind them like long, dancing spirits. If they were marching toward the setting sun, Magdalys figured, that meant they were heading west. West toward the Mississippi, which went straight down to New Orleans where Montez was. Maybe. It all seemed so slow and impossible and hopeless.

"So, you're with us, then, right?" Hannibal said as they passed a group of stegosauruses hauling wagons full of dinofeed amidst a sea of blue-uniformed troops.

"Huh?"

"I'm sure the major general asked you to join up. Everyone knows he's been champing at the bit to get Washington to give him permission to start an air cavalry. And you have dactyls *and* that mystical skill of yours. . . ."

Magdalys frowned, shook her head. "I . . ." She shrugged, knowing that wasn't explanation enough.

"Mags, we —"

"Yes, you need me," she snapped. "He gave me the whole shpiel. I just . . ." Cymbeline's worried face crossed her mind. "I'm just a kid, Hannibal."

"So am I," he pointed out.

"And look: You had to ask someone permission just to walk forward in the line. You can't go anywhere they don't tell you to go, do anything they don't tell you to do. They *own* you, Hannibal."

Shock flashed across his face and then he shook his head.

"It's not the same thing if you're the one who chooses to take part in it."

"I just don't . . . If I muster in . . ."

"How will you run off and save your brother?"

Magdalys looked away, a twist of shame gnawing at her.

"Mags, we all got brothers and sisters in danger."

She thought about David Ballantine in Dactyl Hill, who organized with the Vigilance Committee and had told her just before she left that he'd lost a younger brother. He hadn't elaborated, but he didn't need to — the never-ending ache was right there in his eyes. And Cymbeline's brother, Halsey Crunk, who was probably wondering if she was safe too. "You . . . you got a sibling?"

Hannibal laughed sadly, shaking his head. "Yeah, but that's not what I meant, girl. This thing bigger than you or me. It's not just we, the army, who need you. We," he said again slowly this time, "*all* got brothers and sisters in danger right now, Mags. They need your help."

Those scars crisscrossing Big Jack's back. The plantation they'd flown over the night before. Magdalys sighed, feeling those embers within crackle. *Not now*, she thought, dampening the flames. Without meaning to, she'd shoved the truth of slavery as far back in her mind as she could, if nothing else because the enormity of it felt like it would knock her over if she thought about it too much, like she'd never be able to make it through the day or even get out of bed if she really sat and pondered all the human beings in bondage. And the truth was it made her feel guilty, on top of everything else. Why should she be free when so many of her people were enslaved?

She nodded. Hannibal was right, she just didn't know what to do with that truth. "I know," she finally said, the words woefully inadequate beside the hugeness of how she felt. "I just . . . I don't trust these guys either." They'd passed the stegos and moved into a battalion of paras, stomping along in that smooth, wavy gait of theirs as the riders eyed the surrounding forest. "They're not fighting for us, Hannibal. It wasn't long ago these same folks owned our people themselves. And they don't even pay y'all equal wages!" At the orphanage, Mr. Calloway had told them stories about growing up in bondage on a provisional farm in upstate New York. She still had nightmares about it sometimes. Then again, he never stopped talking about how proud he was that his only son was serving in the Army of the Potomac.

"I know that," Hannibal said. "We all know that. And we don't trust 'em. Well, Octave and I don't. Cailloux probably don't either but he's an officer so he keeps his mouth shut. And sure, Big Jack thinks the Union Army's the best thing to happen since Moses, but they freed him from a plantation outside Baton Rouge, so he can feel however he wants about 'em, far as I can tell."

"Were you . . ." Magdalys's voice trailed off. None of the words seemed right somehow.

"Nah," Hannibal said. "But being who we is, where we are? Might wake up free, find yourself in chains when the sun sets.

I dunno why these cats fighting, Mags." He nodded at the all-white battalion of parariders. "But that's why *I* fight."

The ongoing thunder and clank of hundreds of armored dinos on the march seemed to coalesce into a single steady pulse that Magdalys could feel rattle up her spine.

"Whoa," Magdalys said as they came up on the back end of a huge sauropod plodding along with mounted trikeriders on either side. "I didn't know y'all rolled with a diplodocus!"

She felt the earth shudder with each clomp of the huge dino's armored feet. The diplo was even more gigantic than the brachiosaurus she'd ridden the night of the Manhattan riots, basically running the length of two city blocks. In the Dinoguide, Dr. Barlow Sloan talked about it with undisguised awe and said it was one of the biggest animals to ever live.

"Yeah, that's one of the command dinos. They have to make sure he stay low when we're trying to keep our moves a little undercover though." He pointed to where the diplo's neck stretched straight ahead instead of up into the air. Magdalys spotted a fabric-wrapped chain slung around it just below the head and connecting to the saddle of a trike marching along beneath it.

She scowled. "Can't be comfortable."

"Actually," Hannibal pointed out, "that's the natural position for a diplo. They're more long than tall. It's brachys that like to have their necks sticking straight up."

Made sense that the New York fire brigades would use brachys then, Magdalys thought, to be able to reach high-up windows. Plus, a diplo probably wouldn't fit in the Manhattan streets.

"That's just there to keep them from poking up now and then when they get curious. Can't give the Rebs any more chance to spot us, can we?"

"You know a lot about dinos, huh?"

He shrugged. "I'm in a mounted artillery division. Kinda have to."

Hannibal saluted the guards and led Magdalys up into the saddle. There, Cymbeline stood, shotgun in hand, eyes darting from tree to tree. Behind her, a group of officers gathered around someone slumped over in the chair he'd been tied to.

"Wait here," Hannibal said. "I'll go talk to the major general." He nodded at Cymbeline and walked away.

"Hey," Cymbeline said.

Magdalys pursed her lips.

CHAPTER NINETEEN
BATTLEFIELD SISTERHOOD

"**Y**EAH, WELL . . ." All the sharp retorts she'd been cultivating for this moment fell away. Instead Magdalys just wrapped the older girl in a hug. The boom that ended Sol echoed through her once again as she saw that Confederate falling to his death and the made-up version of his wife and kids sobbing.

"I'm so sorry," Cymbeline whispered.

"You lied to us," Magdalys said, the heat of that betrayal suddenly rising in her again. She stepped back, wiped her eyes.

"I just didn't —"

Magdalys cut her off with a look.

Cymbeline sagged. "I know. I'm sorry. I . . ." She shook her head.

"But?"

"Not but: and."

"Huh?"

"Look," Cymbeline said, one hand landing on her hip, her eyes sharpening. "I *am* sorry I lied, and yes, coming along without telling you I was in contact with the Union Army was a lie, *and* I want, no: I *need* you to understand that I had to."

"*Had* to?" Magdalys's voice stayed just below a yell. The last thing they needed was a bunch of people gaping at them arguing in the middle of a war zone.

"Yes. It's not because I don't trust you, or care about you. Of course I do. *And* I swore an oath *and* me being what I am puts everyone in danger —"

"ALL THE MORE REASON WE NEEDED TO KNOW THAT!" Magdalys exploded, onlookers suddenly unimportant.

"Except that what puts everyone in even more danger than me *being* a spy," Cymbeline growled in a whisper, "is everyone *knowing* I'm a spy. Don't you see, Magdalys? If we were captured, and they somehow figured out what I am, and *you* knew too, they'd then try to get information out of you, out of you all . . . they'd . . ." She blinked away some tears, took a deep breath. "They'd torture you, Magdalys. All of you."

"Then why come at all?" Magdalys demanded, blinking her own tears away. "Why bother?"

"Because you were about to fly into the most danger-ous war zone on the planet all by yourselves and you're only twelve!"

"I . . ."

"And not only that, you want to fly *all the way across* it to the single Union-occupied city in the South — a city entirely surrounded by armies that want you and me dead or in chains. I came because I love you and care about you, Magdalys, and I don't want you to get killed. And I also have my duty and the oath I swore, and that includes not revealing my identity to *anyone*. Sometimes what you love and what you have to do don't get along. If I could've told you, I would've." She put her hand over her eyes and shook her head. "I'm sorry."

Magdalys watched the trikes trodding along below, the graceful swoosh of the duster fans herding those ghostly clouds out into the forest around them on either side, the weary sol-diers. *Sometimes what you love and what you have to do don't get along.* This was *exactly* what she'd been trying to tell Hannibal about why she didn't want to sign her life away. She felt the steady thud of the diplo rumble beneath her. "Does Halsey know?" she finally asked.

"Only because he mustered in with me." Cymbeline wiped her eyes one last time and looked down at Magdalys. "The whole thing was his idea actually. 'We're actors!' he said." She smiled sadly. "'We'll make great spies!' Turns out acting and lying use two different muscles. He's a genius onstage. When there's life and limb on the line — not so much. Plus, they made him pose as someone's slave."

"Oof," Magdalys said.

"Yeah, it was a whole lot. He didn't. . . . It didn't work out too well for him. Kinda messed him up, actually. So he got himself evaluated and they put him on medical leave."

Magdalys thought about Halsey — the smell of alcohol that seemed to stay on him like a cologne, the way he kept sobbing and couldn't pull it together the night of the riots. They'd burned his life's work to the ground right in front of him, so it made sense, but still. . . . He had only sharpened again when he started performing Shakespeare at the Bochinche bar in Dactyl Hill. "But they could call him back in anytime they want," Cymbeline said. "If they decide he's okay enough to be made not okay again."

Without thinking about it, Magdalys found herself hugging Cymbeline. They were even more alike than she'd thought, she realized, taking in her friend's flowery scent and feeling those arms wrap around her. They'd both had brothers wounded by the war and ended up in the battlefield themselves.

"I hate this war," Magdalys whispered.

"I know," Cymbeline said. "Me too. But I hate the world that was before it even more."

Magdalys nodded into her friend's shirt.

"Agent Crunk," Corporal Buford's voice blared out behind them.

Magdalys whirled on him. "How many times does she have to tell you not to broadcast that information across god's creation?"

Buford blinked at her, mouth hanging slightly open. "I ah . . . you, erm, are both requested, your presence, that is, in the major general . . . 's presence." He creased his brow. "Forthwith."

CHAPTER TWENTY
WAR COUNCIL

A TALL, GRIM-FACED SOLDIER passed Magdalys and Cymbeline as they made their way toward Sheridan; the Confederate who had almost toppled off Beans was slung over one of his shoulders, sputtering tearful apologies to no one in particular.

"Yikes," Magdalys said, glancing back, and then all five feet four inches of Major General Sheridan seemed to materialize in a fast-talking blur before them, his eyes all a-twinkle with whatever intrigue was at hand.

"My good young Magadis," he chattered with a head nod, then ran a fast circle around them, appearing in front of Cymbeline before Magdalys could even correct him on her name. "And the renowned young thespian." He kissed her hand with a dashing bow. Sheridan was all decked out in his double-breasted dress jacket. "The battle is anon, my ladies, come this way at once!"

"What battle?" Cymbeline asked.

"That remains to be seen, I'm afraid. But I'm sure we'll find out soon enough." Sheridan led them to a table where several of his commanders stood glowering at each other. The gentle rise and fall of the diplo's thunderous stride had been disorienting at first, Magdalys thought, but already she could feel herself getting used to it; something like the rocking of a boat at sea. None of the officers seemed to notice that their strategy table kept going up and down as they glared at it. Octave and Hannibal stood a little to the back.

"What'd you find out from the prisoner?" Magdalys asked. "Did you ask him about —"

"We'll deal with that presently, my dear," Sheridan cut her off. "First, I'd like you both to be here to hear this report from one of General Thomas's scouts. Go ahead, sir."

"General Thomas leads another division of the Army of the Cumberland," Cymbeline whispered.

A white man in civilian clothes and a wide-rimmed hat stepped forward from behind some of the officers, saluted, and then cleared his throat. "The noble Major General Thomas sends his regards to the great Ma —"

"Yes, yes, get on with it, man," Sheridan snapped. "We're at war, not a royal banquet. And use the map, won't you? Save everybody time."

"Right," the scout said, startled. "We've entrenched on the

banks of the Chickamauga River. Here." He picked up the metal piece tagged *Gen Thomas* and placed it beside a curvy blue line a little ways from where Sheridan's piece was and a few miles below the carved city that represented Chattanooga.

"The enemy has divisions here, here, here, and, according to our other scouts, here." He placed trike and raptor figurines in a tight semicircle wrapping all along the southern front of Thomas's regiment and looping up along the western side. Then he glanced nervously at the worried expressions of the officers around him.

"Sweet mercy," Sheridan said softly.

"What is it?" Magdalys whispered.

Cymbeline shook her head, brow furrowed. "Wait."

"With Longstreet's Confederate trikeriders still on their way by rail, due in some time tonight." He placed a gray triceratops on the railroad symbol between Sheridan's position and Thomas's.

"Card!" Sheridan suddenly yelled, still staring at the map table. "Where's Card? And our other divisions?"

"He's not back from his scouting mission," someone reported.

Sheridan tore his eyes from the map and glared at him. "What did you say?"

"He's not —"

"I heard what you said, you cad. Where's the other Card?"

"He went with him, sir."

"No! The younger one!" Sheridan looked ready to shred

a man with his bare hands. "Do these men have no first names?"

"No one knows them, sir."

"Find Young Card! Immediately!"

"Sir, yes sir!"

"And find me Old Mother Card so I can ask her why she didn't bother naming her children!"

"Right away, sir!"

"It was a joke!" Sheridan called after the departing officer. He shook his head. "Now, where were we?"

The scout had arranged a series of dark blue dino pieces in a scattered mess near Thomas. "The Union positions, sir."

Sheridan shook his head.

"Sir?"

"They're trying to turn Thomas's right flank," Sheridan said, his eyes narrowed.

"Yes, sir."

"If they do, they'll cut us off from Chattanooga and force the whole Army of the Cumberland south. General Braxton Bragg is no longer in retreat."

"He's in full attack," the scout said.

"And if he outflanks us from the north we'll be facing utter annihilation."

"*That*," Cymbeline whispered.

"We must make a fast dash for Chattanooga," one of the officers offered. "If we move quickly we could make it there before Longstreet arrives to reinforce Bragg. With fortifications set up on Missionary Ridge and Lookout Mountain, we'll be unassailable within the city."

"And abandon Thomas to certain destruction?" Sheridan said. "Never."

"We could implore him to retreat as well! Surely the major general will see the —"

"WHERE IS CARD?" Sheridan bellowed.

"Here, sir," the youngest Card said, appearing behind Magdalys and Cymbeline. "I was just with the prisoner that Private Hannibal, ah, handled."

"Has he woken?"

Card tipped his head, eyebrows raised. "Ah, no, sir."

"What did you do to that man, Private Hannibal?" Sheridan demanded.

"A brother in arms was in danger, sir," Hannibal said.

Young Card cleared his throat. "But I did do a search of his person and retrieved something that may be of interest."

Sheridan nodded, seeming to turn inward again as his eyes scanned the various statuettes scattered across the map. "Officers, alert your men: We're to march double-time to the Chickamauga. Thomas will be needing reinforcements. By god's grace we'll get there before the battle begins."

"Double-time?" one of the officers gasped. "The men and mounts are already tired from marching all day, sir, we won't —"

"Then they'll be left behind and shot for insubordination, Corporal. The fate of this entire army hangs in the balance. You have your orders. Dismissed, all of you."

The men began to disperse, some of them muttering beneath their mustaches.

"You stay, Miss Cymbeline," Sheridan ordered. "And you, young Magdalys." He softened, his tense face suddenly growing sad. "If you will. And Privates Hannibal and Rey, remain. Mr. Card, show us what you found."

"It's a medallion, sir." Card pulled a fold of cloth from his jacket and opened it, revealing a golden coin.

Magdalys caught her breath.

On it, the words *K of the G. C.* were inscribed around the image of a roaring tyrannosaurus with rays of lights bursting out from it.

She'd seen that image once before. It was stamped all over the papers of Mr. Harrison Weed, the man who'd taken her out of Cuba when she was a baby and dropped her off at the Colored Orphan Asylum.

Card flipped the coin over; it read *Lieutenant Hardy Luther Hewpat, Class III Dinomaster.*

"K of the G. C.," Sheridan puzzled. "What the deuce does that mean?"

"Knights of the Golden Circle," Magdalys said. "The people who tried to sell the other orphans into slavery."

CHAPTER TWENTY-ONE
MAKE MOVES

"**ARE THOSE DEVILS** still causing trouble?" Sheridan shook his head, inspecting the coin carefully.

Harrison Weed and Richard Riker, along with other Knights of the Golden Circle, were actively snatching black New Yorkers off the streets and shipping them south, then selling them off to slavers. At least, they were until the Dactyl Hill Squad teamed up with the Vigilance Committee. Now Weed's Manhattan headquarters was a pile of ashes and Riker was probably scattered all along the eastern seaboard in the form of Stella the pteranodon's pteropoops.

But the paperwork Magdalys and Mapper had stolen from Weed's office spoke of a huge network, a global organization dedicated to creating a whole new country, the so-called

Golden Circle, spanning South America and the fledgling Confederacy: an empire built on the slave trade.

And now it turned out a Confederate officer who could control dinos was part of the Knights too. The medallion caught the sunlight and flashed across Magdalys's vision as Sheridan held it up. *Class III Dinomaster.*

She shook her head. Of course the secret society was recruiting members who had the same special abilities she did to fight for the Confederacy. And of course they called themselves "masters." When she rode a dino, most of the time it felt like they were having a conversation, like they were agreeing together to do something. She could feel the great reptile's reluctance or excitement, could move accordingly and figure out how to do something the right way. Sure, if it was an enemy mount, the wrangling might involve a little more coercion, but she certainly didn't consider herself the master of any dino. That seemed absurd.

"Did you find out anything from the prisoner you were interrogating just now?" Magdalys asked.

"Just the same sob story they've been told to feed us about how demoralized and hungry their armies are and how they're all about to surrender," Sheridan said with disdain. "They've been fake defecting to our camp for weeks trying to goad us into attacking with that nonsense."

"Uh, sir," Hannibal said. "Permission to speak?"

Permission to speak, Magdalys thought, growling inside

herself. How was she supposed to dedicate her life to a group that demanded such dramatic comeliness?

"Go ahead, Private."

"The prisoner did mention that he was aware Lieutenant Hewpat was a part of a specially designated elite force of dinoriders."

"He meant Forrest's squad, I'm sure," Sheridan snorted. "The fighting finest or whatever they call themselves."

"I believe he meant that Hewpat is what's indicated on this medallion, sir. A dinomaster."

"Hannibal's right," Magdalys blurted out. Everyone turned to stare at her. "Er . . . Private Hannibal. That man managed to take full of possession of Mapper's dactyl and almost killed Mapper in the process. And he flies better than any of the other air cavalry guys. And I couldn't reach his mount to try to keep them from . . ." Her words trailed off as images of the explosion once again flashed through her mind. She rallied herself, feeling the weight of all those eyes on her. ". . . from killing Sol."

Sheridan glared at her for what felt like a very long time. Had she made a mistake, speaking out like that? She had no idea how all these things worked, chain of command and asking for permission to speak.

"You're positing," Sheridan said, very slowly, "that this secret society — the Knights of the Golden Circle — is recruiting an army of dinowranglers with your special skills to help the Confederacy destroy us?"

Magdalys nodded. "That's exactly what I'm saying . . . er, positing."

"Why this is treason of the highest order!" Sheridan snarled. "We must . . ." He paused, turned his sharp glare back to Magdalys. "Does this mean you'll join us, young lady? You see the urgency of the situation now, do you not? It's not just that they have an air cavalry and we don't — the Confederates have superiority in their dinowranglers across the board. And, well . . . if Bragg succeeds in turning Thomas's flank and cuts us off from Chattanooga, we'll be crushed and scattered within days. The entire western theater will be wide open for Confederate expansion, the gains made at Vicksburg and Gettysburg nullified, the Emperor Maximilian will invade from Mexico, and the European powers may well throw their support behind the enemy, tilting the entire balance of the war. Add to that this secret society's elite dinomaster force and the fact that we still have no air cavalry or reconnaissance. . . ."

Magdalys felt Cymbeline's hand land gently on her shoulder — support she hadn't realized she needed as the major general rattled off their dire circumstances and she felt the full weight of the responsibility he was placing on her. She took a step back, shaking her head, said, "What do you need?" in a choked whisper.

"What we need is someone with your abilities to train an elite corps of dinowranglers and their steeds. It's no longer enough to just have a force in the air. We need . . . you." He shook his head. "But even more urgently: We need eyes in the skies!" Sheridan exclaimed as if he'd been waiting his whole life for this moment. "We are running blind through the woods toward a battleground we barely understand. Our ground scouts can barely keep up with the constant move-ment — you saw we had to rely on another regiment's scouts for information just now, and —"

"Wait," Young Card interrupted.

Sheridan blinked at him, astonished at the breach of protocol.

"My brothers haven't returned yet?" Card's reddish face had paled. "I . . . I thought they'd come back."

"No," Sheridan said quietly. "We're still waiting for their report."

Magdalys looked at Card. He was blinking like it would somehow change what he'd just heard, and she could tell their report was the least of his concerns. "They should've gotten back by now."

The middle Card had headed off to check on the enemy position, Magdalys remembered. That must've been the last time he'd been seen.

Sheridan nodded gravely. "I agree." Magdalys imagined the temptation would be to spew some nonsense about how everything would be alright, and she was glad the major gen-eral didn't bother with that obvious lie. Instead he put a hand on the younger man's shoulder. "Your brothers know these woods better than any man alive," he said.

Card looked into Sheridan's eyes, finally stopped blinking.

"Except me." He straightened, seemed to grow several inches as his once-stricken face hardened into a look of grim determination. "Permission to ride out and find my older brothers, sir?"

Sheridan nodded curtly. "But be careful, Card. I can't afford to lose any of you, let alone all three. Bring them back to us alive. Is that clear?"

"Sir, yes sir!" Card yelled with a salute.

Magdalys watched him grapple partway down the saddle and then leap onto his waiting para below and gallop off in a cloud of dust. A deep hunger rattled through her chest, something like longing. Card was doing exactly what she'd been trying to do all this time, but his brothers were so much closer. And it had seemed so simple! Ask permission, off you go. Of course, the Cards had proved themselves invaluable to the Union time and again, that much was clear, and who was Montez Roca to the Grand Army of the Republic? Just another black soldier: good for digging ditches or throwing into the line of fire to hopefully prove his worth in death.

She looked up at Sheridan, who was staring at her. "Permission to speak?" The words felt sour coming out of her, like a lie.

Sheridan smiled wryly. "By all means, young Magdadis."

"It's Mag-da-*lys*, Major General, sir. And I'll help you," she said, and Sheridan's grin widened. "But I'm not mustering in. I'll help scout out the enemy positions at Chickamauga and that's all I can promise." She frowned, then reluctantly added, "Right now."

CHAPTER TWENTY-TWO
FLIGHT PREPARATIONS

"**ALRIGHT, LOOK,**" **MAGDALYS** said, glancing at the four familiar faces of her friends. "We have a mission."

She'd thought they might be excited to do something again, but she hadn't anticipated the wild cheer that went up. Amaya yelled "Finally!" and high-fived Two Step. Mapper hugged Sabeen, who giggled and swatted him.

"Wait, wait, slow down," Magdalys said. "You haven't even heard the plan yet!"

"Don't matter," Mapper said with a shrug. "We in."

"Yeah," Amaya agreed. "Everyone's tired of marching along on trikeback forever and ever."

A fresh buzz of excitement whirred through Magdalys's mind since Sheridan had ordered a faster march. The drudgery of a march to nowhere had given way to a fresh urgency;

there was a battle afoot and the dinos could feel it; they tittered and grunted about it as they rumbled along.

But only Magdalys could sense them. To everyone else, they were just moving somewhat faster, and the endless procession still felt like when the orphanage's old triceratops, Varney, would get stuck in a traffic jam lugging their wagon back through the busy Manhattan streets. The trike beneath them plodded on at a steady jog, but blue-clad troops and armored dinos streamed on and on behind and in front of them, while it seemed like the same mountains and trees passed in an endless cycle on either side.

"What's the plan?" Two Step asked, and Magdalys felt a pang of guilt for what she was about to say.

"It's a scouting mission, and we need an armed escort with us: Hannibal, Octave, and Corporal Cailloux from the Native Guard will act as gunners, plus three riders: myself, Amaya, and Mapper."

"But —" Two Step started.

"We'll take Stella," Magdalys went on. "And then make short distance runs on the dactyls, using Stella as a mother ship. There's a creek up ahead, the Chickamauga."

"Chickamauga!" Mapper exclaimed. "That used to be Cherokee territory."

"Until the army we're about to help out forced them off their land," Amaya said. Everyone got quiet for a few moments. Magdalys didn't know how to respond.

"Both armies are gathering there, but we don't know how many are on either side or what the field is looking like, and . . ."

"Amaya doesn't even like riding dinos!" Two Step said. "Or pteros."

"I kinda do now," Amaya said.

Sabeen put a hand on Two Step's shoulder. "It's okay, man. We'll just —"

"Stop," Two Step said. "Don't . . ."

Magdalys stood. "I'm going to check on Dizz," she said, working her way down the saddle. She stopped, looked at Two Step, her best friend, with the face that wouldn't take no for an answer. "Come with me."

"What do you mean I can't go?" Two Step demanded.

"I didn't say you *can't* go," Magdalys sighed. They were walking along the endless procession of soldiers toward the medical unit. She'd hoped talking it out one-on-one would be better, just in case he—

"What's even the point of my being here if I can't go along with you when you're doing dangerous stuff?"

—lost his cool.

"I just think it would probably be better," Magdalys said, "if you—"

"You're benching me!" Two Stop yelled, his eyebrows

inching closer together as his nostrils flared. "You're benching me because I'm not good enough!"

Soldiers and dinos alike were glancing over with concern now.

Magdalys shushed him and immediately regretted it. "That's not it," she tried to say soothingly.

"Don't shush me, Magdalys Roca!" Two Step yelled. "You don't get to shush me! And who made you the boss of us anyway? Just because we came to help you find your brother doesn't mean you get to just decide what happens to everybody!"

"I'm not bossing you around," Magdalys said, stopping. "I'm worried about you, Two Step!"

He spun around, finger out. "Well, don't!"

"Two Step, you haven't . . ." She shook her head. Any way she could think of to say it, it sounded like she was calling him weak, or saying that he wasn't good enough, but that was the opposite of what she wanted to say.

"Go head," he goaded. "Say it."

"You haven't been the same since what happened that night in the Penitentiary."

They stood face-to-face now, but Two Step looked like the wind was knocked out of him, his eyes glaring at Magdalys's shoes, his shoulders heaving up and down with each labored breath. "Say it," he whispered. "Say what I did."

"Two Step . . ."

"Say it, Magdalys."

"You saved my life."

"I killed someone, Magdalys."

"You saved your own life."

"He's still dead though."

Magdalys shook her head.

"He is. And now you think I'm not good enough to fly."

"No!" Magdalys yelled, taking him by the shoulders. "Listen to me: I love that . . ." No, that definitely wasn't right. She shook her head, tried again, forcing herself to slow down. "I think it's . . . right . . . that it's hard for you. You're not weak, Two Step. You're human. I mean, I don't want you to be hurting and torn up about it, but it would be weird if you were just cool about it too. Nothing is right, none of this makes sense. There is no *right* way to deal with what we've been through, what *you've* been through. And it's even harder because everything just keeps" — she flailed around at the never-ending march of war streaming past — "everything keeps happening! It's only happening more now, in fact! And none of us can catch our breath. But none of us did what you did. And I'm not . . . I won't let you . . . I know I'm not your boss, but I'm not putting you back into a situation where you might go through it all again when you haven't even . . . when you're still dealing with what you've been through."

He stared at her.

"With killing someone," she finally said. "To save my life and yours," she added quickly. "And Mapper's."

"But it's like you said," Two Step sighed. "It's all happening around us whether we like it or not. Look around, Mags. Do you really think you can *stop* me from being in that situation again, at this point? And it's not just because we're here. I mean, it happened in Dactyl Hill, of all places. The one part of this messed-up world where we're supposed to be safe." He shook his head. "And anyway, ever since it happened, all I've done is replay it over and over in my head and wonder if I could've done something differently or should've done something different and all I can think is the only way to find out is to be there again, with a gun in my hand and our lives on the line. And then a day like today happens and part of me just wants to . . ." He clenched his fists and his words trailed off.

"I understand," Magdalys said. "Kind of."

"Hey, the dactyls from Brooklyn girl!" a voice said from behind them. "You looking for your friend?" It was Dr. Pennbroker, now out of his surgeon's coat and wearing a regular dark blue Union Army uniform. They'd walked right past the medical caravan without realizing it.

"Am I ever," Magdalys mumbled.

The surgeon waved them over. "He's right over here. Should be good to go!"

Two Step cocked his head, still in the middle of his storm of emotions, and then stumbled after Magdalys with a curious pout on his face.

Dr. Pennbroker was a tall, thin man with well-trimmed sideburns and an elegant goatee. He flashed a wide smile at Magdalys and Two Step as he ushered them forward amidst the marching dinos. "This is Dr. Pennbroker, the surgeon who was taking care of my dactyl," Magdalys said. "And Dr. Pennbroker, this is my friend Two Step."

"Whoa!" Two Step said, all traces of anger gone. "A black US Army surgeon!"

Dr. Pennbroker chuckled. "Yeah, I get a lot of that. There are about eight of us total; four here with the Army of the Cumberland alone."

"They only let them work on dinos and black soldiers," Magdalys said.

"Technically," she and Dr. Pennbroker added together, both smirking.

"Whoa whoa whoa," Two Step said as his eyes kept getting wider and wider. "I had no idea!"

"Join the club," Magdalys said. "*And* he knows Dr. Sloan."

Two Step looked like his head might explode. "WHAT? The Dinoguide guy? You *know* him?!"

"You could say we go way back," Dr. Pennbroker snickered. "Anyway, here's your dactyl, good as new." He nodded at a wagon being dragged behind a grumbling stego. The dactyl's light blue snout poked up over the side of the wagon, then his whole head. His eyes widened at Magdalys and then Dizz flapped up into the air, landing unsteadily on top of the stego's back.

"Dizz!" Magdalys yelled, running over.

The stego gave a howl of disapproval and reared up. Dizz hopped from leg to leg a few times with what almost sounded like a snicker and then jumped off as the stego's front legs came back down. The dactyl landed in front of Magdalys. He crouched forward toward her, snapping playfully, and she wrapped her arms around his slender neck and squeezed. Around them, Dr. Pennbroker and Two Step chatted and the stomp of soldiers and dinos churned on. "I'm so glad you're okay," she whispered. "Thank you for saving my life."

Dizz unfurled his wings and straightened, lifting Magdalys off the ground. She laughed and pulled herself over his shoulder so she straddled his back as he flapped once, twice, then perched on a wagon next to Dr. Pennbroker.

"Hey, big guy," the surgeon said, amiably stepping out of snapping range. "Tell you what, how bout we do a switch-off, Miss Magdalys? You get your dactyl back, and me and the fellas need another set of hands in the medical tent, and your friend here just volunteered to help out. Sound like a plan?"

Magdalys blinked at Two Step. He nodded, his gaze still on the surgeon.

"Sounds like an excellent plan," Magdalys said.

"Be careful out there," Dr. Pennbroker said.

Two Step glanced at her, anger roiling beneath his tight face, then looked away.

Magdalys opened her mouth but realized she didn't know what to say.

Dizz swung his head around, squawked once, and then hunched low on his knees, preparing to take off. "You be careful too," Magdalys called as Two Step and Dr. Pennbroker and the medical caravan got smaller and smaller beneath her.

CHAPTER TWENTY-THREE
RECONNAISSANCE RUN

MAGDALYS SHOOK OFF the recurring image of Two Step's parting scowl as she surged over the Appalachian treetops on Dizz, Hannibal laughing and howling in the wind behind her and holding on for dear life.

Another haunting to add to her ghost collection. It consisted of both the living and the dead, a nonstop carousel of the missing, the wounded, the silent, the murdered; it was always available to trouble her idle moments or sleepless nights.

Still: the setting sun splashed sharp orange streaks across the comely magentas and darkening blues of the western sky ahead of them, and sent the long shadows of the four dactyls rippling along the dark green forest below.

"I see the joy of flying hasn't worn off yet," Magdalys said when Hannibal paused to catch his breath. They'd rustled up some saddles from the mounted raptor units and adjusted them to fit the dactyls, and it did make flying much more comfortable.

"Man!" he panted. "And I hope it never will! This is the most amazing thing I've ever done!"

"Miss Roca," Corporal Cailloux called as Amaya pulled their mount alongside Dizz. "Would you kindly inform Private Hannibal that we are on a reconnaissance mission and thus under orders to *not* alert the entire Confederacy to our presence?"

Hannibal straightened up. "Duly noted, sir!"

Beans flew up on the other side, apparently just so Octave and Mapper could make sure everyone heard them snickering. Grappler soared up ahead, her long beak moving back and forth slowly as she scanned the horizon for trouble.

"How exactly are we supposed to ascertain the whereabouts of this pteranodon?" Cailloux asked. His voice sounded skeptical but not unkind.

"Magdalys," Hannibal said. "She can do anything."

It was a small statement — just four words! — but it was one of the best things anyone had ever said about her. *She can do anything.* Magdalys wanted to make a talisman of it to dangle around her neck and repeat the words in Hannibal's laughing voice whenever she was afraid. Maybe that would ward off the carousel of ghosts.

"I want you to know, Miss Roca," Cailloux said, "Private

Hannibal rarely has a kind word for anyone, so, though he is a troublemaker, his endorsement carries some weight."

"I take umbrage, Corporal!" Hannibal said. "But you have a point."

And maybe Hannibal was right. The gathering storm of Stella's sweet and lowdown song kept getting louder and fiercer inside Magdalys. Finding her was simply a matter of following the trail of her call. It seemed second nature to Magdalys, but trailing a giant pterosaur through enemy territory would've been daunting to pretty much anyone else.

Maybe she *could* do anything.

"There!" Mapper cried, just as the wail inside Magdalys crescendoed. Something huge crested the mountaintop up ahead, blotting out the sun.

"STELLA GIRL!" Magdalys yelled, and Hannibal let out a wild laugh behind her.

"Remember General Sheridan's orders," Corporal Cailloux said as Magdalys veered Stella south and clicks and clacks of the soldiers preparing their weapons filled the air amidst the caterwauling songbirds below. "We're not to engage the enemy. We're not to fly directly over the battlefield. We're *definitely* not to get shot down. Clear?"

"Sir, yes sir!" Octave, Hannibal, and Mapper yelled in unison. Amaya just nodded.

"Everyone have their security belts secured to both themselves and the saddle?" Cailloux yelled.

"Sir, yes sir!" everyone responded. The corporal had insisted on some security measure in case Stella tipped suddenly, and Magdalys had been glad they'd had the belts handy, although they'd given up sleeping with them attached a couple days out from Brooklyn.

"The Chickamauga heads away from the Tennessee River just north of Chattanooga," said Mapper. Magdalys felt a momentary panic: Mapper was just some kid to these soldiers, not the geographic wunderkind she knew him to be. Who was he to lecture them about geography? But no one chided him or cut him off; they just nodded and waited for him to go on. She breathed a tiny sigh of relief and turned back to the rising and falling peaks around them.

"It runs along the side of Missionary Ridge," Mapper went on, "which should be that high up plateau up ahead."

"So we're in Georgia?" Cailloux asked.

"Probably just crossed into it, yeah," Mapper said, squinting at the imaginary maps imprinted across his brain and then nodding.

"This kid's good to have around," Octave said.

"How do you think we've made it this far," Amaya said with a giggle. Magdalys peeked back again. Amaya never giggled.

"Uh, thanks," Mapper said, looking wildly uncomfortable, the goofiness of his grin turned all the way up to ten.

"I hate to break up the lovefest," Hannibal said, and at the sound of worry in his voice, Magdalys immediately scanned the tree line ahead for signs of trouble, "but y'all hear that?"

Everyone got quiet. Then she saw it: A plume of smoke rose above the trees into the darkening sky.

"I don't hear no—" Mapper started to say, but a low rumble cut him off, then light flashed across the clouds up ahead and a crack ripped out, followed by a ghostly, shuddering afterblast that seemed to flush across the valley toward them.

"Artillery," Octave said. "The battle's already begun."

A gnawing, sinking feeling crept over Magdalys from the inside. They were too late; that was all she could think. But for what, she didn't know. It's not like they had any ability to stop the fighting or turn the tide. Sheridan was already marching as fast as his men and dinos could travel for the battlefront. There was nothing more to do except find out whatever they could, and maybe that was the worst part.

"Stay low," Cailloux said, snapping Magdalys out of her thoughts. "We don't need any of their air cavalry spotting us." More lights flashed across the sky as the rumbling continued at a steady drone, and then the sharp reports of each bursting shell reached them. The sound of death raining down from above, Magdalys thought, veering Stella into a smooth glide just over the treetops.

"Octave, Hannibal," Cailloux ordered. "Hop on dactyls with one of the kids and head in opposite directions. See if you can get the scope of the battlefield and a sense of the enemy numbers."

"Yes, sir!" the two men hollered with a salute. Beans and Grappler were already flapping on either side of Stella; with a quick thought from Magdalys they swung beneath her huge wings. Amaya and Mapper turned to her, and it struck her again that without meaning to or even so much as a vote of confidence, she'd somehow become the commanding officer of this strange, tiny army they'd formed back in Dactyl Hill, Brooklyn. She nodded her approval and Mapper climbed on Beans, Amaya on Grappler, the soldiers mounting up behind them, and they swooshed silently off into the war-torn skies.

CHAPTER TWENTY-FOUR
THE BATTLE BELOW

"**IT'S TERRIFYING, ISN'T** it?" Corporal Cailloux said. Magdalys realized he was watching her as she stared off after the dactyls. She shook her head, somehow smiled. "Which part?"

Cailloux chuckled. "I mean, all of it, of course, but especially this part. Sending men off to what may be their death. Or kids, in this case. Even worse."

Magdalys nodded. It didn't matter that she hadn't given the order and didn't hold any rank to speak of; he'd seen the mar of leadership, the deference they paid her, and he knew what meant, that it mattered more than any chain of command something bad should happen to any of them, Magdalys w carry it with her. "How do you . . . how do you deal with i

Cailloux scowled, eyebrows raised, and made a vague circle with one hand. "I remind myself that this is what they came here for, that this is what we fought for, in fact, and what we're still fighting for: to be able to fight, and maybe die, for a cause we believe in." He paused, his mouth still shoved all the way to one side of his face in a lopsided frown. "Freedom."

For a few moments, they watched the shells paint sudden bursts across the violet-streaked sky. Then Cailloux shouted in a hoarse whisper: "Veer left!"

Magdalys ducked without knowing why and pulled Stella into a sharp curve. "What?" she asked quietly.

"There's a camp right below us," Cailloux said. "Can't tell if it's ours or theirs but I just saw the fires between the trees. Keep veering and take us around closer to the fighting; I don't think they spotted us or we'd have heard shooting by now."

Either side would probably start taking potshots at them, Magdalys realized — there was nothing to mark them as being on one side or the other from below, and anything flying directly above an encampment would probably be presumed an enemy.

Musket fire crackled from the battlefield now, an ongoing barrage that meant countless men were crumbling beneath its onslaught on either side. Magdalys saw the trees light up ahead and more artillery shells crashed through the night.

"We're close," Cailloux whispered, more to himself than Magdalys. "Very close." Then sharply: "Left!" as the whole raging battlefield suddenly opened up beneath them. Men

burst out of the trees amidst the muskets' never-ending pop and crackle. Other men charged forward toward them; it was too dark to make out what color anyone's uniform was. Men screamed, crumpled, muskets cracked, artillery boomed. Torches and bonfires punctuated the otherwise dark field.

"Those are the skirmishers," Cailloux explained as they veered low along the edge of the woods. "Infantry. Each side is testing the strength of the other's front lines."

Testing. It seemed like such a sad thing to die in the service of: a test. But Magdalys knew much bigger stakes loomed behind each tiny movement.

"When they find a weak spot, that's when you'll see . . . there!" A low rumble sounded now, even deeper than the artillery cannons: trikes on the move. Many, many trikes, Magdalys realized, gazing at the sudden rush of movement below. The dinoriders guided their mounts in a thundering charge straight into a collected mass of foot soldiers. It would be a massacre, Magdalys thought, but the infantry fell away in perfect unison just before the trikes reached them, and it was a snarling brigade of raptor riders that took their place.

"Those are our boys," Cailloux said with pride. "General Thomas's 7th Mounted Raptor Squad."

The raptors leapt as one, landing directly in the thick of the trike charge, and then everything became a muddled mass of howls, musket shots, and dinosnarls.

"How can anyone make sense of this?" Magdalys asked.

Cailloux shook his head. "You can't. War doesn't make

sense. Everyone who tries, loses. All you can do is fight as hard as you can and do your best to keep a cool head in the storm."

Artillery bursts rumbled out nearby and then explosions shattered the melee of trikes, raptors, and men.

"Who's shelling them?" Magdalys yelled. "They're hitting everyone!"

"I don't know," Cailloux admitted. "Could be us, could be them. Could be a horrible mistake, could be some terrible strategy at play."

Screams rose from below now as fighting seemed to fade amidst the carnage of the artillery attack, and a thick cloud of dust and smoke covered the battlefield.

"Can you tell . . . if anyone's winning?"

"Not yet," Cailloux said. "Swing further along the edge, I want to see if . . . ah." The field stretched long beneath them, illuminated by the fires of many, many campsites. It seemed to cover the night, that never-ending army in the shadows, and keep going through the mountains and into the sky above.

"Is that the . . . the enemy?"

"Braxton Bragg must've consolidated his whole army. And Longstreet's trikeriders have arrived too."

The darkness itself seemed to writhe with them, and then Magdalys realized why. They were on the march, surging forward into battle.

CHAPTER TWENTY-FIVE
RUMBLE AND CAW

"**W**HAT DO WE do?" Magdalys asked.

"See what they have to say," Corporal Cailloux said, nodding to where both the mounted dactyls could be seen gliding over the treetops toward where they'd perched Stella. "And then send a message back to General Sheridan to let him know what we've seen. Although I'm sure he's already heard the artillery and is rushing his men toward it."

Magdalys glanced back at the approaching dactyls. Night had fully fallen now, the moon just barely peeking out from behind a cloud bank. Something seemed to flicker up into the sky behind where Mapper and Amaya were flying at full speed. Magdalys squinted. Their fourth, unmounted dactyl was gliding a smooth circle nearby, keeping watch, so what . . .

More fluttering shapes resolved and vanished in the darkness. They seemed small, or maybe one huge creature with many moving parts? Magdalys couldn't tell. And then all at once the shapes coalesced into a single, ever-shifting snake that whipped out through the sky; the fires below illuminated a hundred flapping, feathered wings.

Magdalys gasped. The clouds cleared, and the moon revealed a sudden splash of rainbow: brilliant greens, sharp reds, hazy magentas, and stark royal blues all flashed and spun in the air, the breathtaking plumage of these crow-sized creatures on full display.

Archaeopteryx! Magdalys thought, catching sight of those long snouted reptilian heads stretching out from the feathered bodies. All those razor-sharp teeth glinted in the moonlight as nearly four dozen mouths opened at once. *Although small,* Dr. Barlow Sloan noted about the archaeops, *and deceptively beautiful in their plumage (if not their hideous faces and wide, eager eyes), these little fellows are some of the fiercest and smartest dinos known to man! Beware!*

With a hissing squawk, the snaking limb of archaeops dispersed and they seemed to cover the whole sky behind Beans and Grappler.

"FLY!" Magdalys yelled, her hoarse cry almost buried by another eruption of gunfire below.

Amaya leaned forward, urging her mount into a mad scramble, but Mapper glanced back just as the archaeops converged again, now into two whiplike shapes. Both curled up into the sky and then dove.

Someone was controlling those dinos, Magdalys realized. And whoever was doing it was really, really good. There had to be almost fifty of them, all wielded in perfect unison as a single, unstoppable weapon. But where was the wrangler? She scanned the treetops and skies, but barely had time to look before the two attacking archaeops streams bore down on Amaya and Mapper.

Shots rang out — Hannibal and Octave letting loose from each dactylback, surely. Winged shapes screeched and were flung backward and then down with each shot, but there were more than anyone could hope to take out one by one.

"What are those things?" Corporal Cailloux asked, constructing some kind of contraption on Stella's saddle.

"Archaeops," Magdalys said. "Hold tight to whatever you're setting up. We're about to fly."

"Hang on," Cailloux said through gritted teeth. "Let me just . . ." He heaved a long, fierce-looking gun with several long barrels onto his contraption.

"Hurry," Magdalys said. "They're almost on them."

Grappler had surged ahead but the attackers were closing on Mapper.

With a click and snap, Cailloux growled, "Okay, go!" and at a signal from Magdalys, Stella unfurled her forty-foot wings to either side and launched into the air.

"Roll up on 'em and then swing her to the side," Cailloux commanded as Grappler came barreling forward full speed. The caws of the pursuing archaeops grew louder. Amaya and Hannibal jumped off Grappler and landed on the saddle. Magdalys sent Stella directly at the approaching swarm. "Now!" Cailloux yelled, and she spun Stella off to the right. An earsplitting barrage burst out behind her: *BRADAGA-DADAGA-BRADADAGA-DAGAGA!!* and Magdalys found herself grasping the huge pteranodon's neck as the bonfires and battles veered past below. For a second, she thought she'd been hit herself, the gunfire rattled so viciously through her core.

But no: Up ahead, the archaeops swarm had been decimated — limp, bullet-riddled dino bodies tumbled from the sky and a passing breeze carried hundreds of multicolored feathers out over the trees. Magdalys gasped. Sure, those creatures were bent on attacking them, but . . . that *machine* had seemed to tear apart the sky and sweep them away by the dozens in a matter of seconds. Wholesale slaughter. She should've been celebrating, but those creatures had clearly been wrangled — it wasn't their fault some Confederate dinomaster snatched them up and hurled them into battle.

There wasn't time to mourn though — Hannibal was right.

"What *is* that thing?" Magdalys demanded as she picked herself up.

"It's a Gatling," Amaya said, gazing over Cailloux's

shoulder with a glint in her eye. "I've never seen one in action before."

"HELP!" Mapper's voice carried to them over the wind. Magdalys swung Stella around just in time to see the other swarm descend on Beans, enveloping him, Mapper, and Octave in a bright and lethal rainbow.

"No!" Magdalys gasped as Stella swung into a turn so sharp it almost tipped them all over the side, and then surged forward. In a matter of seconds, she'd gone from feeling bad at the archaeops being slaughtered to wanting them all destroyed to save her friends. And even worse, now they couldn't be without making everything worse.

The swarm screeched and cawed and three gunshots from within sent a couple archaeops spiraling away. Then a long gray beak appeared, followed by Beans's face, his eyes narrowed with determination. One of his wings broke free, blood flowing freely from gashes the smaller dinos had torn in it, and then the other. Finally, Beans merged fully from the swarm, Mapper and Hannibal crouching with their faces covered on his back.

"Mapper!" Magdalys and Amaya cried at the same time. Beans flapped unsteadily — cuts lined his whole body, Magdalys now saw — and then fell into a wobbly glide toward them.

BRIGAAWWWW!!!! came a wretched, high-pitched screech from somewhere below.

Cailloux swung his Gatling toward the treetops a moment

too late: a brilliant flash of color leapt up into the sky between Stella and Beans.

It was shaped like the other archaeops — same shimmering plumage and bare reptilian head, same wide, wild eyes and sharp pupils — but this thing was much, much larger. On its back, a pale woman — no, she was a *girl* — sat riding side-saddle in a full ball gown. She didn't look much older than Magdalys, maybe sixteen. Another swarm of smaller archaeops fluttered up into the sky around the huge one. The girl's face curved into a triumphant grin. *This* was who'd been commanding those legions of archaeops?

Cailloux swung his Gatling up toward her.

"Don't shoot," Amaya said. "You'll hit Mapper and Hannibal!"

"I won't," Octave said, lifting his rifle, but the girl had already kicked the spurs on her pink-and-white raptorskin boots, sending the giant archaeop into a swooping charge. "On, Rathbane! Attack!" she shrieked. The two swarms surged forward around her.

Even with their heavy firepower, a pteranodon and three dactyls could never best that many archaeops, especially with that huge one leading the pack. They were outnumbered and probably doomed, but trying to escape would be a disaster: The dactyls they had were already worn out and wounded, and Magdalys wasn't sure Stella could outfly that feathered monstrosity.

Fine. She narrowed her eyes and urged Stella straight

ahead into the oncoming assault. Behind her, the clicks and clacks of Hannibal, Octave, and Cailloux preparing their weapons sounded. A shape rose in the sky beside them, then another. Magdalys glanced over.

Dactyls!

They weren't the Brooklyn squad Magdalys knew, these were other ones. Was there a Union wrangler helping them out from below? More likely her own crew had somehow recruited these local ones. Either way, she didn't have time to worry about it — they were on her side, that much was clear, and that was all that mattered. They stood a fighting chance after all.

Rifle shots sang out from behind her. Archaeops fell from the sky to either side but there were too many. And then, with a calamitous rumble and caw, the two sky giants smashed full into each other as the dactyls and archaeops clashed in the air around them. Stella went right for the archaeop's neck, just missing it as the smaller creature dug all four of its claws into Stella's neck. A clutch of smaller archaeops followed suit, each cutting long red gashes along her hide.

Stella let out a howl that must've reverberated across the valley, but the deeper one shuddered inside Magdalys. It was the first time she'd felt panic from her humongous friend. Rathbane had latched on to a part of the pteranodon's chest that she couldn't reach with her huge claws.

Magdalys climbed up Stella's neck. Gunfire burst around her as Mapper, Amaya, and the soldiers fought off the attack.

In the sky just ahead, a small clutch of archaeops swarmed one of the new dactyls and slashed its wings, sending the creature into a shrieking plummet toward the trees. Magdalys shuddered — the poor thing had come to save her and now . . .

She blinked away tears, shook her head, and peered over the pteranodon's shoulder. The girl stared up with a defiant grin. "So you're the Union's new dinomaster. Just a child, I see. And a Negress at that." She shook her head pityingly. "I guess they're determined to prove to the world how pathetic their sham ideas about equality are."

Magdalys had no idea what to say to that. All she knew was that people and dinos were being massacred all around her, and blood was pouring out of the creature that had saved her life. Another desperate caw rose inside Magdalys and Stella heaved suddenly to the side.

"Whoa!" Hannibal yelled behind Magdalys.

"I'm about to destroy your pitiful air cavalry," the girl said, pulling out a chain with a grappling hook at the end and sending it into a swing over her head, "but you can be comforted in knowing you were defeated by the greatest dinomaster that ever lived, Elizabeth Crawbell. I'm sure you've read about my exploits."

"I haven't," Magdalys said. "I have no idea who you are." Stella had swung them away from the battlefield, and now the dark Appalachian forests filled the world below them.

Elizabeth looked a little put out, then just shrugged and sent her grappling hook flying up toward Stella's crest. With all the others busy fighting off the archaeops, there was only one way to dislodge this arrogant girl and her beast.

Dive! Magdalys commanded. The last cohesive thought Magdalys had before the terror of a sheer plummet took hold was that she hoped the others had remembered to secure themselves to the saddle.

CHAPTER TWENTY-SIX
DIVE

MAGDALYS WAS PRETTY sure she was screaming. Someone definitely was. Or maybe many someones. Or maybe it was the wind, shrieking the sound of Magdalys's panic as the line where the earth met the sky steepened.

Stella's urgent caw slid into a grittier, more determined growl and the giant ptero sped at full velocity toward the treetops.

Elizabeth's chain-hook had swung wide and then dropped uselessly to the side at the sudden change of trajectory, and now the Confederate dinomaster was clinging desperately to the neck of her mount, teeth clenched. "It won't work, you fool!" she howled over the wind.

Magdalys glanced back. Mapper and Amaya had both grasped Hannibal and were holding each of his hands as his legs flew out in the wind behind. Cailloux and Octave had been thrown to the back of the saddle but then managed to secure themselves. Archaeops and dactyls still grappled above them.

Back on Stella's chest, Elizabeth was peering nervously at the fast-approaching treetops. Finally, just as the dark leaves began to take shape behind her, she snarled and spurred Rathbane to release. The giant archaeop swooped away, tearing a few new gashes in Stella's hide as he went, and Stella evened out into a smooth glide over the forest.

BRADAGA-BRAGADA-BRAGADA-BRAGADA Cailloux's Gatling sang, but when Magdalys turned, it was Amaya behind the turret. Out in the sky behind them, Elizabeth swung Rathbane into a dazzling series of evasive maneuvers and then, when Amaya's barrage didn't let up, simply turned tail and sped off into the night followed by what was left of the fluttering archaeop swarm.

Magdalys exhaled, then glanced over Stella's shoulder at the still bleeding gashes.

Come on, girl, she thought, *let's get you on the ground.*

"What . . . was that?" Mapper gasped once they'd found a clearing and brought Stella down for a bumpy, lopsided landing.

Magdalys, already on the ground and approaching Stella's wounded hide with caution, shook her head. She'd been thinking the same thing, over and over, since the wrangler behind that impressive archaeops swarm had revealed herself. There had to be at least thirty dinos flying in perfect coordination at one time, Magdalys thought. People were impressed with Magdalys summoning a dactyl here or there, but that was all cute parlor games next to what this girl could do. "Elizabeth Crawbell, she said her name was."

"Ugh," Hannibal said. "The one and only. If I hadn't been busy fighting off her little beasties, I'd have gotten a shot off and Abe Lincoln himself woulda pinned me with the Medal of Honor for ridding the world of that traitor."

Six large claw cuts formed a spiraling bright red crescent from Stella's jaw to the top of her wide chest. They didn't seem to be bleeding anymore, so that was good, and hopefully meant they weren't too deep. The pteranodon, settled into a precarious squat that reminded Magdalys of a nesting hen, gave a feeble caw and shook her massive head. "I know, baby girl," Magdalys said, rubbing small circles on her smooth hide. "She seemed to think I should've heard of her — Elizabeth, that is."

"Yeah, the papers have been covering some of her so-called exploits," Octave said, sliding down from the saddle. "Oop, hang on." He stepped a few feet away and then ralphed a full day's worth of hardtack into some bushes. "Man . . . I gotta get used to this flying thing."

Hannibal chuckled. "You good, Private Rey?"

Octave waved him off. "I'll be alright. That was some fast shooting, Amaya."

Amaya nodded her head, conceding the compliment without a word, and went over to stand beside Magdalys.

"She got you for your Gatling, Corp," Hannibal laughed.

"She did indeed," Cailloux acknowledged. "Where'd you learn to do that, young lady?"

Mapper piped up, "Her dad's a super-famous commander in the a —"

"Mapper!" Magdalys snapped as Amaya's hand wrapped around hers and squeezed. "Shut it."

Mapper's eyes went wide. "Oh. I thought —"

"You thought wrong," Magdalys said.

The soldiers traded glances, then shrugged and went back to checking their equipment.

"You okay?"

Amaya shrugged, still holding Magdalys's hand in a death grip. "Let's get these wounds cleaned up."

"Anyway," Hannibal said, "the young Miss Crawbell ain't even a Southerner. She from Connecticut or something."

"DC," Octave corrected him.

"Whatever," Hannibal said. "Ain't the South. But she wanna be Southern so bad. Well, Confederate Southern, that is. Not us Southern, obviously."

"And her daddy's a big-deal secessionist politician," Octave added. "The Pinkertons arrested him for aiding and abetting the enemy a couple times but the charges never stick."

"She's part of the reason General Sheridan's so pressed about having an air cavalry of our own," Cailloux explained.

"And he ain't wrong," Hannibal said, with a pointed look at Magdalys.

A familiar cawing cut the night, and then Beans, Grappler, and Dizz flapped out of the sky followed by a handful of those new dactyls. Magdalys caught her breath. "You guys alright?" she called, running over as they landed.

The three from Brooklyn seemed to be, besides some cuts and bruises (Beans had been slashed pretty badly when they'd surrounded him, and he looked extra ready to get back out there and whup more archaeops). But one of the Tennessee dactyls came in for a calamitous landing and then just lay there, barely breathing. The others gathered around, nudging him with their beaks.

Everyone stopped what they were doing and watched. For a few moments, they kept murmuring to each other and poking their fallen brethren; then a quiet understanding seemed to descend on them. The wounded dactyl's body stopped rising and falling; he lay still. The others bowed their heads; one swept a single wing over the body and then they all turned away sadly.

Magdalys watched in horror. It was just one life, and a dactyl at that, and the cannons and rifle fire still boomed across the valley around them as many hundreds of human lives were snatched from existence, but . . . that dactyl had shown up in the nick of time to help, and now he was dead. They all had. Sure, she hadn't summoned them, but they'd still come and she definitely would be summoning more before this was all over. In her mind, she saw the dozens of bloodied archaeops cascading from the sky amidst Cailloux's withering Gatling fire. And how many more people and dinos would die around her? Because of her?

"Breathe," Amaya's voice whispered in her ear, and Magdalys realized she hadn't been.

She blinked, exhaled, tried to pull in air but it was like there was none. She'd been bested. Elizabeth Crawbell was still out there, and now she'd be looking for Magdalys. And she had whole battalions of archaeops ready to strike at her command.

"Breathe," Amaya said again.

Magdalys nodded, pulling harder. Around them, everyone had shaken their heads sadly and gone back to what they were doing. The world kept turning. Life flickered out and all there was to do was keep moving, keep moving, headlong into more destruction.

"Breathe," Amaya commanded quietly.

Magdalys nodded. Let a shaky breath out and pulled in another. She couldn't keep throwing dinos to their doom. And what would happen when it was one of her friends who was hurt or killed? If it was this hard with a dactyl she'd never even met before.

Beans, Grappler, and Dizz hopped over to Stella, who gave an appreciative coo, nuzzling each of them with her big head, and then settled back into having her wounds cleaned.

They were okay. They were more okay than Magdalys,

from the look of it. She exhaled a shivering chuckle and Amaya eyed her. "Just . . . sad. About all this," Magdalys said.

Amaya nodded.

"Can they fly?" Corporal Cailloux asked, stepping up to where the other dactyls had now gathered around Stella.

"Seems like they're okay," Magdalys said.

"Good. We have to get back out there. Sheridan's column will be entering the fray anytime now, if they haven't already. Can you guys fly?"

The soldiers had already finished gearing up and dusting themselves off. They'd just been through the worst smashup Magdalys had seen yet — she'd barely caught her breath — and they were ready to jump back into the thick of it. She glanced at Mapper and Amaya, found they were looking at her expectantly. They were already clicking into the relentless rhythm of war, she realized. But she wasn't sure if that was a good thing or not.

She nodded to them, and they started gearing up.

"What about Stella?" Amaya asked.

Magdalys looked over the towering pteranodon. For a few moments back there, she really thought they might both be destroyed by that horrible girl and her beast. Hearing that giant yelp of panic inside of herself had been terrifying. But more than that, the existence of Elizabeth Crawbell meant more than ever that the Union was vastly outmaneuvered in the one area Magdalys had the power to help.

She looked up at Stella, who was lashing her long tongue

along her freshly cleaned wounds. "How bout it, girl — you ready to get back in there?"

Stella shot her such a fierce and brittle glare, Magdalys didn't have to wait for the roar to erupt within her to know how the ptero felt.

Ready.

She only wished she could say the same about herself.

CHAPTER TWENTY-SEVEN
A ROUT AND A RUN

MAGDALYS WASN'T SURE if it was that it was her second time, or that the field had been brightened by even more torches, but as Stella approached the raging calamity of soldiers and dinos below, it all seemed so much clearer than it had earlier that night.

There were the skirmishers up at the front of both armies. Foot soldiers and raptor riders both rushed forward in quick, desperate pushes toward each other's lines and then fell back suddenly, or sometimes just seemed to shatter where they stood and be swept away by the ravenous tide of battle. Row after row of trikeriders and stegos stretched away from the front lines in either direction, occasionally punctuated by the long body and swooping neck of a command sauropod; these were the reserve units, waiting for a break in the line or the need for reinforcements.

And there, out in the dark woods at the far end of the corpse-strewn battlefield, the moonlight caught the momentous dust cloud rising around General Sheridan's weary soldiers as they surged forward toward the fight.

"Can you tell how it's going?" Magdalys asked, taking Stella in a wide arc around the edge of the woods and staying low. Surely their fight earlier had attracted some unwanted attention, which meant they'd be on the lookout now, and the air cavalry would probably be lurking somewhere nearby, if not Elizabeth Crawbell and her archaeops. She didn't seem like the type to sit and nurse her wounds for very long, if she'd even gotten any.

Hannibal shrugged. "Could go either way. Think they've got us outnumbered now that Longstreet's trikeriders showed up, but not by much. And Sheridan will help even it out some more. But if they turn that right flank" — he pointed to the far edge of the fighting, where smoke hung over the battlefield like a huge angry ghost — "it might well ripple all the way down our lines and then they'll get behind us and block our retreat to Chattanooga."

Magdalys shuddered. She didn't plan on staying in Tennessee much longer, but the thought of the whole Army of the Cumberland being cut off from their supply line and any hope of escaping north . . . they wouldn't stand a chance.

"That's why the Confederates are trying to build up on that end. But Thomas won't let 'em, see?" He nodded toward a small plateau in the center where a battalion of blue-clad soldiers on paraback were launching attack after attack on the Confederate line. "He keeps hitting 'em over here so they can't mass their forces over there. Wait, something's happening . . ."

Magdalys brought Stella even lower, felt the cool wind against her face as her heartbeat triple-timed against her ears. "What is it?"

"The Ohio 7th is advancing!" Corporal Cailloux yelled further back on the saddle, where he'd set up a spyglass. "They're pushing away that stego unit."

"That's the right flank!" Hannibal said just as they came around from behind a tall row of pines and glimpsed the full battlefield. The Confederate resistance was indeed falling away as the Union fighters pushed forward, but it wasn't in disarray. Instead, it looked like they were gathering at the center of their line.

"Uh-oh," Amaya said.

One of the Union battalions near where Thomas was fighting was in motion too, but instead of rallying around the embattled soldiers on the plateau they headed the opposite direction, toward a far flank.

"What's happening?" Magdalys yelled, trying to quell the panic rising in her.

"I don't know," Hannibal said. "It's impossible to tell from outside the fray, really."

"And even harder from inside," Octave said, shaking his head.

There was a terrible pause, like the night itself just needed to stop and take a deep breath away from the ever-mounting carnage. That gaping hole in the Union line glared up at Magdalys — it must've been glaring out at the Confederate generals too. The whole world seemed suddenly so quiet, and Magdalys imagined that maybe they'd all just realized how futile this whole thing was and decided to call it quits.

Then a terrible howl rose — the Rebel yell — and the whole mass of gray lurched forward as one, its focus right on that opening in the lines.

Another sound rose up now, but it wasn't the desperate yells of men in battle or the grunts of combat. This was something far worse, Magdalys realized as the blue army seemed to scatter like blown dust in the night: the cry of retreat.

CHAPTER TWENTY-EIGHT
CATCH AND CARRY

ONE REGIMENT REMAINED.

It had all happened so fast. After so much back and forth, hours and hours of death and destruction but no real gains one way or the other, virtually the whole army had simply vanished in a matter of moments.

Magdalys blinked at the rush of men across the battlefield as the last retreating Union soldiers disappeared into the woods toward Chattanooga. She'd read that nearly as many men died getting stampeded by fleeing dinos during a retreat as did in actual battle. Already, trees were collapsing throughout the forest amidst the rumbling escape.

She took in a gulp of that crisp mountain air.

One regiment remained: General Thomas's men, still on

that plateau that had once been the center point of a whole sprawling army, now alone in a sea of gray.

She narrowed her eyes on the position.

Thomas had spread his men out just enough to block the main escape route the others had taken. A few squads of trike-riders had slipped past and were in hot pursuit through the woods, but the rest of the army seemed to be kept back by these few men holding their lines.

They had remained so the others could get away.

The Confederate advance checked, they now hurled squad after squad of raptor riders crashing against the rapidly thinning Union lines.

For the second time that night, Magdalys sent Stella into a headlong dive that she wasn't at all sure they'd make it out of alive. Her heart thundered away as the wind rose to a shriek and the blasting of muskets grew louder.

"Incoming!" Octave yelled from behind her, and then the smell of gunpowder filled the night and shots erupted around her. "Air cavalry!"

More blasts rang out — the others returning fire probably — and then the Gatling's ear-shattering staccato song.

"There's too many of 'em!" Hannibal yelled.

The shooting got even hotter now as Stella swooped low over the colliding armies and then something high-pitched whistled over Magdalys's head and exploded behind them.

Artillery.

She glanced up and almost burst out laughing. There was Big Jack standing tall atop his trike, the howitzer still smoking. They'd pulled up behind the crumbling Union lines and immediately jumped into action.

"Nice shot!" Hannibal yelled. "Scattered 'em!"

"WOOHOO!" the men below yelled as Magdalys swung Stella into a half moon over their heads and more artillery shells screeched up into the night.

Already, the Confederate cannons grew louder as the growls of their mounted raptor units rose up over the celebrating troops. Sheridan's column may have arrived just in time to reinforce Thomas's beleaguered last stand, but they were still vastly outnumbered.

"Those trikeriders are getting ready for another charge," Cailloux said. "Set her down in that clearing, Magdalys."

Musket balls whistled through the air around them — the skirmishers had probably caught their breath long enough to take some potshots. Magdalys eased Stella into a landing on a trampled-down open area behind the Union line and squinted out at the dust cloud of combat nearby.

It was impossible to tell what was going on; all she could make out was a rustling sea of blue uniforms pressed together between the back ends of trikes and stegos. Every once in a while the sea would push back and then surge forward as shouts, gunshots, and dinogrowls filled the air.

"Major General!" Cailloux said, sliding down from Stella and snapping to attention.

Sheridan rode up on paraback as his men streamed past him in a steady flow into the fray. He saluted Cailloux and then his eyes went wide as they traced from Stella's humongous claws up past her folded wings to where Magdalys sat near her neck. "My heavens! Is that the . . ." He shook his head, the grim rictus of battle momentarily lifted from his open face. "She's a wonder."

Magdalys smiled and patted Stella.

"Sir," one of the officers nearby said, and then he nodded at something approaching in the darkness above. Sheridan held out his arm for a tiny flapping minidact, which landed on it and held out a roll of parchment in its beak. The general unraveled it and squinted at the writing, shook his head. "Heavy fighting on Missionary Ridge and Lookout Mountain, but they'll hold out. Those positions are well fortified. These lines, on the other hand, won't last much longer." He looked at the entourage of scouts and officers around him. "Tell General Thomas we have arrived and await his counsel." A uniformed man saluted and scurried off and Sheridan turned to Cailloux. "Report, Corporal."

"Aerial surveillance revealed a pretty evenly matched fight for most of the evening. The air cavalry has been out, including Miss Elizabeth Crawbell, who we had quite a scrap with. Just now though, the enemy charged our center as an opening was created, causing both flanks to collapse. General Thomas's men have been holding out to provide cover for the retreating men."

Sheridan shook his head, one hand idly stroking his goatee. "It's what I feared. Still . . ." One eyebrow rose, and Magdalys imagined this was the face he made every time he was about to leap into action. "We'll have to pull back to Chattanooga. From there, we'll regroup, and with coverage from Lookout Mountain and Missionary Ridge we'll be able to make forays into the valley and push Bragg's men back once more."

"Sir." A ragged voice came from the other side of the steady stream of soldiers still pouring toward the battle. Magdalys looked up just as a few of them cleared out of the way for a limping parasaurolophus.

"Card," she gasped.

It was the middle brother, and the older Card rode up just behind him. Both wore bloodstained clothes, their faces even more sullen than usual.

"Good god, man," Sheridan exclaimed. "Where have you been? I sent . . ."

Card silenced him with a shake of his head.

"Oh no," Sheridan said.

"Partisan guerrillas caught him over by Bellham's farm," the eldest brother said. "Hanged him from the tree outside our daddy's house."

"We're going to . . ." Middle Card said in a choked whisper that sent chills up and down Magdalys's spine. He cleared his throat, sent his deathly glare at the ground. "We're going to kill them all. Every last one. I've already put out the word."

The war had snatched someone else's loved one. Once

again, Magdalys was struck by the heartbreaking absurdity of caring so much about one life when hundreds and hundreds were being vanquished just feet away from them, but she had met Young Card. He'd been kind to her, saved her in fact. And anyway, nothing made sense. Not in the world, and especially not at war. She blinked away tears that she didn't even fully understand and the battle seemed to close in around her, around them all, the whole terrible war. One death amidst so many. . . . She shook her head.

"Card," Sheridan said firmly. "I know you have to do what you have to do, but . . . we need you. We're about to get run off this battlefield entirely and it's a miracle we weren't pressed into enemy territory. We're barely scraping by, man. I must . . . I must command you to put off your revenge until *this* fight, which you have sworn an oath to see out, is finished."

Card looked slowly up at the general with all the cool ferocity of a raptor about to make a kill.

"And by order," Sheridan added, meeting his scout's glare with a firm one of his own, "I mean, ask you, as a friend."

The older Card put a firm hand on his brother's shoulder. They exchanged a look, the slightest of nods. "We will honor our oath," he said. "And then we will do what must be done when this wretched war is over."

Sheridan closed his eyes. "I thank you."

"General!" A voice rose from the fighting. "General Sheridan!"

What now? Magdalys thought. A thickly framed man with

a short beard and harried scowl hurried over amidst a small gaggle of attendants.

"Thomas!" Sheridan said, dismounting and rushing over to him. "What news, man?"

General Thomas shook his head. "We've held as long as we can. We must pull back. They've overrun our positions on Lookout Mountain and Missionary Ridge!"

Sheridan boggled. "What?"

"I just got word. If we don't move now, we'll be cut off from the rest of the army."

Bugles erupted around them — the signal for retreat. Magdalys looked on in terror as the ocean of blue began drifting toward them. But it wasn't an ocean at all, she realized, just a very thin dam, and it was barely holding off the real ocean of gray that raged just on the other side. She gulped down a wave of panic, looked to Cailloux, who yelled to Sheridan, "Sir! We need to get you out of here. Now!"

CHAPTER TWENTY-NINE
FLIGHT

"**TAKE HEART, MEN!**" Sheridan yelled into the wind as Magdalys brought Stella low over the heads of the retreating soldiers. They stumbled along in a bedraggled, shambling shadow of the glorious parade they'd been just a few hours ago. Men limped and dragged each other; some all-out ran as cannon fire erupted behind them. A few straightened up and cheered when they heard Sheridan's voice, then gaped at the humongous pteranodon he rode on. Others just kept shuffling, heads bowed.

"Sir," Corporal Buford urged nervously. "I'm not sure you should be hanging quite so far over the edge of the saddle like that."

"Nonsense," Sheridan scoffed, leaning even further to prove his point. "How else will the men see me? And anyway,

I'm quite secured by these straps. Magdalys, take us around again, dear."

"You want to go *back*?" Buford gaped. "Back toward the advancing Confederate Army that just smashed us to bits? General . . ."

"That's quite enough, Corporal. If you don't like it, you're welcome to get out and walk, you know."

Magdalys wasn't wild about the idea of getting anywhere near the advancing Rebel lines, but she smirked to herself at Buford getting put in his place yet again. "C'mon, girl," she whispered, steering Stella up over the tree line and then into a wide turn back toward the rearguard of the retreating army.

Sheridan had insisted on taking a ride to encourage his men and wouldn't be swayed by the other officers urging him to use the opportunity to remove himself from the battle-field. Mapper and Amaya had stayed on board, and Hannibal and Octave trained their weapons to either side in case of an ambush. Cymbeline rode up front with Magdalys.

"I was worried about you," she said.

Behind them, Sheridan was encouraging Buford to shout his own heartening words to the troops below. It wasn't going well.

"I was worried about you too. I've lost track of all the peo-ple I'm worried about," Magdalys said with a frown. "People keep . . . people keep dying. And dinos too."

Cymbeline grimaced. "I know. This is . . . it's been bad the whole war, but I guess . . . after Gettysburg and Vicksburg, I thought things had turned around. This . . . this is really bad."

"Good job, men troops!" Buford yelled shakily. "Er . . . troop troops! Soldiers! Keep . . . keep at it! Excellent retreat!"

"What happens now?"

"That," Sheridan said, startling both of them, "is precisely why I joined you on this magnificent creature." He'd somehow made his way up front without either of them noticing.

"Stealthy, aren't you, sir," Cymbeline said wryly.

He leaned back and yelled over his shoulder, "Keep going, Buford, you're doing great!" then leaned forward conspiratorially and whispered, "He's not."

"You have a plan?" Magdalys asked.

Sheridan shook his head and the brave, unflappable veneer came suddenly crashing down as his face creased into an anguished frown. "I . . . There is no plan. All I know is this: We need General Grant. Without those two mountain outposts, we'll be starved out of Chattanooga in a matter of days. And then we'll be crushed. Grant has an army at his disposal and he's the only general with the tactical genius to get us out of this."

Cymbeline looked stricken. "Isn't Grant in —"

"New Orleans," Sheridan said, leveling a look at Magdalys.

Her eyes went wide, but Sheridan quelled the yelp she was about to release with a raised hand and a solemn shake of his head. "What is it?" she asked.

"Of course, I would rejoice at this seeming coinciding of our needs and yours, but . . ."

Magdalys's heart sank. The US Army needed an air cavalry

now even more than ever, and without someone who could connect directly to pteros, what good would they be against a wrangler like Elizabeth Crawbell?

From not too far away, the booms of artillery shells concussed the night. The battle was still raging even as the Union Army did everything it could to escape. If the Confederates decided to pursue them it could be an all-out massacre.

Magdalys closed her eyes. "I . . ."

"This pteranodon is the only way we can get someone to Grant fast enough," Sheridan said.

"I know," Magdalys said, eyes still shut. A mounted dactyl would have to keep stopping for breaks and risk capture every time. A minidact would probably never make it. And traveling by land through that much enemy territory was far too dangerous.

"But without someone who can reach the dinos the way you do . . ."

"There is someone," a voice said.

Stella let out a bellow that Magdalys was pretty sure was triumphant.

Magdalys's eyes sprang open. Dactyls rose in the air all around them. Not just the Brooklyn dactyls — the Tennessee ones who'd helped them out earlier against Crawbell too. They glided silently up from the dark forest below, their eyes narrowed with determined intent.

"I can do it," Hannibal said.

"What?" Magdalys, Sheridan, and Cymbeline all burst out at the same time.

"This . . . you're doing this," Magdalys said, waving at the squad surging around them. "And that was you who called them to help us earlier!"

"Remarkable!" Sheridan exclaimed.

Hannibal smiled but his eyes were sad. "That was the first time I'd actually got up the courage to try it. Every other time, it's just sort of . . . happened. I . . . I've always known. I just didn't have it in me to admit it. Not to anyone. I was afraid. I mean . . . I'd never met anyone else who could do that. And sure there were stories, legends really, but even knowing what I could do, I still didn't believe it could be me . . . like, why me? I'm just some street kid from Tremé, you know? I thought I had just lost my mind, even though I knew I hadn't. And then . . . and then I met Magdalys."

Magdalys just stared at him, understanding where this was going but unsure how to take it in.

"And you," Hannibal said, shaking his head and blinking away tears. "You're just so . . . you know who you are, you know your power. And you embrace it. I . . . I want to be like that. I want to be like you, Magdalys. Or maybe I should say: I *am* like you, Magdalys, and for the first time, I know that's something to be proud of."

"Remarkable," Sheridan said again, this time in an awed whisper.

Cannons boomed below them, and artillery tore the sky, its ragged echoes shuddering across the valley.

"Thank you," Hannibal said, his eyes meeting Magdalys's.

She grinned. "Anytime, freak."

"In that case," Sheridan yelped, "we have not a moment to lose! Cymbeline!"

"Sir?"

"You will accompany Miss Magdalys. Borrow a uniform from one of the men. You will pose as a Union soldier now, my dear. Can't have you that deep in enemy territory as a woman. You are to cut your hair and find a man's name. Is that clear?"

She nodded, eyes wide. "Actually, Cymbeline *is* a —"

"Never mind all that," Sheridan said. "I'm sure it can be done! Why, just last week, we discovered not one but *two* of our men bathing in the Tennessee River, and do you know it turned out they weren't men at all!"

"That's not what I was —"

"Indeed!" Sheridan yelled. "Apparently it's quite common. Now, Private Rey!"

Octave looked up from his position scanning the battlefield below. "Sir!"

"You are to accompany Cymbeline and Magdalys on their mission to retrieve General Grant. Keep them safe at all costs and alert the general to our present circumstances. He'll know what to do. Is that clear?"

"Sir, yes sir!"

"And give him this." Sheridan passed Octave a sealed envelope. "It's my report. Already vastly out of date by the sudden turn of events, of course, so you'll have to fill him in on the rest yourself."

"Very good, sir."

"Magdalys!" Sheridan barked. "You are not one of my men, er, girls, ah, you know what I mean. I humbly ask that you fly this pteranodon to New Orleans to help us retrieve General Grant."

Yes! Everything in Magdalys yelled. But the thought shattered almost immediately: Sabeen and Two Step were down there somewhere, running for their lives. "Is there any way . . . the rest of my friends . . ."

"There's no time for that, I'm afraid," Sheridan said, and Magdalys felt a tiny shattering feeling in her chest. She'd known there was a good chance that would happen, that any time they separated it might be for good, but . . . it still hurt more than she'd thought it would. "These two may go along, of course," Sheridan added, "but that's all. You must trust that your other friends are in the best of hands and we'll do everything in our power to keep them safe."

Two Step's hurt, furious face flashed through her mind again. What if that was the last time they saw each other? She shook away the thought.

"Will you accept the mission, Magdadis?"

Sure she'd been about to take off on her own just the night before but . . . some part of her hadn't really thought through what it would feel like to actually be separated from her squad for real. It hurt. Magdalys gulped back the sadness. Then she stood and saluted as best she could. "Sir, yes sir!"

"And," he added with a sly wink, "I sincerely hope you find your brother while you're down there."

The grin that crossed Magdalys's face rose from a place deep inside her.

"Now!" Sheridan spun around, facing Hannibal. "Young man! Why don't you use some of these special powers you've been concealing to get us safely out of here so these folks can set off on their mission, yes?"

Hannibal flashed his cockiest smile. "I've been waiting my whole life to do that, sir!"

CHAPTER THIRTY

DARKNESS OVER THE DEEP

TINY, SHINING GLIMMERS of light danced in the darkness below — the moon again, winking at them by way of the Mississippi River to let them know that even as the stifling night closed in around them, they traveled the right path.

"I don't trust him," Amaya said, clipping another strand of Cymbeline's hair.

"Who?" Magdalys asked. She had the comb held out but Amaya didn't seem to need it.

"Sheridan."

Instinctively, all three of them looked to the front of the saddle, where Private Octave Rey sat scanning the dark horizon beside Mapper, rifle ready.

They'd passed through Georgia mostly in silence, with the exception of Mapper's occasional notes pointing out where this or that land had once belonged to the Cherokee or Creek. To Magdalys it seemed like the echoes of mortar blasts and those endless barrages of musket fire only got louder as the thrill of battle fell away and left behind only that rumbling, roiling dread. *What would happen now? Where were Two Step and Sabeen?* At sunset on the second day, Magdalys had looked out across the treetops and glimpsed what Mapper explained must be the faraway lights of Atlanta shimmering in the sky, and she'd realized they'd witnessed firsthand the army of a nation bent on enslaving them crush the army of a nation that wanted to free them. Or at least it claimed to. But even that nation had once enslaved them too. And it didn't even seem so enthusiastic about freedom so much as it was about preserving its precious union. She'd shaken her head, turned away from the illuminated sky, back toward the gathering night, and let out a deep, exhausted breath as the cannons and muskets boomed through her memory once again.

Now, two days later, Magdalys watched Amaya chop away at Cymbeline's thick hair and wondered: If all that had happened in just a few short hours, how much more had already happened since they'd left? And would Two Step ever forgive her for leaving him behind? It seemed like no matter what Magdalys did, she was letting someone down.

"You shouldn't," Cymbeline said with a sniffle. "You shouldn't trust any of them."

Magdalys looked at the older girl, caught a flash of moonlight reflected in the two streams that slid down her face. "Cymbeline . . . what's wrong?"

Cymbeline shook her head, ran a hand beneath her nose and snorted.

"It's the hair," Amaya said. "We carry it with us everywhere we go for so long, and then suddenly it's gone. Like losing our own shadow. My mom told me once we cut our hair when we're mourning or during times of great change. So . . . makes sense, I guess."

Cymbeline nodded, sniffled again, then shrugged. "Right. It's a good kind of sadness. I feel . . . lighter somehow. Like I just threw away a big suitcase I've been lugging around for ages. But also, I . . . I love my hair." She cradled some of the curls Amaya had let fall in her lap and then threw them up into the air for the wind to take. "Loved."

"It'll grow back," Magdalys said, knowing that wasn't much help.

"It's also that . . . I'm scared. For all of us. Why don't you trust Sheridan, Amaya?"

Amaya scowled, handed Magdalys the scissors, and pulled out her bowie knife. "Hold still. Because I grew up around those types."

Cymbeline scoffed. "Overexcited short men in uniform who will promise the stars and sky then turn their backs on you in the blink of an eye?"

"Pretty much just described my dad," Amaya said. "Except

he's six three. But yeah. And I get it: Winning the war is top priority, but that's just it. Everything else is expendable."

"Including us," Magdalys said.

"You guys are black and I'm Apache," Amaya said. "I don't think they know how to see us as anything but expendable." She sliced away some errant clumps of hair, then tilted Cymbeline's head to the side to get a better angle.

"Whether there's a war going on or not," Cymbeline agreed.

"Exactly, and anyway, there's a whole other war going on that nobody wants to talk about it. A perpetual one. The beloved savior Lincoln hanged thirty-eight Dakotas in a single day at the end of last year, and that's not even to mention the ones who were massacred in the run-up to that."

Cymbeline nodded sadly.

"I . . . I didn't know," Magdalys said. She tried to reconcile the gnawing sense of doom and betrayal with the beautiful world around her. The evergreen and pine forests of Georgia had given way to Louisiana's murky swamplands below, and now the shimmering moonlight danced not just through the wide river but sudden stretches of lake and bayou amidst the trees.

And still, dactyls plummeted over and over again through the sky in her mind, as hundreds and hundreds of men collapsed beneath thundering cascades of rifle fire. She couldn't keep dragging dinos and pteros into this bloody horror show. She wouldn't.

She clenched both fists, watching the forest slide by below. She would get to New Orleans and find her brother and then together they'd run off to somewhere safe. Cuba maybe, or even further safe. Somewhere with no cannons or troops marching to their death, where she wouldn't have to call upon giant reptiles for anything more dangerous than a grocery run.

Yes.

"And you're done," Amaya said, brushing away the last couple of strands from Cymbeline's shaved head. "Did you come up with a boy name yet?"

"That's what I was trying to tell the general," she said, standing and wiping herself off. "Cymbeline *is* a boy's name. He was a king in a Shakespeare play."

"Alright, Private King Cymbie," Amaya said, saluting with a wry smile. "Dismissed."

Cymbeline rolled her eyes, returned the salute, and headed over to the front of the saddle.

Magdalys and Amaya sat beside each other in silence for a few minutes as Octave admired Cymbeline's haircut and Mapper explained to her how she should walk to seem more like a man.

Amaya scoffed. "As if Cymbie needs acting lessons from that clown."

"You know," Magdalys said, and then the full hugeness of Amaya's life and strange father seemed to materialize in a heavy cloud around Magdalys and she didn't know what to say.

Amaya looked at her. "What?"

Magdalys dragged a hand down her face and realized how tired she was. "I just . . . we're already scattered. You should . . . when we get to New Orleans . . . you should go."

"Oh."

"Find him, I mean. See what it is he's going on about."

They both turned back to the front, where Cymbeline was pulling one of Octave's blue army jackets on.

"She was a cook at the Citadel," Amaya said so softly Magdalys barely heard her over the wind. "My mom."

Magdalys nodded very slightly, eyes still ahead. Off to the side, Grappler, Dizz, and Beans squawked and swooped back into formation from a hunting run.

"She used to take me aside late at night and tell me about what it was like back home, in Apache Country. About her family . . . *our* family. My older brother from her first husband, and all my cousins. The elders. She smelled like dish soap and a faraway flower and she said every word in English so carefully, like it was a fragile object she didn't want to mishandle." Amaya smiled; tears glistened at the edges of her eyes. "Mama tried to teach me some Lipan — that's our language — but . . ." She shook her head, shrugged.

I'm sorry, Magdalys wanted to say, but what sense did it make? Words were so useless. She didn't have any memories of her own mom, who was still somewhere in Cuba probably. She'd find her one day though. She would.

"One night," Amaya said, "when I went to look for her in the kitchen after hours, she had tears in her eyes. She hugged me extra tight and when I asked what was wrong she just shook her head and told me to do what my father asked of me, *everything*, and to learn everything I could, and in time I would understand. Then she said the name of a place, an important place, she said, but it wasn't that I was supposed to go there, not right away anyway, just that I should know it. Like" — she shook her head — "like one day I'd understand, I guess? But if she's there . . ." Tears welled up. Amaya brushed them away. Magdalys wrapped an arm around her and squeezed. "If she's there, I just want to go there, whenever we get out of this mess. I don't want to go see my dad. But I also know that's what my mom wanted me to do. She said if I wanted to help her, to help us, she said, I'd do what my father asked of me, even if it didn't seem to make sense."

Magdalys didn't need her to say it to know that was the last time Amaya had seen her mom.

"And it wasn't just her telling me to be obedient. There's a lot I don't know about my mom, but I know she was about more than just accepting the lot she was given. I mean . . . it felt like she was planning something. For me, I mean. Like, I was part of her grand plan somehow. But . . . that's all. Then she hugged me tight and sent me to my room. And all I was left with was an order to do what the General says and a name of somewhere I've never heard of." She scowled, wiped a few more tears away.

"So I did what she said. I became the best at everything there was to get good at. Practiced every move I saw them learning in combat class for hours and hours. Aced every test, memorized the ins and outs of each weapon I could get my hands on. But . . . I still don't even know what I'm supposed to understand, and now . . ."

And now the war has broken up the squad, Magdalys thought, watching the swaying swamp trees below and wondering where Two Step and Sabeen were and if they were okay.

Amaya threw her hands up. "I don't trust him. I don't think I love him, even though he's my dad. I don't know what I'm supposed to do."

She put her head on Magdalys's shoulder and day broke slowly across the Southern skies around them.

PART THREE

LOUISIANA

CHAPTER THIRTY-ONE
CRESCENT CITY

A **LOW, RASPY DRONE** sounded and a thousand paras galloped in their strange halting gait across a sun-streaked field as brittle, yellowish hills rose from the ground around them. The paras poured forward, trampling everything in their path. Magdalys swooped closer; she could hear them speaking — not that inner voice that let her know a dino's thoughts — no, these were human voices, discussing the weather, the state of the war and the world, some indecipherable coming crisis . . . and beneath it all, that strange buzz droned on and on, rose and fell, simmered and then suddenly lifted into a startling, urgent shriek just as Magdalys realized those yellow hills were made from hundreds and hundreds of bones.

"Mags!"

Magdalys woke with Mapper's face way too close to hers, his eyes worried as he shook her.

"What happened?" The dream lingered; the buzzy drone still sounded all around her. Thick warm air clung to her as she shoved Mapper away and sat up. "Where are we?"

"Nothing, it's just . . ."

To the east, a pinkish haze swept away the dark blue sky. Below water stretched out to either direction. Stella was gliding low, just over the surface of the lapping waves. "We're over the ocean?" Magdalys blurted out. "We've gone too far!"

"No," Mapper said, and she could tell it was taking all he had not to get snappy with her. "That's Pontchartrain. The *lake*. We made it."

The others were up front, all gazing at the horizon ahead.

Magdalys blinked. "We . . . what?" A surge of something — was it sadness? — rose up in her and she gulped it back, shaking her head. "We're . . . here?"

"New Orleans sits between a curve in the Mississippi River — that's why they call it the Crescent City — and a huge lake called Pontchartrain. In fact, it was founded by —"

"There it is!" Amaya yelled from up front.

Mapper gasped and ran over, and Magdalys stumbled after him. She put her hands on Amaya's and Cymbeline's shoulders and squeezed in between them, gazing out at the stretch of water ahead of them.

"Home sweet home," Octave sighed. "Ain't no place like it."

Rooftops lined the far shore. They mostly just looked like dark lumps from this far away in the half-light of dawn, but they were definitely the beginnings of a city. New Orleans.

They'd made it.

Everyone cheered. Magdalys exhaled a breath that she felt like she must've been holding for months. Cymbeline and Amaya squeezed her into a tight hug as Mapper tried to teach Octave one of his overcomplicated handshakes.

"What is it?" Amaya asked, finally letting go of their hug and taking in Magdalys's solemn face.

Montez was here somewhere, probably. They crossed onto the shore and suddenly tiled rooftops and spiraling Victorian mansions and busted old shacks rushed past beneath them.

"I guess I just . . ." She shook her head. "I don't think I really thought we'd ever get here somehow."

New Orleans meant she would finally have an answer, one way or another, and she wasn't totally sure, even after all they'd been through, that she was ready for that. Even with the riots and the prison yard scuffle with the Kidnapping Club, the world had seemed much simpler in New York, more stable somehow. Sure, people were trying to kill and capture them at every turn, and even their well-meaning organizations meant to protect them were mostly criminally inept, but still . . . newspapers crowed about the US Army's sweeping victories and all those towering buildings offered at least the illusion of some kind of invincibility, however corrupt and unfriendly.

Tennessee and the Battle of Chickamauga had taught Magdalys that the world was just a tinderbox waiting to catch fire, and any life could be snuffed out by a bullet or bomb in fractions of a second. She'd seen it happen up close and then over and over again from above.

The possibility that Montez hadn't survived had seemed to grow large and long while she wasn't looking, a silent, towering shadow. And now, soon, she would have her answer.

Cymbeline squeezed Magdalys's shoulder, catching her eye. "Hey," she said. "We're with you."

Magdalys nodded.

"So, I figured we'd head to the Saint Charles Hotel," Octave said, looking out across the rooftops to where the winding coils of the Mississippi curved through the heart of the city. "That's where General Grant is staying while he's here. From what I've heard about the general, he'll probably be wherever the troops are, but at least the hotel could probably let us know where that is."

"Alternately," Mapper said in a voice that made it clear a Mapper-Knows-All moment was in the pipes, "we could follow the masses of Union troops gathering below."

"Huh?" Octave said, and they all glanced down to the streets below, where blue-coated soldiers worked their way past scowling old ladies and kids playing in the street toward one of the main tree-lined throughways.

Magdalys banked Stella to the side so they could catch a better view. All along the promenade, Union soldiers stood at attention beneath the long, wandering oak branches. Another group moved along slowly from the far end of the avenue, and Magdalys heard the distant strains of trumpets rising over the incessantly buzzing drone.

"A PARADE!" Mapper yelled.

CHAPTER THIRTY-TWO
AMBUSH MUSIC

MAGDALYS WATCHED AS Cymbeline and Amaya mounted up on Grappler and then went swooping away from Stella over the rooftops. Up ahead, Mapper and Octave were already bringing Beans down for a bumpy landing on the bell tower of an elaborate stone church.

"Get somewhere safe, Stella," Magdalys whispered, wrapping her arms around the huge pteranodon's neck. "Thank you for carrying us all this way." Stella snorted and grunted her acknowledgment and Magdalys felt a loving sadness inside that she knew belonged to both her and the ptero. "I know, girl. I know." She patted that smooth, sun-soaked hide one time and then stood.

Dizz stood in the middle of the saddle, his head cocked to one side, and lifted one foot then the other impatiently.

"Alright, buddy, I'm coming," Magdalys said. Music was rising from below, a sweet, wild, and relentless march that made her miss Two Step. She crossed the saddle at a run and leapt onto Dizz, then felt the air whip around them as he carried them off Stella and away. Magdalys glanced back, caught a final nod from her huge friend as the pteranodon banked off toward Lake Pontchartrain.

Other pteros and flying dinos speckled the thick warm air over New Orleans. They glided and tumbled, flitted around playfully and swooped in long arcs across the city, some paired up, others in massive flocks, many by themselves. A few had that determined look that minidactyls get when they're on a mission, but most just seemed to be wandering free. That was different. New York was a way bigger city, with taller buildings and everything packed tightly together, like it had been shoved into a jar it didn't quite fit. But there weren't nearly as many reptiles flying through the air, and the ones that were usually looked like they were on the way somewhere, not just idly flapping about.

New Orleans looked more like it had been splattered outward from the riverbanks, with low houses speckling the outskirts and tighter clusters along the avenues downtown. None stretched so violently into the sky as those New York monstrosities though, Magdalys thought as several sauropods lifted their long graceful necks over the rooftops nearby and started munching on the leaves of a palm tree.

"It's beautiful," she said, and Dizz's *fubba-fubba* reply seemed to be in agreement. A warm, wet breeze tickled her face and the thick swampy air seemed to hug her somehow, keep her afloat. She closed her eyes, allowed herself a few moments to take it all in. That music rose around her — those soaring trumpet notes calling back and forth to each other like sauropods and the heavy thump of the bass drums speckled with a ferocious *brat-da-tat-tat* of the snares — and Magdalys smiled. Somewhere down there, Montez might be marching. He was a new person now, a sharpshooter apparently, and maybe, just maybe, they'd get out of this mess together and make it home alive.

Magdalys opened her eyes and sent Dizz into a spiraling dive toward the church tower.

Paramounted soldiers paraded down the wide stretch of Saint Charles Avenue, followed by a trike unit and two huge brachys, each carrying elaborate officer's quarters. Folks had gathered on either side of the block, Magdalys noticed, but none of them were cheering. Most just watched in stony silence; a few jeered and threw things.

"Occupation," Octave said, passing his spyglass to Magdalys. "The Confederate garrison emptied out as soon as our gunboats showed up on the Mississippi two years ago. Gave up the city without a shot fired. Now it's just an uneasy type of truce here. At least between the white New Orleanians and the US soldiers. Our folks though, heh, well, see for yourself."

Octave pointed further down Saint Charles, where the marching band approached behind three brightly colored . . . were those dancing archaeops? Rainbow feathers covered the figures, sprouting down their long wings and along those tall necks. But they were stomping and shimmying in time to the music and marching on two feet like humans. Magdalys had seen stagedinos before — Cymbeline and Halsey used them in their Shakespeare shows all the time — but they usually just functioned as clowns or elaborate parts of the scenery, and couldn't be trained to do much more than come and go on cue or play fight. They'd certainly never danced.

"What on earth?" Mapper said, taking the spyglass Magdalys was holding out to him and squinting through it for a better look. "What kind of boogie-down dinos are those?"

Octave laughed. "They're not. Those are Mardi Gras Indians. It's regalia."

Amaya perked up. "Indians? Gimme the spyglass. Do you know what tribe?"

"Well," Octave said, "I'm not sure it's really that they're with a particular tribe. They're more like paying tribute to the Indians that helped some of our folks get free from slavery at different times, and the cultures kind of combined into something new."

"Oh," Amaya said, not sounding *too* disappointed. "They're beautiful."

The music got louder as the band marched past. Magdalys could make out the thick, shimmering coils of a tuba wrapped around a tall black man as the driving *oompah-oompah* rounded out the swirl of trumpet and trombone calls. It sounded like they'd taken a regular military tune and thrown it up into the air so all the notes suddenly landed in different places, but you could somehow feel the melody moving along underneath. Magdalys had never heard anything like it — this brand-new swing with those rasping, soaring trumpets, this rumbling, weeping, caterwauling song that was both sad and happy at the same time, that made her want to cry and break into a shimmy.

"There go the Native Guard!" Octave yelled, his voice brimming with pride. "That's my boys!" Amaya passed him the spyglass.

"Wonder if the Louisiana 9th is with 'em," Magdalys said, squinting down at row after row of blue-clad soldiers marching in formation.

"And there's General Grant!" Octave said.

The general sat astride a tall, aging dino that looked like a tyrannosaurus but with small spikes lining its snout. An allosaurus, Magdalys realized, and a bright red one at that. It strutted proudly along, slightly hunched over and squinting impassively at the crowd like it had seen all this before. General Grant wore a tattered blue jacket and busted brown hat with a wide rim. A cigar stuck out from his bearded face and he seemed to regard the whole world somewhat like his steed did, with a kind of weary acceptance. A feisty-looking microdactyl sat on his shoulder and cast a sharp glare at the buildings around them.

A flutter of black from a rooftop across the avenue caught Magdalys's eye.

"*That's* the general that the whole US Army is resting its hopes on?" Mapper asked. "He looks kinda over it. Lemme see the spyglass."

Crows. They'd been perched along the balcony rail of a pillared mansion and suddenly took flight in a splash of dark feathers.

Something had spooked them.

Magdalys squinted at the balcony, then the rooftop. A figure, tall and feathery, rose; then another.

Those weren't the Mardi Gras Indians though. Those were mounted lizards. She could see the sun glinting off the rifle barrel of one of the riders. They wore hooded cloaks, just like the Kidnappers Club members back in New York.

"It's an attack," Magdalys said, already making a dash for Dizz. "We need to —"

A sharp crack ripped through the air, its echo rumbling like thunder across the city of New Orleans.

CHAPTER THIRTY-THREE
ATTACK!

MAGDALYS BARELY PAUSED as the shock of the blast rumbled through her. Montez might be down there, and even if he wasn't, the general definitely was, and whoever those attackers were they were probably gunning for him. Dizz was already extending his long wings and crouching down, ready for flight. Magdalys grabbed his neck and heaved herself onto his back.

"Go!" she yelled, and the church tower fell away beneath them.

Soldiers and civilians scattered through the streets below. Smoke rose from the sidewalk in front of the mansion those mounted riders had appeared in. But where were they? And where was the general? Magdalys pulled Dizz into a steep climb and then circled back down toward Saint Charles.

There! That tired ol' allosaurus still had plenty of fight in it, she realized. The dino had charged down the avenue full throttle, using those front horns to smash any obstacle — a small parade vehicle, an ice cream stand, a fallen tree — out of its way. General Grant had both reins in hand and was bouncing up and down in the saddle but didn't appear especially bothered or afraid.

Two trikes rumbled along in their wake, each mounted by a cadre of frantic-looking blue coats — the general's guard detail, Magdalys assumed.

Another flicker of movement caught her eye and the two flying dinos burst into the air from a nearby rooftop, spread their brown, gray, and black feathered wings and soared toward the street below. Sinornithosaurs. Those things could kill with one bite because of the venom hidden in their razor-sharp teeth. Magdalys launched after them. The trikeriders had their eyes on the surrounding streets, totally oblivious to the attack careening down from above.

"Look out!" Magdalys screamed.

Their faces all turned skyward at once and their rifles followed suit. Magdalys gasped and swung Dizz into a barrel roll out of the way as the bullets blasted past. One of the sinorniths screeched and tumbled, sending its rider screaming toward the ground; the other swung deftly out of the way. Magdalys glanced back. The rider who hadn't fallen landed his mount on a nearby balcony and was prepping his rifle. Across the street, Cymbeline burst into the air on Grappler's back. Octave rode in the saddle behind her, already hurling shot after shot at the attacker.

So that was handled. Magdalys turned back toward the general. She swooped low past the trikes and was about to swing skyward when something slammed into Dizz from the side with a growl and the world did a somersault. Gravelly pavement scraped her arms as she skidded off to the side amidst flailing dactylwings and snapping jaws, and then she was up, not too hurt, and backing away from a snarling green raptor.

It scrambled to its feet with a growl, dust flying up around them, and then lowered that long snout, eyes wide, and took a slow step toward them. Dizz had tumbled a few feet behind her and was still trying to get himself together, and Magdalys had sworn she wouldn't drag any more dinos into this war on her behalf, she'd *sworn* it! But this one, although riderless, was clearly already involved. And anyway, he was about to eat her. She reached out with her mind and . . . nothing.

Blocked again!

That meant that somewhere out there, another Confederate dinomaster was lurking, watching, controlling things.

The raptor rose up, and then swung his head low again, sniffing loudly, eyes narrowing. One razor-sharp claw scratched a line into the gravel.

Magdalys backed another step away. If she ran, it would simply snatch her up. She reached for her pistol but knew there wouldn't be time to load it before the raptor pounced.

A bright flash of color suddenly took over the world in front of her. A whole rainbow seemed to parade before her wide eyes now. The Mardi Gras Indians!

"HA!" they yelled in one resounding voice amidst a shimmer of tambourine bells and deeper drum hits.

The raptor recoiled.

"HA!" Louder now. And again: "HA!" And they advanced as one, their feet gliding across the pavement in smooth circles. The raptor backed up uneasily, glancing to either side at these strange new opponents. They stepped forward.

Magdalys gaped at them. They weren't in the raptor's head — there was no way. They were just collectively wrangling it away from her, with nothing but drumbeats and the sound of their voices. She'd never seen anything like it.

"Th-thanks!" she said, probably not loud enough for them to hear. Then Dizz gave a startled caw just as Magdalys felt the ground rumble. She looked up just in time to see one of the security trikes barreling toward her, now with only a single rider on top. He wore a US Army uniform and had a long red goatee. He was glaring at Grant. The rest of the soldiers who'd been on it lay scattered on the ground, looking stunned.

The Confederate dinomaster! It had to be!

She dove out of the way as the trike thundered past, was already running as she rose and then leapt onto Dizz's back and they took off after it.

CHAPTER THIRTY-FOUR
THROUGH THESE BROKEN STREETS

GENERAL GRANT HAD his sidearm out and was glancing around wearily, oblivious to the trike charging from the rear.

"General Grant!" Magdalys yelled. "Behind you!"

He spun around, face clenched and eyebrows arched, with the trike just a few steps away and closing fast. That red allosaurus sidestepped just enough so the trike's long horn scratched along its haunch instead of impaling it clean through. The beast roared and swung its head around, chomping a nice chunk out of the trike's upper thigh as it passed.

"Whoa!" Magdalys yelled.

The trike shrieked and swung hard to the left, bustling down a side street as Grant let off a series of pistol shots after

216

it. "Go, Samantha! After them!" he hollered in a gravelly voice, and the allosaurus lurched forward in a lopsided canter.

Magdalys blinked, veering Dizz into a wide turn behind the general. "I didn't see *that* coming," she said.

Fubba-fub, Dizz agreed.

Up ahead, the trike crashed down a ragged mud-strewn street beneath winding oak branches and palm fronds. It was definitely favoring the side that hadn't been chomped, but the beast had still managed to reach an impressive gallop. Samantha wasn't far behind though, and she wasn't letting up. Grant leaned forward in the saddle, both hands on the reins now.

Something stirred in the shadows of an alleyway and then a finback hustled out into the street from behind a shotgun shack. What was it doing? That tall sail along its spine rocked back and forth as the dimetrodon stopped just in front of Grant's charging allosaurus.

The dinomaster, Magdalys realized. He was wrangling anything he could get his mind on and sending them in Grant's path.

Samantha didn't even pause, just sent the finback tumbling out of her way with a sharp kick and kept it moving. The finback rolled a few times and then got up, shook itself off and headed back to the alleyway, dazed.

But now a whole pack of long-necked, slender-bodied dinos fell into stride on either side of Samantha. They pranced along on their back two legs, snapping at her with long snouts and squealing. *Struthiomimus*, Magdalys thought. *The ostriches of the dinoworld*, Dr. Sloan called them, *in form, attitude, and general demeanor.* They posed no threat to a huge beast like Samantha, of course, but they might slow her down.

Magdalys swooped Dizz into a long dive and came up fast behind them, knocking the skinny running dinos to either side with ease.

Grant urged his mount on, barely noticing, and pulled out his service revolver again as he got closer.

Up ahead, the red-bearded rider glanced back, face wide with fear, and snarled, turning just in time to see the tremendous pothole in the street ahead of him. "Aiigh!" the dinomaster yelled, and the trike seemed to crumple beneath him as it stumbled, then crashed with a tremendous explosion of dust into the broken concrete disaster area. The Confederate catapulted forward, tumbling a few times, and then sprung to his feet. "Up, fool!" he screeched, but the trike couldn't right itself.

Magdalys urged Dizz up and forward, hoping to swoop down on him from above, but Grant was already lobbing shot after shot at the man, as Samantha lowered her horned snout and broke into a full-on charge.

"No!" he yelled, stumbling back a few steps and then dashing into a nearby alley as gunfire thudded into the street on either side of him.

Samantha skidded to a halt beside the downed trike just as two more mounted sinorniths launched skyward from another mansion rooftop. The sinorniths had begun their dive, but Grant was still squinting toward where the Confederate had disappeared into the alley. "General Grant!" Magdalys called, spurring Dizz into a dive. "Behind you!"

He cocked his head at her, blinking, then spun just as the first sinornith leveled into a straightforward glide-charge down the street toward him. A single shot sang out and the rider went flying backward with a scream as the sinornith veered suddenly away. Magdalys hadn't even seen Grant raise his pistol.

The second attacker was still coming fast and now a third leapt from a nearby rooftop, glide-diving toward Grant with a shrill caw.

He would never be able to fend them both off.

One snap from those jaws and the general on whom the Union's hopes rested would be a dead man.

"C'mon!" Magdalys grunted into Dizz's ear, and he flapped harder, surging forward as the ornate mansions and twisting oak trees became a blur on either side. Grant fired again but the shot went wide, and then they were rushing up from behind and the sinornith riders swept toward them.

Magdalys leapt from Dizz's saddle, crashing into General Grant from the back and throwing them both out of the way as the allosaurus roared and snapped at the sinornith in front of her, grasping one wing in her mighty jaws and wrenching him from the sky.

Magdalys felt the wind rush out of her body as she landed

on the uneven cobblestones with a nasty thwack. The whole world flashed bright white and then grew hazy. Magdalys was pretty sure she saw the other sinornith land on that bright red allosaurus neck with a terrifying screech, its jaws opened wide, all those glistening, lethal teeth on full display. Then General Grant heaved himself into a squat beside her, raising his pistol so it was almost point blank against the sinornith's chest, and a single shot cracked out just as everything became nothing at all.

CHAPTER THIRTY-FIVE
THE SAINT CHARLES HOTEL

THAT BUZZ.

Or was it a growl?

Either way, those paras were stampeding again, loping along with desperate, thundering strides across the valley, hills made of yellowed bone on either side.

They hooted and barked, and then they spoke in quiet, concerned tones to one another about politics and military strategy, and even from way up above them where she soared, Magdalys could somehow tell that their hands were human hands, pink and brown and long-fingered, and their lips were human lips.

And then the growling buzzing droning murmur grew louder and louder and suddenly the ground itself seemed to open in a gaping maw and the stampeding paras slipped in by the hundreds, their voices, unperturbed, warbling on and on as they tumbled into the darkness.

Magdalys flew higher, glanced down, gasped in awe as the earth and grass peeled away from either side of the brand-new crater to reveal a gigantic set of very human teeth.

The hole kept getting bigger — or was she falling toward it? Either way, soon the world was in darkness and all she heard was that dissonant, chirping murmur until, ever so slowly, the twittering song of a morning bird accompanied a gentle breeze and the smell of magnolias and jasmine.

Magdalys blinked.

An ornate ceiling came into focus, all flowery plaster motifs and elaborate paisley wallpaper. New Orleans. She could already recognize that warm, swampy air and the hooting calls of so many dinos passing by on foot and overhead.

And beneath it all that never-ending murmur, which Magdalys had come to think of as a song unto itself. She didn't know if it should frighten or comfort her, but whatever it was, it wasn't going anywhere.

She was in a bed, and a dull ache pulsed through her, and by the soft gray light she guessed it was very early in the day. A brass frame rose above her and there was a shape clutching it, no, a figure, she realized, squinting through her aching, blurred vision. A microdact, its little claws grasping the crossbar, its wide eyes glaring into her own.

"Gah!" Magdalys yelled, wishing the thing gone, and with a screech the tiny beast flung across the room, bashed into the far wall and then fluttered with a squawk to the top of a dresser, where it perched and eyed her angrily.

"So it's true then," a gruff voice rasped from the window.

Magdalys sat up.

General Ulysses S. Grant sat at a small desk, plume poised over a messy stack of papers. One of his legs had been swathed in bandages and was resting on a fancy pink ottoman that seemed utterly out of place beside the general's rumpled blue slacks and off-white button-down shirt.

"Good morning? Sir?" she said. "I'm . . ."

"Magdalys Roca," Grant finished for her, more or less nailing the pronunciation. He spoke with the long, matter-of-fact sigh that she'd come to expect from folks from the Midwestern states like Ohio and Illinois. His gruff face widened into a magnificent grin that then quickly vanished again behind that shabby brown beard. "I've heard all about you already. Mind if I smoke?"

"Uh, no. And what's true?"

He struck a match and lifted it to the cigar already perched between his lips. "I can't even get Giuseppe to fetch me a newspaper from the chair beside me."

"Giuseppe?"

Grant cocked an eyebrow and nodded at his microdact, who still scowled at Magdalys from atop the dresser. "You sent him across the room without moving a muscle."

Magdalys furrowed her brow. He was right — she hadn't even meant to, or realized she'd done it, but the creature had startled her so much, the shock must've translated into a command that he had . . . been forced to obey. The idea gave her a chill. This was what those Confederate dinowranglers were doing, of course: mastering and dominating their mounts, making them servants instead of partners. That's not what Magdalys wanted to do.

Still.

She threw her legs over the side of the bed and stood. "Yes, it's true." It wasn't a bad skill to have handy in a bind. "What . . . what happened?"

"Well, for one thing," Grant said, letting a gigantic musty mountain of smoke out, "you saved my life, young lady."

"I . . . I did?"

"And Samantha's too, for which I'm eternally grateful, of course. Made my security detail look a touch incompetent though, so they may be a bit salty with you. But that was the Bog Marauders' play, it seems."

"Who?"

"The Bog Marauders are a paramilitary group of Confederate supporters who patrol the swamplands across southern Louisiana. They've been giving our troops a whole lot of trouble out in the wilds, but they hadn't been bold enough to strike within New Orleans." He twisted his mouth and sighed. "Until yesterday that is. That fellow we were chasing was Earl Shamus Dawson Drek."

"What a name," Magdalys said.

Grant nodded. "Indeed. We'd been tracking his moves as best we could for the past year, but what we didn't know until your intel came through was that he's a Knight of the Golden Circle. What they call a Class II Dinomaster."

Magdalys sat up very straight.

"Seems these Knights have been traveling to different hot zones, bolstering the combat troops or partisan guerrillas as needed by the Rebs. Causing political trouble in places like Kansas and Kentucky." He scowled. "Bad business. I was hoping to wing him at least and then bring him in for questioning."

"But?"

"That area of the Garden District he escaped into is well-to-do and white, I'm afraid, so when our boys got there for pursuit, nobody had seen anything." The general rolled his eyes. "Perils of a Union-controlled city in Confederate territory, you know. Drek has protection and he's probably back out in the Atchafalaya Swamplands by now." He looked up. "Anyway, they were certainly trying to kill me. And they would've too, if it hadn't been for you."

"Oh," Magdalys said. "I . . ."

Grant waved her wordlessness away. "That's alright, Magdalys, I never know what to say to people either. Wouldn't mind if folks just left me alone altogether, if we're being honest. But by the look of things, that's not going to happen anytime soon."

Magdalys shook her head. "No, it's probably not."

"Sheridan sent a letter along, you know," Grant said. "An excitable little fellow, that one, but he's not an easy man to impress."

Magdalys still didn't know what to say. She reached over to the tray of breakfast food someone had left on the bedside table and held one of the rolls out to Giuseppe, taking care not to accidentally demand he come to her. "I . . . I just want to find my brother."

Giuseppe eyed her suspiciously for a few moments, then flapped down to the foot of the bed.

"Yes," Grant drawled, "he mentioned that. I've sent my man Parker to make some inquiries about the Louisiana 9th."

Magdalys looked up, her heart racing, and Giuseppe took the opportunity to hop over and snatch the roll from her hand, then flap back to his perch on the bedframe.

"Quite a regiment," Grant continued. "They really came through for us at Milliken's Bend. Took a serious beating too. Up to that point, I hadn't been sure if . . ." His cigar-stained voice trailed off. If Negro troops would be of any use in battle, the rest of the sentence went. He didn't have to say it. "Well, you know."

"Did . . . do you . . ." Magdalys stuttered.

"Don't know anything yet, but I'll let you know as soon as I do." The general adjusted himself on the chair to face her more directly, cringing slightly as he moved. "But listen, Magdalys, if I may . . ."

"Yes, sir?"

"I've also been updated about the situation at Chattanooga."

Magdalys nodded and tried not to look away. She knew where this was going.

"I'm not going to lie and say the US government is fighting this war just to free your people," Grant said matter-of-factly. "In fact, there are a good number of folks up north who would just as well call it quits right now and let the South keep their slaves, as I'm sure you know."

She nodded, staring at him.

"And to be plain, at one time it seemed like the path to victory might include such a concession, and I was all for it if that's what it took to win this war." He frowned, shaking his head. "I'm not a savior, nor a liberator. Not an abolitionist, although I think the whole matter of slavery is a cursed endeavor."

Giuseppe flapped across the room and perched on Grant's shoulder, glancing uneasily out the window and then around the room.

"But that's no longer a possibility, and as many lives as it's cost, I do think the world will be a better place for it in the long run. We need to crush the South to end this rebellion, and that includes ending slavery. And we need your help to do it. All of you . . ." He waved his cigar in little circles, searching for the word. "Your people. But especially you, Magdalys."

She tightened her lips.

"I know it's not fair, to put that burden on one so young. Especially one who has already been through so much. I won't pretend any of this is fair, or noble, or glorious. It's war, and it's ugly, and it'll snatch your whole soul away if you let it. And it's the world we've inherited, and I intend to make this place a better one than it was when I got here, and if you can help me do it, well, it'll be that much easier, is what I'm trying to say." He exhaled, seemed to deflate some now that he'd gotten that off his chest. "You've had a run-in with Miss Crawbell and her archaeops, I heard?"

Magdalys nodded.

"Then you know what we're up against. If the Knights of the Golden Circle are as well organized as your friends and the Pinkertons have told us, this whole war could be won or lost on their whim. I don't plan on letting that happen, and for that I need all the dinowranglers I can get to help me."

Magdalys felt a lump gather in her throat — the damp, heavy weight of disappointing yet another person who was doing everything they could to win this war. "I'm not . . ." She'd promised herself. She wouldn't drag any more lives into this sinking pit of a war with her. She wouldn't. And if she wasn't willing to wrangle dinos, what good was she to the Union cause? She was just some kid, was all. And anyway: She had to find her brother. And as soon as she signed up, she'd have to do whatever they told her. "I'm sorry, sir," she said in what sounded like a tiny, faraway whisper. "I just —"

"You're worried about having to do what you're told, aren't you?"

"Well . . ."

"That you'll never see your friends again, or your brother, because once you sign up you'll be beholden to whatever order your given, on pain of death."

"That's definitely part of it, yeah," Magdalys admitted. It was nice to have someone else say it for her, even if it kinda sounded like a threat. And anyway, what good did it do? The general understanding her predicament didn't change it.

Grant leaned forward, winced, then squinted directly into Magdalys's eyes. On his shoulder, Giuseppe did the same. "What if I were to tell you that you could be in charge of your own special regiment of dinowarriors."

Magdalys blinked at him.

"A team that you could put together yourself and have total authority over, answering only to me. Let's call it a counterbalance to the Knights of the Golden Circle. Heck, you can even name it if you want. I'm sure you'd think of something better than anything I could come up with."

"Is that even . . . possible?" Magdalys managed. "I mean, do you . . . can . . ." There was no way to ask the question without sounding like it was undercutting the president's favorite fighting general.

Grant leaned back, chuckled. Giuseppe kept squinting at Magdalys, but she thought just maybe he was smiling now. "You mean" — he pulled on his cigar — "how could I possibly have the authority to do such an audacious maneuver?"

"I . . ."

He smiled and shook his head. "It's a good question. As it

happens, the president has seen fit to name me commander in chief of this entire army." The general looked uncharacteristically pleased with himself. "A brand-new position, in fact, with unprecedented powers. Just went through Congress. Probably hasn't even hit the wires yet."

"Whoa," Magdalys said. "Congrats."

"Heh." He nodded his acknowledgment, long crow's feet stretching away from his smiling eyes. Then his face grew serious again. "I don't like it, mind you. I don't mean the position — that's fine. I don't like young people being in the line of fire. Not now, not ever. But when I accepted the position I told the president I'd do whatever it takes to win, that I'd meet any force they brought to bear on us with an even greater fire that would smash them into submission, and that's exactly what I intend to do. Now, we may have another dinowarrior of your skill within the ranks of this army, but if we do I'm not aware of it and we simply don't have the luxury of being able to go looking for him right now."

Giuseppe squawked and flew over to land on Magdalys's shoulder.

"Or her," Grant said. "And anyway, I imagine you in more of an administrative capacity. Overseeing and training and such."

A moment passed.

"So, what do you say, Magdalys?" the general said. "How would you like to have the full weight of the US Army at your back so we can stop these Rebels in their tracks?"

"I don't know what to say," Magdalys said.

Grant nodded. "Good. It's a big decision. You shouldn't rush it. Giuseppe."

The microdact squeezed Magdalys's shoulder once and then stuttered across the room, snatched a sealed envelope off the desk, and delivered it to Magdalys.

"See," Grant said. "Exactly what I wanted him to do. That never happens. He's trying to impress you."

"What's this?" Magdalys asked.

"A document stating exactly what I just said to you in no uncertain terms. If you should decide to join us, just show it to the nearest commanding officer and they'll sort you out. All I ask is that you don't tear it up. Could come in handy."

A knock came at the door and then some scuffling noises. Magdalys pocketed the envelope. "Ah, sir?" someone called from the other side. "There are some, ah, people . . . here."

"Come in," Grant said gruffly.

The door flew open and Mapper and Cymbeline rushed in, followed by Octave and a tall, stout officer with light brown skin and a wispy goatee. "Magdalys!" Mapper yelled. "You're alright!" He rushed over and threw his arms around her while Cymbeline stood by, her expression sad.

That wasn't like Mapper.

"What is it?" Magdalys asked. "Where's Amaya?"

"She's gone," Mapper said, and squeezed her even tighter.

CHAPTER THIRTY-SIX
PLANS AND PARTINGS

"**AND THEN SHE** just . . ." Mapper shook his head, staring at his hands. ". . . just. . . ." He shrugged. "She gave me a big hug and said she was sorry and walked out the door. That was it."

They stood on either side of Amaya's empty bed. In the other room, Cymbeline, Grant, and the officer, Colonel Ely Parker, conferred quietly.

"You gonna open it or do I have to do it for you?" Mapper said, nodding at a crisp envelope on the pillow with Magdalys's name written on it.

She scrunched up her face, somehow dreading what she'd find. The scrap of paper inside just had three words:

Tamaulipas — Esmeralda Crusher

"What's that mean?" Mapper demanded. He'd hurried over to where Magdalys was standing and was reading over her shoulder. "Is that a name? Sounds like a name kinda."

"I have no idea," she said. Was it the place Amaya's mother had whispered to her before she'd disappeared? Had Amaya gone there instead of off to find her father? The information felt sacred somehow, something she wasn't even supposed to tell Mapper. Not yet anyway. And she had no idea what to make of Esmeralda Crusher.

"Tamaulipas looks Spanish," Mapper said, his voice harried. "You speak Spanish, right, Mags?"

She shook her head. "Yeah, but . . . not perfectly and it's nothing I recognize. I . . . look, whatever the word means, what this really means is she's gone." The Dactyl Hill Squad was truly in the wind now, scattered like seeds across the battle-torn country. Magdalys sniffled. Everything they'd built with each other — this war had just shredded it to pieces.

"We gotta . . ." Mapper threw his hands up. "We gotta go look for her. She might be —"

"No," Magdalys said. "She wasn't snatched off the street, Mapper. She left."

"I know." He hugged Magdalys. "I get it. But . . . why?"

"She . . . she's doing what her mom wanted her to," Magdalys said. "Something she has to do. And it won't be easy, whatever it is. But we can't go after her, Mapper. I . . . I'm sorry." She put a hand on his shoulder and he hung his head and covered his eyes.

"We're all over the place," Mapper sighed. "I didn't think this would happen. Not this fast, anyway."

"I know," Magdalys said. "Me neither." She knew she'd told Amaya to go, but it still hurt. Way more than she'd thought it would. She tucked the note in her pocket. She'd have to figure out whatever it was Amaya was trying to tell her later.

Mapper looked up. "Are you okay, though? We were worried about you."

Cymbeline came in and sat on the bed beside her. "We were really worried. You were . . ." — the actress's eyebrows rose and then she tipped her head — "*very* brave."

Magdalys shrugged. "I'm alright. Aches and pains."

"They said you might have a concussion," Cymbeline said.

Now Grant limped in on a crutch, his finger fidgeting endlessly with the buttons on the jacket he'd just pulled on, Colonel Parker just behind him. "Ah, young people?"

Magdalys stood, because she wasn't sure what else to do with herself. "What is it?"

"We . . ." Words seemed to fail him again, and Magdalys was about to yell at him to spit it out when he managed to do just that. "Your brother's medical convoy was attacked while they were en route to New Orleans."

Magdalys gulped and her legs seemed to give out from under her. She felt Cymbeline's steadying hand on her shoulder, felt the bed beneath her, felt a wide, impossible emptiness stretch out inside her.

"He and his fellow soldiers have been declared missing in action, but . . ."

"We have to go find him!" Magdalys blurted out.

"The area where they went missing," Colonel Parker said, stepping up beside the general, "the Atchafalaya Swamplands, is a vast, almost impossible terrain that is completely under the control of the Bog Marauders."

"That's where you said Earl Shamus Dawson Drek probably escaped to," Magdalys said.

Grant nodded. "Indeed. And . . ." He looked around, flustered. "It is said to be haunted by the phantoms of long-dead dinosaurs. But that's just silliness, of course."

"And the convoy was lost over a week ago, I'm afraid." Parker shook his head. "I don't think —"

"I don't care what you think," Magdalys snapped. She was standing again, her finger raised, aimed directly at Parker. Cymbeline's hand stayed on her shoulder, and Magdalys felt like without it she might just float away on a torrent of her own wrath. "It doesn't matter how many Marauders there are or what the terrain is, we *have* to —"

"No," General Grant said, not unkindly. "I'm sorry, Magdalys. I can't authorize a rescue mission into the swamplands. I've ordered Sherman to march overland for Chattanooga and bring all available corps from the Army of the Mississippi."

"But . . ."

"And Emperor Maximilian is massing troops at Matamoros

on the Mexican border and they'll tilt things toward the Rebels if they have a chance, so General Banks has already marched out with whatever units he has left to deal with that and the mosasaurus-riding blockade runners." He shook his head. "I'm sorry," he said again, his sad eyes meeting hers.

She turned. Shrugged. Shook her head. She wouldn't cry. This wasn't the time for that. She had a mission to prepare for. "Doesn't matter," she said, heading for the door. "You may need my help to get the job done" — she shot Grant a long, sharp glare — "but I don't need yours."

The door slammed on a cacophony of yells and questions behind her.

The churches, mansions, and run-down shacks of the Garden District stretched to either side of her. The buildings got taller and fancier and then slid back into dilapidated one-stories, on and on throughout the city.

The sun had risen on a muggy purplish morning as huge tortoises lumbered up and down Saint Charles Avenue with dark green streetcars hitched to their harnesses. They stopped every few blocks to let off and collect passengers; nodded solemnly as they passed one another.

A bakery opened its doors on the far side of the block, and the smell of fresh bread reached all the way up to where Magdalys stood on the hotel roof with Dizz, Beans, and

Grappler perched on either side of her. She thought she'd come up here to cry, but no tears had come. Maybe she didn't have any left; all that was left inside her was fire — that never-ending flame she'd first felt flying over that Tennessee plantation.

But even the fire had been reduced to a quiet, crackling sizzle. She'd told it to cool and it had, tamped down by the shock of Cymbeline's lies and then the confusion of all that army protocol and tough decisions and the suddenness of battle. And with no tears and barely any fire, all Magdalys felt was empty.

Sol had been killed before her very eyes. There was nothing even left of him, no body to send home or bury. The youngest Card had died that same day, and countless others. Sabeen and Two Step were trapped in a strange city, surrounded by enemies who wanted to kill or enslave them. Amaya had run off to find out what twisted destiny her father had in mind for her, and how it all fit into her missing mother's plan.

The US Army was on the verge of total destruction, it seemed. And Montez . . . Montez was lost in the Atchafalaya Swamplands, probably dead.

Magdalys shook her head. She'd come all this way, crossed the whole country from north to south just about, only to find that he was still gone, just gone.

And no one would go look for him except her.

She heard the rooftop door creak open and then slam closed — someone coming to convince her it was alright somehow, that she should just give up and go along with Grant to Chattanooga.

"Magdalys," Cymbeline said from behind her.

Magdalys shook her head. "I'm not going."

"I know," Cymbeline said. "I'm not asking you to go. The general knows you're not going too."

She raised her eyebrows. "He does?"

Cymbeline came up beside her; Grappler edged a few inches over to make room. "He's no fool, Magdalys. And neither am I, by the way. I don't think you should go out there by yourself, but I know I can't stop you. I don't think anyone could stop you from doing anything you've set your mind to, Magdalys Roca. And I'm not totally sure that's a good thing."

Magdalys acknowledged the point with a surly shrug.

"I don't know what you're going to do," Cymbeline said, "or how you think you're going to do it. But I know what I have to do. I have to help this army win this war."

Magdalys wished it could feel so simple for her, and the wish tasted bitter, wrong somehow. Because it wasn't simple for Cymbeline either, or Hannibal, or any of them. And still — the feeling remained, worming its way through her thoughts without permission. "They're taking you with them back to Tennessee?"

"I have orders, Magdalys. New ones. I'll be taking the general to Tennessee, yes, and then I have to head back up north from there. There's an operative in New York they need me to . . . handle."

Magdalys wanted to scream but instead she just leaned against Cymbeline and put her head on her shoulder.

Cymbeline wrapped an arm around her. "I'm sorry," she whispered.

"Don't be," Magdalys said. "I understand, just like you understand me."

"Yeah. Doesn't make it any easier, does it?"

Magdalys shook her head, sniffed. "Nope."

A moment passed, that never-ending murmur rising and falling amidst the sounds of the city waking up for another day. Magdalys reached out with her mind, past the clutter of commuters and beggars, the snorts of giant tortoises and grumbling dinos.

There.

She turned to Cymbeline. "Listen," she said, found herself smiling. Somehow, the path was clear. She didn't know what it meant or why, but she knew what to do. At least in this moment, if no other. This must've been what Hannibal had felt like, carrying that secret and then suddenly seeing how he could put it to work.

"What?" Cymbeline asked.

"I have something for you."

Then yells erupted from below and a huge shadow passed over them. Cymbeline gazed up, mouth open.

Magdalys's smile grew bigger. "Some*one*, I should say."

"Stella," Cymbeline gasped as the magnificent pteranodon landed with a thud on the rooftop and looked around languidly. The three dactyls squawked a joyful song and waddled over to nuzzle her.

"How else were you going to make it back there in time to save Chattanooga?" Magdalys said.

"But —"

Magdalys cut her off. "These guys are all I'll need."

"You mean all *we'll* need," Mapper said from the doorway.

"Wait," Magdalys said. "What?"

'I'm coming with you, Mags." He was lugging a whole bunch of saddlebags. "Did you really think I'd just let you run off to save the day on your own? I said I had your back from the beginning and I meant it. Now give me a hand with these ammo cases General Grant asked us to hold on to for him while he's away!"

CHAPTER THIRTY-SEVEN
INTO THE SWAMPLANDS

THE DARK GREEN and murky brown forest swamps blurred past beneath Magdalys and Mapper. New Orleans had become a scattering of cabins and occasional clustered tents as they flew west, and eventually the wilderness became the world and sparkling bayous snaked through vast oak and pine forests.

"Atchafalaya," Mapper said, but Magdalys could tell his usual excitement was dimmed some.

"Go on," she said, after a few moments passed of just the whistling wind and burps, chirps, and yelps of swamp life around them. "I'm listening."

"It's a Choctaw word. But there are tons of different nations besides the Choctaw that were and are on this part of the state: the Houma, the Chitimacha. . . ."

"How —"

"Books, Magdalys." Mapper's voice wasn't cold exactly, but it certainly wasn't warm either. "We had a whole library at the orphanage, remember? And sometimes the newspapers report on different nations around the country."

"Gotya."

That murmur only grew louder the further they got from the city: a deep, chortling burble that sometimes swung upward into an all-out wail. Magdalys had just gotten used to it. The sound was either the collected calls of the many, many dinos of the Louisiana bayou country or it was . . . she shuddered. Grant had said the Atchafalaya was haunted, but he was right: that was silliness.

Still.

The swamp gave way suddenly to an expanse of trimmed grass and hedges. A few busted shacks speckled the edge of the property and two grandiose pillared mansions faced each other from either end.

Magdalys shuddered, felt that familiar rage start to build up in her again, but this time when she told it to go it listened right away, eased back to a sparkly simmer and then dispersed entirely, leaving only sadness in its wake.

"I know," Mapper said, watching her face go from clenched to resigned. "Me too."

She glanced across the open sky to her friend.

It had been a while since she'd really taken the time to look at Mapper, or anyone for that matter — everything kept happening so fast, pausing seemed like a luxury. But no one was shooting at them right now; in fact, no one was around at all. Besides the never-ending murmur and the hoots and caws of swamp dinos below, they were alone. The world was theirs, and, of course, very much not at the same time.

Mapper smiled a sad smile. His face looked older somehow, more solid. The past few weeks had shoved them all much closer to being grown women and men than Magdalys wanted to think about.

"You really . . ." she started, then just sighed. She would say he didn't have to come and he would say of course he did. What was the point? "Thank you," she finally settled on. "I'm not sure what I'd do without you, Mapper."

He tipped the Union cap that Octave had given him before they left. "Anytime, Mags. We should probably give them a rest soon, huh?"

"Yeah." She'd been about to suggest that anyway. Grappler's weariness had begun tugging at her and she knew they'd all need to be careful of the dactyls' flagging energy if they wanted to get out of this alive. Or be ready for an attack.

"What's the . . . ah, plan, by the way?" Mapper asked as they circled toward the treetops.

Magdalys laughed ruefully. "Ah, Mapper. Always with the plans." She shook her head. "We fly around till we find my brother and then we get him and leave."

"And the other soldiers he's with? We gonna leave them behind?"

"I . . ."

Mapper sighed. "Ah, Mag-D. Never with the plans." They brought Beans and Grappler down on a sturdy branch and Dizz flapped down with the saddlebags a few moments later.

Magdalys started unstrapping the bags so Dizz could rest. "Ugh! You have one, don't you? See — this is why no one comes up with plans around you, Mapper. Because why bother? You're just going to come up with one anyway. This is just like in Manhattan. . . ."

"When I saved you and Miss Du Monde *and* made sure that evil guy's fancy office got a generous helping of pteropoop?"

"Well . . ."

"Greatest plan ever, honestly. You're welcome."

Magdalys rolled her eyes. "Alright, alright, what you got, man?"

"Actually, not much. But I figure, wherever they are, they're probably gonna need ammo and supplies, right? So we got those. And there is a rail line not too far outside the Atchafalaya Swamplands, buuut it's Confederate controlled right now, so that might get sticky. I figure the best way to get a bunch of people back through Rebel territory to New Orleans is on the water. A lot of these bayous lead to major riverways. And then there's the ocean, or gulf technically. If we travel overland we could make it to the coast in a few days and then . . . er, we'd have to figure out something from there, but with your mad dinowrangling skills . . . Mags?"

A plume of smoke rose over the canopy of trees up ahead. It didn't look like an explosion, and Magdalys hadn't heard anything. But then what was it? Magdalys started loading the saddlebags onto Grappler.

"What are you doing?" Mapper demanded.

"That could be him . . . them," Magdalys said. "We gotta —"

Mapper's hand wrapped around Magdalys's wrist and she swung around, her mouth already curled into a growl.

"Don't even think of telling me off," Mapper snapped, and the words caught in Magdalys's throat. "It's one thing to get all righteous with a Union officer and then storm away in a huff. But I'm your friend and I've come all this way with you and . . ." Tears filled his eyes; he wiped them away angrily. "And I'm not about to let you run headlong into what might be a whole nest of Bog Marauders on a worn-out dactyl with no escape plan."

Magdalys blinked at him. He was right. She knew he was right. Still, her whole body thrummed with that ravenous hunger to do something. Anything to make this whole mess be over so she could get her brother and get out of there. And hopefully not have to get any more dinos or people killed in the process.

"He could be . . ." she whispered, then closed her eyes and let her fists unclench, her snarl simmer away, her frenzy disperse.

"I know," Mapper sniffled. "Slow down. Take a breath."

She did — a long deep one that eased her aching mind some. "Sit."

"So bossy," Magdalys grumbled, but she did it anyway, easing herself down beside Grappler on the winding oak tree branch. Spanish moss dangled in wispy beards around them, swaying slightly in the thick marshy breeze.

Mapper sat next to her, put his head on her shoulder. "Do you think she'll be alright?" he asked after a moment.

The snarls and hoots of swamp dinos filled the air over that sweet breeze and the still-churning murmur.

"I don't know," Magdalys said.

CHAPTER THIRTY-EIGHT

ATCHAFALAYA TIROTEO

THE SUN SAT smack in the middle of an almost cloudless sky as Magdalys and Mapper soared over the swamplands toward the billowing smoke.

Magdalys tried to slow her racing heart, failed over and over. It was Grappler's turn to carry the supplies. Magdalys had let Mapper stay on Beans, since they seemed to understand each other better than anyone else understood either of them, and she rode Dizz.

Mapper had insisted they have their carbines out and ready, but the thing just felt like a heavy, awkward burden in her hand. Magdalys hated guns. She'd been pretty ambivalent about them for most of her life, and during the riots, Cymbeline's shotty had saved their butts more than a few times. But after hearing that barrage after barrage of musket fire during Chickamauga and seeing what happened to Sol . . . she couldn't stand the feel of firepower against her skin.

Still, she wouldn't turn Mapper down, not after all he'd done for her. And anyway, he was probably right. Again.

Mapper waved at her from up ahead and then veered off suddenly to the side.

She urged Dizz forward and took in the view below.

A group of wooden houses stood on stilts over the murky water of the bayou. On a nearby island, several men wearing brown and gray conferred quietly on sinorniths beside a smoking pile of trash and foliage. The Bog Marauders. Magdalys and Mapper skirted the edge of the clearing, but one of the sinorniths let out a shrill caw and all the men looked up. "Hey!" one of them yelled. "Come back here!"

The shrieks of pursuing dinos filled the air. *The sinornith is a glider*, Dr. Barlow Sloan had written in the Dinoguide. (Sloan reminded her of that surgeon who knew him, Pennbroker, who reminded her of Two Step, who she prayed was okay and didn't hate her, but there was no time for that now!) *They launch high into the air and then come sailing down on unsuspecting prey, immobilizing and killing them with a single venom-filled bite that causes slow agonizing death. Although essentially obedient, sinorniths are incredibly stupid and make terrible pets.*

She looked over at Mapper. His brow creased low over his eyes and his fists clenched the reins. They could outrun these things for a little while, sure, but soon they'd have to stop and let the dactyls rest. He turned to her, nodded, then raised his carbine, balancing his elbow on one of his knees the way Octave did, and started shooting.

Magdalys glared into Beans's wide eyes. *Stay steady, B*, she thought toward him. *You too, Dizz.* She sent Grappler flying low and out of the way.

Cr-crack!! sang Mapper's carbine.

Then she scooched back in the saddle and turned herself around, breath coming faster with each passing second, raised one knee in front of her and placed her own elbow on it, leveling the carbine at the riders surging toward them across the open sky.

One let out a scream and tumbled into the forest below as his mount flapped in a lopsided spiral. The other four had drawn their own weapons, old muskets from the look of them, and now muzzles flashed amidst the crackle of return fire.

Mapper shot again, missing, and then again, and another Bog Marauder was flung backward and into the trees.

A bullet screamed past Magdalys. She felt its horrible whispering whistle as it went, just inches from her face.

And then she was pulling the trigger again and again as the whole sky caught fire around her and the world became an endless succession of bangs and billowing smoke.

Up ahead, a rider screamed and fell and Mapper was shooting too and then one of the sinorniths screeched, its wing shredded by several shots, and plummeted toward the trees.

Magdalys blinked through the smoke. Something was burning her hands. The carbine. She threw it down on the saddle, almost leaping backward away from it. Had she been hit? She glanced down at her body. No. Of course not. She would've known if she'd been shot, wouldn't she? She had no idea.

Another crack sounded from across the sky. She'd thought they were all gone. The last Bog Marauder had let off a final, parting shot and was turning his mount around, guiding it into a smooth glide back into the forest.

She was alive. She'd taken life. Probably. She glanced over at Mapper. He nodded toward a nearby oak tree that spread over the other trees like a huge multiheaded sauropod.

Yes. Somewhere to rest. Good idea. But he was alive. He hadn't been hit. They had made it, this far at least. She guided Dizz to the closest branch, her hands still trembling, her breath finally slowing, and set him down. Mapper perched Beans alongside her and Grappler flew up from behind them.

Magdalys slid off the saddle and stood on the thick branch, blinking.

"Hey," Mapper said, climbing down next to her and putting a hand on her shoulder. "Hey."

Magdalys nodded. She was okay. Sort of. She would be. She knew that, somehow.

She knew this moment would come; it had to. And she'd wondered if she'd even survive it, and she had. She had. She looked up at Mapper, trying to get her hands to stop trembling.

"It's alright," he said. "You're alright. You did what you had to do."

Magdalys let out a sad, jittery chuckle. "Pretty sure I said the exact same thing to Two Step when he was all messed up after he shot that guy in Dactyl Hill."

Mapper nodded. "I believe I was asleep at that particular moment. I did thank him later though. Thought it might help him cope a little better, but it just made it worse to bring it up again."

"Yeah," Magdalys said, relieved to be talking about something else, anything else. "Wait, why are you so calm after your first time taking a life?"

Mapper raised his eyebrows. "What makes you think that was my first time?"

Magdalys opened her mouth but nothing came out except a soft gurgle. "What?" she finally managed.

Mapper shrugged and looked away. "I came up on the streets, Mags. The streets of New York. I was born in the Raptor Claw. I wasn't out there robbing random citizens or nothing — I was fighting for my life. Where I'm from, you don't get to be the one who walks away alive without some blood on your hands. I'm not saying I'm cool with it, or that I don't think about it a lot. But I did what I had to do to survive."

"I . . ."

"Why do you think I always have to know exactly where I am? Did you think it was just a random cool skill I developed for fun?"

Magdalys just stood there. That was *exactly* what she had thought.

Mapper laughed. "When people get lost in the Raptor Claw they get found the next morning as a body. That's it. So I swore I'd always know where I was. And turned out the habit was hard to kick, even when I was safe and sound in the orphanage."

"I . . . I don't really know what to say," Magdalys said.

Mapper smiled. "Then don't say anything. It'd probably be corny anyway. I know how you feel; that's what matters." His face got serious again. "The real question is: Why didn't you do your dinomagic back there and just make them all fall off like ol' boy almost did to me back in Tennessee?"

"I . . ." Magdalys faltered. Truth was: It hadn't even occurred to her to wrangle them. She'd already managed to put her own skills so far out of her mind. And anyway, she'd promised herself. "I'm trying not to?" she said, but it didn't come out right at all.

Mapper cocked his head. "Trying not to use the one skill you have that might keep us alive?"

"No, it's just . . . I . . . That night of the battle . . . Elizabeth Crawbell and . . . I've never been bested before." She shook her head. "I don't know if . . . and . . ."

Mapper tensed, then softened, shook his head. "Sometimes I forget you're just a kid like the rest of us."

"What's that supposed to mean?"

He fixed her with a stern look. "It's not losing you're afraid of."

"What's *that* supposed to mean?" she demanded.

Gunfire erupted from out in the swamplands ahead. Magdalys looked up, heart thundering. A few scattered musket shots became a cascade of blasts rippling over the trees. Mapper was already climbing onto Beans, scanning the horizon with a concerned frown. Magdalys grabbed Dizz's reins and heaved herself up. She thought it was coming from somewhere beyond a series of jungly hills rising out of the bayou water.

"That way!" Magdalys yelled. They zoomed out across the treetops.

CHAPTER THIRTY-NINE
JUH

FAR UP AHEAD, the shooting tapered off and then started up again.

Montez. Why else would there be a firefight out here in the middle of nowhere? And if not Montez, at least what was left of the Louisiana 9th. It *had* to be. She was so close!

Beneath them, the hills rose and fell like a giant forest-covered tide that had been frozen in place.

Magdalys took Dizz higher until the whole of Atchafalaya seemed to spread beneath her. The hills went on and on and right up to the edge of a lake, and there, on the far side, a crowd of figures surrounded a decrepit pink mansion. Another series of shots rang out and Magdalys saw smoke rise into the air. "I see it!" she yelled. "Come on!"

Montez. The 9th had survived the ambush somehow, and they'd made their way through the wilderness and found shelter in that big busted old house. And now they were hemmed in by the Marauders, fighting for their lives. It made sense!

"Our friends are back," Mapper called, nodding behind them. "And there are more of 'em." A full two dozen sinornith riders glided toward them, screaming that Rebel howl. They were a good ways back but approaching fast. Magdalys shook her head and urged Dizz onward.

Montez. His name a pulse within her, matched only by that buzzing murmur that seemed to rise around them the deeper they flew into the swamplands. They banked sideways to avoid an especially tall hill and then swooped over a swampy field and headed toward the lake. Microdacts fluttered here and there, some of them probably carrying messages between the Marauders.

"There!" someone yelled from below. "Stop them!"

Magdalys barely had time to look before gunshots ripped through the air around them. Grappler squealed and fell into a swirling dive up ahead. "No!" Magdalys yelled, sending Dizz into a swerve after her.

Montez. She was so close. She wouldn't fail him. Not when she'd come so far.

"Mapper!" Magdalys yelled. "Head for that hill!" Grappler had steadied her dive some but still careened listlessly downward at an ever-sharpening angle. Magdalys swung Dizz underneath her, his tummy just grazing the tops of the trees below, and pulled Grappler onto the saddle. The dactyl collapsed against her with a sigh. "Okay, girl," Magdalys whispered. "I got you." Dizz wouldn't be able to carry them both for much longer.

"I'm coming!" Mapper called from behind. A few more shots burst out and whizzed past her into the sky. The tangled underbrush sloped upward, became forest and then a towering hill. Still clutching Grappler, Magdalys brought Dizz down through the canopy and they landed in a mulchy grove beside a winding bayou.

"Is she alright?" Mapper said, bringing Beans down nearby and running over as Magdalys eased Grappler to the ground.

"I don't know," she said. A bullet had passed through her right shoulder near where the wing connected and burst out the other side. The holes weren't too big and the bleeding wasn't bad, but that didn't mean she'd be okay. "I don't know," Magdalys said again.

Mapper bit his lip. "We gotta . . ." He looked around, drawing his carbine.

"I know," Magdalys said. "I just don't . . . I don't know what to do."

Juhjuhjuhjuhjuhjuhjuhjuhjuhjuhjuhjuhjuhjuhjuhjuh went the never-ending murmur in her ears. *Montez*, sang her broken heart. Both siren songs had grown even louder and clearer once they'd touched down on the swamplands, and Magdalys could barely think straight.

"What is it?" Mapper asked.

Magdalys shook her head, squinting through the rising and falling tide of noise within her. "Some dino . . . chatter . . . might just be that the ones out here are . . . louder."

Mapper frowned. "Whoever shot us down will be —"

"I know," Magdalys said. What Mapper had left unspoken boomed through her: She would need to wrangle some help if they were going to get out of there alive. "Maybe Grappler and Beans will have to take turns . . ."

JUHjuhjuhjuhjuhjuhjuhjuhjuhjuhJUHjuhjuhjuhjuhJUHjuhjuh

It sounded like some cruel swamp god was mocking her.

"Uh-oh," Mapper said. Magdalys followed his pointing finger. A single, rippled semicircle cut the dark bayou water. It was headed their way. Another fin emerged beside it. Then another. They were striated with shades of brown and dark green and topped with sharp notches.

Mapper took a step back from the edge of the water. "We gotta get Grappler loaded back up on —"

"Already on it," Magdalys said, heaving the inert dactyl on top of Beans and strapping her in with one of the cords. When she turned back, the fins were closer and there were what looked like bamboo shoots gliding along through the water behind each one. "What are those?"

"I don't know," Mapper said, "but let's fly."

A caw sounded above them and the dark shapes of sinorniths crisscrossed the sky overhead.

Something way too close to her growled and then a long

toothy snout and two beady yellow eyes emerged from the water in front of that fin, followed by a spiny neck and three-fingered claws. Another head emerged beside it, then a third, and all three lifted up out of the bayou, revealing their thick bodies and the tall sail-like fin stretching across their backs. Spinosaurs.

Each wore a metal collar with a chain leading into the water. With a splash, three soaking-wet men rose from the swamp. They'd been clutching those bamboo shoots in their mouths, breathing through them.

JuhjuhjuhJUHjuhjuhjuhjuh the forest caterwauled within her, but it wasn't any louder now than it had been, so it couldn't be these foul creatures.

"Well, well, well," one of the men said, shaking his head.

"Run!" Mapper yelled, and then a shot rang out and the man who'd spoken flew backward with a shocked look on his face and splashed into the swamp. The spinosaur he'd had on the chain launched forward and Magdalys tensed her face, reaching out ever so slightly.

Locked and blocked. Someone was manipulating these dinos. Earl Shamus Dawson Drek. It had to be. She took another step back, glancing around. Sinorniths landed in the branches above, but she couldn't make out if any had riders through the branches and glaring sunlight.

The spinosaur lunged, snapping. Mapper shot again, blasting it in the leg, and then again as Magdalys and the dactyls backed away up the sloping hill.

"Mapper!" Magdalys yelled over the gunfire. "Come on!"

He let off two more shots. The spinosaurs had splashed out of the way and two of the men were simply gone, swallowed by the swamp, while the third hid behind a tree rising out of the water.

"Mapper!" she yelled again.

Mapper shot once more, the bullet smashing into the tree, and then turned and ran.

"Where do we go?" he yelled.

Magdalys didn't know. She had no answers, only sheer terror and the never-ending *juhJUHjuh* of the swamp around her and the sheer magnetic force of her brother's name, tugging at her from closer than it had been since she'd seen him last. "Up," she gasped. At least from there they'd get a view of what was going on and maybe see somewhere they could take shelter.

The crackling of branches sounded from somewhere above and behind them — those sinorniths getting ready to attack, surely. She pulled out her carbine, hating it, needing it, hating to need it, and fired up at the trees.

Mapper reached her and glanced back too. The dactyls scrambled ahead. "Keep climbing," he said as the hill grew steeper. "We can see what things look like from the top."

One of the spinosaurs snarled, already clambering after them, and Magdalys heard the splashing of several more emerging from the water and angry hoots and growls calling back and forth. They were coming. Drek was orchestrating a whole deadly symphony of dinos to close in around them. And he was doing it all from some safe hiding place. The coward!

Magdalys seethed at the thought. This Confederate, this self-anointed Knight, would destroy them without even lifting a finger or having to show himself.

No.

The sizzling embers popped and snarled inside her.

Montez.

Below, the foliage rustled.

JUHjuhjuhjuhJUHjuhjuhJUHjuhjuhJUHjuhjuhJUHjuhJUH juhJUHjuhJUH. It was getting louder now. Magdalys and Mapper reached the top of the hill, shoving through a grove of bushes and dangling vines behind the dactyls, and stopped to catch their breath.

Up ahead was the lake, and beyond it that decrepit pink mansion where she was sure her brother was holed up with his comrades, he had to be! There were a lot more Bog Marauders surrounding it than she'd thought though — had to be at least a hundred of 'em. She could hear the crackle of the muskets and see an occasional muzzle flash from the broken windows of the mansion. She tried not to imagine Montez in there some-where, taking cover as bullets blasted around him through those old wooden walls.

A crowd of shapes filled the air above the lake though: sinorniths. The Marauders around the mansion must've sent their mounts to help Drek finish her and Mapper off. The dinos hurled skyward, wings spread, and then sailed down, landing on small islands in the lake and launching up again, closer and closer.

Somewhere nearby, Drek lurked.

Just a little down the hill, the spinosaur snarls grew louder.

Magdalys glanced around, fear rising up within her amidst the sizzle of a newly birthed flame.

JUHjuhJUHjuhJUHjuhJUHjuhJUHjuhJUH

Images of her own death, of Mapper's, flashed through her mind. She tried to shake them away but it was all she could see. Those sinorniths, their gnashing teeth and glinting eyes — all it would take was one bite. And they had almost reached the hill where Magdalys stood now; she could make out the striations along their dank feathered wings, those claws. They would all be under Drek's powerful dinomastery by now — it was no use trying to get at them.

But maybe . . . if she could reach some other dino.

Beyond the panic, a sorrow rose up in her. She'd barely been able to keep her promise more than a couple days.

It came to survival. That was all there was to it, really. They'd forced her hand. She passed Mapper her carbine. "Just try and buy me a little time," she said, and he nodded, face tense, frown severe. As she closed her eyes, the last thing she saw was Mapper turning both barrels toward the sky.

KaBLAM kaBLAM!! Blam! Blamblamblam!

With everything she had, Magdalys reached. She imagined hundreds and hundreds of reptiles clambering through the woods toward them.

*JUHJUHJUHJUHJUHJUHJUHJUHJUHJUHJUHJUH
JUHJUHJUH*

More dinos than she could even grasp. She reached out even further with her mind than she had before, linking with that ever-rising murmur that had been growing inside her since they'd approached New Orleans.

And then she reached further, felt herself coming unmoored from her own body as the *JUHJUHJUH*s rose around her, within her, and then the soil itself seemed to take a breath and cede away, welcoming the tendrils of her mind that burrowed through them, uprooting ancient, forgotten relics and impossible shapes amidst the churn of swamp water and tree roots and all that life . . .

*JUHJUHJUHJUHJUHJUHJUHJUHJUHJUHJUHJUH
JUHJUH*

It became everything: sight sound feel smell.

All that power — there had to be dinos all around them, surely. And they'd poke their heads between the trees and then flush down the hillside and out into the sky and overwhelm the spinosaurs below and sinorniths above.

But when she opened her eyes, the surrounding forest was still empty. They were all alone.

Then the ground beneath them began to shake.

CHAPTER FORTY
FIRE

JUHJUHJUHJUHJUHJUHJUHJUHJUHJUH

The murmur grew to a yell; it seemed to open up inside her, carve a whole new sparkling expanse within her.

"What's happening?" Mapper yelled.

JUHJUHJUHJUHJUHJUHJUHJUHJUH

Magdalys tried to steady herself against a tree but the whole thing uprooted and went crashing down the hillside. The sinorniths pulled back in a scattered panic, suddenly without a safe landing area.

Beans and Dizz were huddled together while Grappler, still strapped to Dizz's back, glanced around nervously. Great chunks of soil dislodged themselves on either side of them and cascaded off the hill, taking trees and bushes down with them and splashing into the bayou along with a rumbling pile of boulders.

"Hold on!" Magdalys called, finding another, larger tree and pulling Mapper over to it. A family of herons took flight, shrieking as they lifted off. Then the whole front part of the hill gave way before them and Magdalys and Mapper stared out at the open sky.

JUH!!!!

The murmuring burst into a sudden fierce blast that seemed to echo out across the swamp around them.

"Uh, Mags," Mapper said.

Magdalys looked around. "I think . . ." The hill had taken on a moist, dark green shine where the soil had fallen away. It sloped down around them in lumpy, shining mounds. "I think this isn't a hill," she finally blurted out.

Two enormous yellow eyes opened on either side of where they stood.

"No kidding!" Mapper yelled. "What tipped you off?"

JUH!!!! the gigantic toad insisted inside Magdalys. From far away, another call responded: *juhjuhjuhjuh*

"Whatever it is," Magdalys said, "there are more of them."

"Look!" Mapper called. The next hill over wasn't a hill either — the swamp water churned beneath it as trees and soil billowed off to reveal a huge mouth and two long folded-up legs. Slime-covered vines and tendrils dangled from its dripping neck folds.

JuhJUHjuhJUHjuhJUHjuhJUH

In the sky above, the sinorniths were already regrouping. Magdalys spied a figure riding a crimson dactyl of all things, that long red beard visible from the hill where Magdalys stood. Drek waved his hands around him, directing the sinos like a frenzied flying conductor.

"Are you . . ." Mapper asked. "I mean, can you . . . ?"

"I . . . I think so," Magdalys said.

JuhJUHjuhJUHjuhJUHjuhJUH

"You should probably do it now, if you can," Mapper said. "Those guys are coming our way again." Drek was browbeating the sinorniths into a tight formation up above.

Attack! she thought to the toad. *Smash them!*

juhJUHjuhjuhjuhJUHjuhjuhJUH came the warbled reply.

"Mags . . ."

"I know," she growled. "And I don't know . . . I don't know what's happening!"

juhjuhjuhJUHjuhjuhJUHjuhjuh

"STOP JUHING AND DO SOMETHING!" Magdalys yelled. The toad nodded its head slightly but otherwise: nothing. Despair curled around her heart. She had done *everything* — broken her own promise even — and they were still there, trapped and doomed on top of some giant warty amphibian in the middle of a swamp. The growls of the spinosaurs sounded in the forest around them.

JUH!!! A resounding call, a wide-open space within her.

Magdalys hurled a desperate plea at the toad: *We need your help!* And in the stillness that followed, Hannibal's words echoed back to her: *They need your help.* Magdalys blinked. Montez needed her, if he was still alive even, but it wasn't just about Montez anymore. *We all got brothers and sisters in danger right now*, he'd said. And he was right: They needed her help. And she had wanted, still wanted, with everything inside of her just to run away. But she couldn't. There was no away to run to, not really. She was bound to the destiny of her people, no matter what she did or where she went. And her people were in chains. And the whole Confederacy was to blame. As long as it existed, was armed and organized, she would never be safe.

The Confederacy must fall, she thought, stomping her foot, and the idea seemed to ricochet through that cavern inside her and then, suddenly, explode.

Fire.

She had suppressed it, that fire. Shoved it away. Back in Tennessee, flying over that plantation. Then again and again since. The worry she felt every time she thought about what might've happened to Montez. Big Jack's torn back.

FIRE.

These horrible, jeering men closing in on her and Mapper. On the mansion across the lake. On Chattanooga, where Two Step and Sabeen were probably preparing for another onslaught with the Native Guard, with Hannibal, waiting for General Grant.

The flames roared to life within her, crackled and shrieked and rose.

How would you like the full weight of the US Army at your back? The general's words rumbled through her. Alone, she could rain down some havoc and probably get destroyed in the process. But with an army . . . with an army, she could win, crush the Confederacy forever.

FIRE.

She could win. The thought was terrifying somehow — what that would really mean, the destruction it would entail. She'd forced it away from her mind. Refused to even consider it. Mapper was right: She hadn't just been afraid of losing. It was winning she feared most, her own strength. The true ferocity of her power unleashed.

But no more.

"Give me your knife," Magdalys said.

Mapper passed it over handle first without a word.

She reached back, grabbed her bun with one hand, pulled the blade hard along her head just where the hair was tied, felt the whole thing come free and whoosh away in the wind.

Fire.

"Mags!" Mapper yelled, and then his carbine burst to life again and a sinornith went careening out of the sky with a sharp caw.

As the spinosaur growls drew nearer around them and Mapper let off shot after shot at the sinorniths above, she narrowed her eyes and reached outward with her mind. Men and dinos would die. But she would not.

She found the spinos — there were four — felt that

now-familiar shield that had kept her out of their minds. She shook her head, reached further. Resistance, resistance, the pressure built within her, but the fire raged stronger.

She grunted as sweat broke out across her forehead, glimpsed the four long snouts emerge from the underbrush around them. That fire: she released it, felt it hurl along the pathways she'd opened, shred through the blocks that had been holding her back and then with a snap, all four spinosaurs stood at attention, blinking rapidly.

Awaiting her command.

She waved her arm once and they turned and fled.

"What the — ?" Mapper gasped.

Magdalys didn't have time to explain. She whirled around, faced the army of sinorniths descending from above. Magdalys held up one open hand as Mapper's carbine blasts picked off a few here and there.

Fire.

She stretched her mind across the length of that plummeting horde, felt the grim determination, the need to bite, to kill, that Drek had driven into them. She clenched her fist, obliterating it all, and the horde scattered, sinos spinning off course, bumping into each other with caws and squawks, suddenly confounded and lost.

Fire.

Magdalys let out a long breath of air and stepped back. Mapper blinked at her, then they both glanced upward: Many of the sinos had fled, but plenty remained and the Marauders who'd been approaching from behind weren't far off now.

JuhjuhjuhJUHjuhJUHjuhjuhjuhJUH, the toad sang.

Magdalys was out of breath but she wasn't done yet.

"Impressive," a voice yelled from above. Drek. He was a ways up, the coward, and further than she'd ever been able to reach with her mind, but maybe . . . "But you can't keep breaking through all of my mastered dinos, girl."

"Watch me," Magdalys whispered, but already she felt her energy waning.

"We have you surrounded, you know. And we'll give you a chance to be taken alive, whoever you are."

Something big thrashed in the underbrush to Magdalys's right. She spun around, arms and mind outstretched just as an alligator the size of a train car lumbered forward, jaws open.

No! she thought, pinpricks of fire exploding inside. The gator's mouth slammed shut and it looked around, confused. Breaking Drek's hold on dinos was getting easier and easier, but still, she couldn't hold out forever.

"Up above!" Mapper yelled, letting off one shot then another. The sky had darkened; twenty more sinorniths converged above them and dove.

She unleashed, sending the imaginary sword of her mind dancing in wild loops across the sky, smashing easily through Drek's hold on them as dinos scattered and spiraled away in confusion.

That crimson dactyl.

Magdalys reached her burning thoughts toward it, but the rebuff was stronger than with the others. It wasn't just Drek's dinomastery that was driving that creature: The thing was there by choice. It was his companion.

JuhJUHjuhJUHjuhJUHjuhJUH

The woods around them rustled again and a bristling, screeching pack of microraptors leapt out of the underbrush. Magdalys sent a few scrambling and Dizz and Beans snapped and whacked away the rest with their wings.

Up above, another pack of sinorniths clouded out the sun, preparing to dive.

Out across the lake, a sudden barrage of musket fire erupted.

Montez! The pulse of his name clamored suddenly louder, ferocious amidst all those flames within her. His face flashed through her, squinting even with glasses, reading his books late into the night by candlelight. Everything that had happened to him since he left. He *had* to still be alive.

And she had to get to that mansion before it was too late.

With a roar of her own, Magdalys sent half of the sinos colliding into the other half, causing enough confusion to throw off the attack for at least a few moments. Then she directed her mind back to the humongous toad beneath them.

juhjuhjuhjuhjuhjuhjuh

This thing was very, very old. It wasn't like any dino she'd ever made contact with. That croaking murmur within her felt like a murky bottomless pit, something slippery and almost beyond this world. But it had heard her when she reached out, had answered her call, even if it had then ignored her when she needed it most. And now . . . now she'd opened up something new inside herself. If she could break through Drek's control, maybe she could get through to this humongous beast.

juhjuhJUHjuhJUHjuhjuhjuhJUHjuhJUH

She knelt. Placed her hands on its slimy, lumpy skin. Reached. Felt the tendrils of her thoughts slide into that dank and gargantuan consciousness below, felt its ambivalence and beneath that, a grudging curiosity, felt that curiosity grow as the toad recognized the fire she wielded her thoughts with. And then Magdalys felt the full, ragged attention of the ancient creature focus on her.

Help us, Magdalys thought, hearing again the echo of Hannibal's plea to her a few days earlier.

A pause, then a murmured reply: *Juh.*

Take us across the lake. Smash their armies.

Something inside the toad seemed to light up.

For my brother. For all our brothers and sisters.

The *juh*s resolved into a deep, burbling growl.

"Might wanna hold on to someth —" Magdalys started to say, but the toad cut her off with a final, ferocious *JUH!!!*

And then it leapt.

CHAPTER FORTY-ONE
EARTHSHAKER

THE WIND WHIPPED through Magdalys so suddenly she didn't even realize they'd launched into the air until she caught her breath and saw the swamp recede and the lake passing beneath them.

JUHHH!!!!

For a moment the whole world seemed silent.

Then gunfire rang out up ahead, and Magdalys could make out the tiny flashes from the muzzles and then, as she sped closer, the terrified expressions of the Bog Marauders.

"AAAAAAAAAAAAAAAAAAAAAAAAAAAAAAAA AAAAAAAHHH!!!" Mapper yelled.

"Brace for impact!" Magdalys called as the ground rushed up to meet them.

KAFWOOOM!!! They landed at the far shore of the lake with a tremendous boom, sending dust and debris and a few Marauders flying to either side.

"Rally!" someone yelled from below as Rebel yells shrieked into the sky. "Take down that thing!"

Magdalys and Mapper peered over the edge of the toad's gigantic mouth. The Marauders swarmed over the now demolished shoreline, taking up positions with their backs to the mansion and aiming their muskets at the toad.

"Get down!" Mapper yelled, but then the sound of breaking glass sounded from one of the high-up windows.

A voice called out: "Hit 'em with everything ya got, boys!" and the whole front of the house seemed to burst with flashing muzzles.

The Marauders didn't know where to turn. Several screamed and collapsed; others turned their guns back toward the mansion; a few took potshots up toward where Magdalys and Mapper watched in awe.

A dactyl caw sounded from behind them. Drek.

Do something, Magdalys insisted again to the toad as she stood and whirled around. The sinoriding Marauders had caught up with the free-flying ones now, and the whole swarm of them were just reaching the far side of the lake. Drek fluttered along on his crimson dactyl in their midst. Magdalys ran between the two bony, wart-covered ridges over the toad's eyes to its lumpy back.

But those two other toads were still there, staring expectantly at Magdalys from across the lake. Their immense bellies pulsed, sending ripples of dark water out around them.

She narrowed her eyes.

Break them.

One of the toads seemed to cock its head slightly, then looked away. The other glanced once at the pack of smaller dinos screeching past, then leaned forward and opened its humongous mouth. Something pink unfurled and flashed out across the sky, sending the cloud of sinos scattering. It was gone again in barely a second's time: slurping back into the toad's gaping jaws with a squawking sino in its grasp.

The other toad looked up now, blinked, and released its tongue with a croak, blasting two sinos out of the sky and snagging a third for a meal.

Magdalys gaped, then nodded her thanks and ran back between the eye ridges to where Mapper was crouched, aiming his carbine at the fighting below. She peered over his shoulder. "How we looking?"

"Getting there," Mapper said. Caught between a giant toad and an onslaught of fire from the mansion, the Marauders had all but dispersed entirely. Only a small group remained holed up behind a makeshift trench, and it looked like they were setting up some kind of cannon. "But they'll be regrouping before long."

He was right, and those toads behind them had probably

only put a small dent in the sino brigade. Plus, Drek was still out there somewhere.

Magdalys growled at the massive creature beneath them. "Can you just for once —" she started to say out loud, but then the toad lurched forward, knocking her and Mapper on their butts. That giant tongue flitted out, shattered the trench, and sent the cannon hurtling through the air in an explosion of dirt and debris.

"Aiiii!" the last Marauders yelled as they booked it triple-time into the underbrush.

"Whoa!" Magdalys and Mapper said at the same time. Then they looked up as the dust cloud cleared. Faces appeared in the smashed windows of the dilapidated old mansion. Most of them were various shades of brown and wore blue caps. One had a mustache and an eyepatch and a wide grin. "Ahoy! Who goes there?" the man yelled with a chuckle. "I'm Corporal Wolfgang Hands, commanding officer of the Louisiana 9th, Mounted Triceratops Division, United States Army, although we're fresh out of trikes I'm afraid, and ammo too, after that last barrage. And whoever you are, we owe you some whiskey and a night on the town!"

"Uh . . . hi," Magdalys called back. "I'm looking for —"

"MAGDALYS!" someone yelled directly across from where she stood.

She knew that voice.

Magdalys looked up, tears already welling in her eyes. The

attic window was open and Montez Roca's long, bespectacled face was poking out of it with the biggest smile she'd ever seen.

"What are you doing here?" he called. Then his eyes narrowed. "And what'd you do to your hair?"

He was alive. Montez was alive. And she'd found him.

All her memories of who he'd been came crashing into the sudden vision of who he'd become: a soldier. Hardened by battle, sure, but still somehow glowing with that excitement for life she knew so well. It wasn't just that she feared he'd been killed, she realized; she didn't know who he'd be after all that had happened, even if she could reach him.

A feeling swelled in Magdalys: waves of sadness and joy seemed to have smashed into each other and were rising.

She didn't know how to meet Montez's gaze, this bookworm turned sniper who was her brother, like somehow if she locked eyes with him the whole moment would go up in smoke, become another fever dream of bone hills and gaping maws in the earth. She'd fought so hard to get here and still, none of it seemed possible. But there he was, alive and in the flesh. One of the lenses in Montez's glasses was cracked and he had a bruise on his forehead, but otherwise, he looked pretty okay.

"We came to get you out of here," Magdalys said, as more faces emerged from the darkness behind shattered windows. "All of you."

"Hey, Montez," Mapper yelled.

The caws of approaching sinorniths came from not far away,

and from even closer, more shouts from the Bog Marauders, already regrouping.

"Did General Grant send you?" Wolfgang asked. "Are you with the Union Army?"

Magdalys shrugged. "We weren't when we started out, but somewhere along the way, I think we may have mustered in." She looked over at Mapper. He nodded enthusiastically. "I have a letter from the general that'll explain everything."

"Excellent!" the corporal yelled as a cheer rose up from the mansion. "There should be a division of General Banks's army heading west from New Orleans to dislodge some Confederate blockade runners in Brownsville, Texas, and spook Emperor Maxwell's forces out of Matamoros, across the border. We were hoping to link up with them. Of course, we gotta bust out of here first, and to do that we'll need all the help we can get, but especially the kind that comes sauntering into battle on the back of a giant toad!"

"Now that that's settled," Magdalys said, finally meeting her long-lost-could've-been-dead-apparently-a-sharpshooter brother's eyes, "let's fight our way out of this swamp together."

A NOTE ON THE PEOPLE, PLACES & DINOS OF THE DACTYL HILL SQUAD

Once again, let me get this out of the way right off the bat: **There were no dinosaurs during the Civil War era!** In fact, there were no dinosaurs at any point in time during human history. The Dactyl Hill Squad series is historical fantasy. That means it's based on an actual time and place, events that actually happened, but I also get to make up awesome stuff, like that there were dinosaurs running around. So some of the people, places, and events are based on real historical facts, some are inspired by real historical facts, and some are just totally made up. Throughout this note, I've given some recommendations on books that helped me pull all this together; some of them were written for adult readers, so make sure they're the right ones for you before diving in.

PEOPLE!

Magdalys Roca and the other orphans are not based on any specific people, but there was indeed a Colored Orphan Asylum, and their records speak of a family of kids mysteriously dropped off from Cuba without much explanation. That was part of the inspiration behind this book. You can read those stories and more about the Colored Orphan Asylum in Leslie Harris's book *In the Shadow of Slavery*.

Cymbeline Crunk and her brother, Halsey, are inspired by Ira Aldridge and James Hewlett, two early black Shakespearean actors who performed in New York City. Hewlett cofounded the African Grove Theater, the first all-black Shakespearean troupe in the United States. Halsey and Cymbeline Crunk are entirely made-up characters. You can read more about Hewlett in Shane White's book *Stories of Freedom in Black New York* and more about Ira in *Ira's Shakespeare Dream*, by Glenda Armand and Floyd Cooper.

General Philip Sheridan was a famous Union general known for his charisma and aggressive military tactics. He would go on to lead the cavalry division of the Army of the Potomac in the last year of the war. He wrote about his life and his time in the Civil War in the autobiography *Personal Memoirs of P. H. Sheridan*.

The **Card brothers** were real scouts under General Sheridan who proved crucial assets during the Tennessee campaigns of the Army of the Cumberland. Much of what happens to them in the book is taken from real-life events, although it has been condensed and the dates moved around.

General Ulysses S. Grant was the leading commander of the US Army by the end of the Civil War and went on to become president of the United States. During the war, he quickly became one of President Lincoln's favorite generals for his unwavering commitment to victory and determination under fire. While he was never known to have an allosaurus named Samantha or a microdactyl named Giuseppe, he did spend time in New Orleans just after the fall of Vicksburg and suffered a riding accident while reviewing troops that left him bed-bound and in a cast at the Saint Charles Hotel for several days.

Big Jack Jackson was a real US soldier who was liberated from slavery by the Union Army and fought valiantly at the Battle of Milliken's Bend, where he was killed in action.

Both the **Louisiana 9th** and the **Louisiana Native Guard** were all-black divisions of the US army. The Native Guard didn't fight at Milliken's Bend but were involved in a famous assault at Port Hudson. While the soldiers we meet here are entirely made up, many of their names are taken from actual soldiers who fought in those units, including Cailloux, Octave Rey, Hannibal, and Solomon.

In the case of the Louisiana Native Guard, the word *Native* refers to natives of Louisiana, not Native Americans, as Amaya at first thinks. It's unclear when the word *Native* became commonly used for Indigenous people. At this time in American history, the US Government was fighting a war of extermination against the many Indigenous nations, many of whom they'd already forced to relocate during the Trail of Tears a few decades earlier.

You can read about the Native Guard in *The Louisiana Native Guards: The Black Military Experience During the Civil War* by James G. Hollandsworth, Jr.

While **Dr. Pennbroker** is a fictional character, over a dozen black surgeons served in the US Army during the Civil War, including Dr. Anderson Ruffin Abbot and Dr. Alexander T. Augusta.

General Ely Samuel Parker was a real-life Seneca lawyer, engineer, and diplomat. Both Harvard University and the New York Bar Association refused him entry because of his race. He eventually went on to become a key engineer and general during the Civil War and one of General Grant's right hand men. After the war, he went on to be the first Native person to hold the position of Commissioner of Indian Affairs.

Allan Pinkerton founded the Pinkerton National Detective Agency in 1850, and the organization went on to serve as President Lincoln's bodyguard and intelligence service during the Civil War. It later became the largest private law enforcement agency in the world, and was notorious for violently disrupting the Labor Movement.

Elizabeth Crawbell is entirely made up, though she was inspired by two real-life Confederate spies: Belle Boyd, a teenager who became a famed courier and secret agent, and the widow Rose O'Neal Greenhow, who monitored Union troop buildups and coordinated spies from her Washington, DC, residence. Both were captured by the Pinkertons. You can read more about them and two women who worked for the Union side, Emma Edmonds and Elizabeth Van Lew, in Karen Abbott's *Liar, Temptress, Soldier, Spy: Four Women Undercover in the Civil War.*

Corporal Buford, Lieutenant Hardy L. Hewpat, Earl Shamus Dawson Drek, and his crimson dactyl are totally made up.

PLACES & EVENTS

Dactyl Hill is based on a real historical neighborhood in Brooklyn called Crow Hill (modern-day Crown Heights), which, along with Weeksville and several others, became a safe haven for black New Yorkers escaping the racist violence of Manhattan. You can find out more about Weeksville at the Weeksville Historical Society and in Judith Wellman's book *Brooklyn's Promised Land.*

The **Colored Orphan Asylum** was on Fifth Avenue between Forty-Second and Forty-Third Streets in Manhattan. It was burned down in the New York Draft Riots. All the orphans except one escaped, and the organization relocated to another building.

By the second half of 1863, when this book takes place, the Union Army had just achieved two major and decisive victories after two and a half years of the Civil War. At Gettysburg, the newly promoted General Meade repelled General Lee's Army of Northern Virginia, effectively ending the Confederate invasion of Pennsylvania; and in Mississippi, General Grant sacked the fortress city of Vicksburg after a prolonged siege. Starting earlier that same year, the US government finally allowed black soldiers to be mustered into service, although they insisted on paying them significantly less than their white counterparts. From Maine to the Midwest all the way down to Louisiana, many thousands answered the call anyway. Besides fighting valiantly in combat, they agitated successfully for equal pay, and eventually made up 10 percent of the Union Army. You can read more about the famed Massachusetts 54th and 55th regiments in *Thunder at the Gates* by Douglas R. Egerton and *Now or Never! Fifty-Fourth Massachusetts Infantry's War to End Slavery* by Ray Anthony Shepard. *A History of the Negro Troops in the War of the Rebellion, 1861-1865* is also a fascinating historical overview written twenty years after the war by a former soldier and one of the first African American historians, George Washington Williams. There are numerous other books about the Civil War, but one of the best is *Battle Cry of Freedom* by James McPherson.

The Battle of Chickamauga took place over several days (not one like it does here), just south of Chattanooga, Tennessee. While some of the details depicted are made up, a few major parts really did happen that way, including the wider strategic questions the Army of the Cumberland faced once they'd chased General Bragg's Confederate forces out of Tennessee. After a vicious back and forth, the near-stalemate was broken when a miscommunication on the Union side led to one regiment being moved out of the way just as the Confederates charged, which then divided the Federal forces in half and collapsed their front lines. General Thomas famously held out, covering the retreat of the other units, a feat that earned him the nickname "The Rock of Chickamauga." General Sheridan's division was cut off from the rest of the army during the rout, and then regrouped and made their way back to try to reinforce Thomas as night was falling, although it's unclear how much help they were able to provide.

The Battle of Milliken's Bend, which Montez was wounded in, was indeed an important moment in the victory at Vicksburg, as the 9th Louisiana Regiment of African Descent and others repelled an attempt by the Confederates to reinforce their besieged troops.

The song that Sabeen sings, "**John Brown's Body**," was a popular Civil War marching tune in the US Army. John Brown was an abolitionist who led a raid against Harper's Ferry in 1859. The original melody comes from an old folk hymn called "Say, Brothers, Will You Meet Us." Soldiers in the black regiments sang a version too — the one Magdalys hears them sing while marching through Tennessee. Julia Ward Howe wrote the most famous rendition of the song — "The Battle Hymn of the Republic" — after visiting Union soldiers in 1861.

The **Knights of the Golden Circle** were composed of various pro-slavery advocates throughout the Americas who were dedicated to bringing an expansion of the slave states into the Caribbean and Central and South America that they dubbed "the Golden Circle."

Federal naval forces led by General Farragut took over **New Orleans** very early on in the war and the city remained in Union control the whole time. A city known for delicious food and a mix of cultures, New Orleans is considered the birthplace of jazz, which grew in part out of the second-line funeral tradition that Hannibal tells Magdalys about.

The **Mardi Gras Indians** are a New Orleans cultural tradition dating back to the nineteenth century, when black Americans wanted to honor the Native Americans who had helped them out during slavery. To this day, the different Krewes create brightly colored, feather-adorned regalia and parade through the streets of New Orleans on certain days of the year.

DINOS, PTEROS & OTHER ASSORTED -SAURIA

Of course, a lot less is known about dinosaurs than about the Civil War–era United States. Because of this, and because this is a fantasy novel, I took more liberties with the creation of the dinosaurs in this story than I did with the history. Experts can make intelligent guesses based on the fossil data, but we don't really know exactly what prehistoric animals looked like, smelled like, or how they acted. In the world of Dactyl Hill Squad, the dinos never went extinct, but humans did subdue and domesticate them as beasts of burden and war.

The **brachiosaurus** was a humongous herbivorous (meaning it ate plants) quadruped (meaning it walked on four legs). Its long neck allowed it to eat leaves from the tallest trees. It lived during the Late Jurassic Period and probably didn't hoot the way the ones in the Dactyl Hill world do.

Sauropod is a general term for the gigantic quadrupedal dinosaurs with long necks, long tails, and relatively small heads. In the Dactyl Hill Squad world, they are used for transportation, cargo carrying, and construction.

As Magdalys points out, **pterodactyls** weren't dinosaurs, they were pterosaurs, flying reptiles closely related to birds. They flew through Jurassic-era skies munching on insects, fish, and small reptiles. Generally about the size of seagulls, they weren't really large enough to carry a person. A group of pterodactyls is not called a squad (although maybe it should be!) and scientists don't suspect them to have been pack dependent as described in the book. But who knows?

Raptors were a group of very intelligent, bipedal (meaning they walked on two feet) carnivores (meaning they ate meat). They had rod-straight tails and a giant claw on each foot, and they hunted in packs during the Late Cretaceous Period.

Triceratopses were herbivorous quadrupeds about the size of an ice cream truck that roamed the earth during the Late Cretaceous Period. They had three horns: one protruding from the snout and two longer ones that stuck out from a wide shield over their eyes that stretched out over its neck.

The **diplodocus** was one of the longest known sauropods and it roamed the North American plains toward the end of the Jurassic Period. It was over ninety feet long! Basically the size of a nine-story building turned on its side.

Pteranodons were large, mostly toothless pterosaurs without long tails. In fact, their name means "toothless lizard." Quetzalcoatlus, the largest of pterosaurs, was big as a fighter plane — forty-five feet long. They ruled the skies of the Late Cretaceous Period.

Archaeopteryx, which means "Old Wing," are considered to be the oldest form of bird. About the size of a raven, these Jurassic-era dinosaurs had sharp teeth, a long bony tail, and hyperextensible second toes called "killing claws." Yikes!

Sinornithosaurs were Cretaceous Period birdlike dinos once believed to have a venomous bite, although experts now don't believe that to be the case. They glided and hunted through the skies of what we now call China, and their name means "Chinese bird lizard."

The **parasaurolophus** were Late Cretaceous Period plant eaters that walked on both four and two legs. They had a long bony crest that extended from the backs of their heads.

Dimetrodons, also known as finbacks, were short, four-legged synapsids (creatures that roamed the earth forty million years *before* the dinosaurs) that were recognizable for the tall sails protruding from their spines. They are related to modern mammals.

Spinosauruses were large theropods that hunted the wetland areas of the Cretaceous Period. They had long, crocodile-like snouts, and the bony spines extending from their vertebrae were probably connected by skin to give a sail-like look.

A NOTE ON WEAPONS

In this messy, broken time of mass shootings and state violence, it's important to note that guns almost always create more problems than they solve. More than that: Young people suffer with trauma from those problems in increasing and heartbreaking numbers. This is an adventure story, and it takes place during a war, in an era when folks were being kidnapped and sold into slavery and an invading rebel army threatened the nation's capital. Guns are one of the parts of life in that time that I chose to include in this story, but I hope that a) the dangers, both physical and emotional, of gun violence ring loud and clear on the page, and b) we one day live in a time when gun violence doesn't exist anymore at all.

Rifled muskets are enhanced versions of the old Revolutionary War firearms. The rifled muzzles gave these weapons greater precision, and their caplock mechanisms made them easier to load and fire than their flintlock ancestors. Rifled muskets, both Enfields and Springfields, were the most commonly issued guns on both sides of the Civil War.

Many rifled muskets were armed with a **bayonet,** a sharpened sword attached to the muzzle that could be used to stab an attacker.

The **carbine** is smaller and lighter than the rifled musket, with a shorter barrel. Because they are breach-loading, meaning you insert the bullets at the middle of the gun instead of into the muzzle, they are easier to shoot from horseback (or dinoback) and thus were favored by cavalry (mounted) units.

The **Gatling** is a multibarreled rapid-fire gun invented by Richard Gatling, a North Carolinian who, horrified that more soldiers died of disease than from combat during warfare, decided to invent a weapon that would "supersede the necessity of large armies." Which doesn't totally make that much sense and definitely didn't work out that way, but hey . . . He sold his new weapon exclusively to the US Army, but it didn't see too much action during the Civil War as it had only just been invented.

The **howitzer** is a short-barreled smoothbore mobile artillery cannon that could fire shells of twelve, twenty-four, and thirty-two pounds in a high trajectory. They were used as defensive weapons and to flush enemies out of their entrenched hiding places.

ACKNOWLEDGMENTS

I am deeply grateful to Nick Thomas and Weslie Turner — we did it again!

Thank you to the whole team at Scholastic, who have been amazing throughout this process, especially Arthur A. Levine, Lizette Serrano, Emily Heddleson, Tracy van Straaten, Rachel Feld, Isa Caban, and Erik Ryle.

Thanks to Erika Scipione, Gavin Brown, and Fay Koh who created the online Dactyl Hill Squad game, Rescue Run. It! Is! So! Awesome!

Nilah Magruder has once again brought Magdalys and the crew to life and it's always such a breathtaking wonder to see her translate my words into images. Thank you, Nilah! And a huge thank you to Afu Chan for the terrific Dactyl Hill Squad logo and to Christopher Stengel for bringing it all together with such grace and precision.

To Eddie Schneider and Joshua Bilmes and the whole team at JABberwocky Lit: you are wonderful. Thank you.

Many thanks to Leslie Shipman at The Shipman Agency and Lia Chan at ICM.

Leigh Bardugo talked me through a key plot point on speaker phone as I drove in circles through the foggy streets of New Orleans late one night, and for that I am forever grateful. And Brittany Nicole Williams came through in the clutch and caught me trying to squeeze in an unearned reveal. Thank youuuu!

Dr. Debbie Reese was terrifically generous with her time and wisdom and analysis. She gave detailed notes after reading both this and Book One, and I'm deeply grateful. Her work at American Indians in Children's Lit is always a crucial resource and necessary reading.

Thanks to Mark Norell and Derek Frisby! All incorrect historical or dinofactual matter is my own fault and it's probably on purpose, unless it's in the appendix and then it's totally my bad.

Thanks to the kind clerks at James H. Cohen & Sons Inc, a rare antique weapons shop on Royal Street in the French Quarter, who were extremely helpful when this writer came in asking about which Civil War–era guns would be best shot from dinoback.

Thanks always to my amazing family, Dora, Marc, Malka, Lou, Calyx and Paz. Thanks to Iya Lisa and Iya Ramona and Iyalocha Tima, Patrice, Emani, Darrell, April, and my whole Ile Omi Toki family for their support; also thanks to Oba Nelson "Poppy" Rodriguez, Baba Malik, Mama Akissi, Mama Joan, Sam, Tina, and Jud and all the wonderful folks of Ile Ase. And thank you, Brittany, for everything.

Baba Craig Ramos: we miss you and love you and carry you with us everywhere we go. Rest easy, Tío. Ibae bayen tonu.

I give thanks to all those who came before us and lit the way. I give thanks to all my ancestors; to Yemonja, Mother of Waters; gbogbo Orisa, and Olodumare.

ABOUT THE AUTHOR

Daniel José Older has always loved monsters, whether historical, prehistorical, or imaginary. He is the *New York Times* bestselling author of numerous books for readers of all ages: for middle grade, the Dactyl Hill Squad series, the first book of which was named a New York Times Notable Book and to the NPR and Washington Post Best Books of the Year lists, and the second of which was named a Publishers Weekly Best of Summer Reading; for young adults, the acclaimed Shadowshaper Cypher, winner of the International Latino Book Award; and for adults, *Star Wars: Last Shot*, the Bone Street Rumba urban fantasy series, and *The Book of Lost Saints*. He has worked as a bike messenger, a waiter, and a teacher, and was a New York City paramedic for ten years. Daniel splits his time between Brooklyn and New Orleans.

You can find out more about him at danieljoseolder.net.

READ ON FOR A SNEAK PEEK OF MAGDALYS AND THE SQUAD'S NEXT THRILLING ADVENTURE IN . . .

"A mind-bendingly original series."
—*New York Times Book Review* on *Dactyl Hill Squad*

TOAD, TOAD, TOAD

FOR A FEW moments, a strange quiet settled over the Atchafalaya Swamplands. Magdalys Roca, standing on top of a gigantic toad, looked over to her brother, Montez, whom she'd traveled all the way from New York City to rescue. He stared back at her from the shattered fifth-floor window of a dilapidated mansion; peeling pink shutters dangled off rusty hinges on either side. He carried a sighted rifle, the kind the sharpshooters used, and that made sense: He'd become a soldier in these past couple months of war, a sniper. He'd taken lives, and now, so had Magdalys. And she was a soldier now, just like him.

"Um," Corporal Wolfgang Hands said from a window a few floors down. He was a big man with a dashing mustache, light brown skin, and a black eye patch. He'd gotten his men to the safety of this swamp mansion after their medical convoy had been ambushed, and this was where Magdalys and her friend Mapper had found them, hemmed in by Confederate Bog Marauders with more on the way. Magdalys had sent the enemy scattering when she'd brought her giant toad crashing down from across the lake. But she could already hear the rustle and yells of the swampland guerrilla soldiers regrouping. "You do know how to control that thing, don't you, young lady?"

"Sure seems like she does," someone yelled. "Unless it just happened to take her to us and scatter the Marauders."

"The other two are still giving 'em a good lickin' out on the lake," a young soldier with a nasty scar down the center of his face pointed out. The others scoffed and rolled their eyes. "No pun intended!"

Magdalys smirked. Last time she'd looked, the two toads behind them had been lashing out at an attacking brigade of mounted sinornithosaurs with their humongous tongues, swallowing a few and knocking others out of the sky in wild spirals. She looked Corporal Hands dead in the eye. "I do control these toads, sir," she said. "My name is Magdalys Roca and I'm the greatest dinowrangler in the world."

"And I'm Mapper!" Mapper said. "I mean, I'm Kyle, but they call me Mapper."

"Wait, you wrangle dinos?" Montez said.

"Wait, as in the famous Magdalys Roca that Razorclaw over here won't shut up about?" Corporal Hands said.

"Wait, as in the Magdalys Roca who I sent that dactyl-gram?" another soldier yelled.

Magdalys gaped at him. That gram — the matrons of the Colored Orphan Asylum had given it to her the night of the Draft Riots back in July; the night everything changed. "Private Tom Summers?"

He nodded. "The same! Glad you made it! But I didn't mean for —"

"Enough chitter chatter!" the corporal hollered. "Those Bog Marauders'll be back here any minute, and remember, with only one bite from one of their sinosteeds you'll be —"

"Dying slowly in a pool of your own vomit and drool," the other five soldiers all groaned at once.

"We remember," Montez said. Then he hoisted his rifle up, squinted through the sight, and let off a shot that Magdalys heard whiz past her and then land with a distant juicy thunk. She whirled around as the caw of a sinornith rang out, saw it plummeting from the sky, its rider already splashing into the lake below with a yelp.

"Whoa!" She looked back at her brother, blinking. "You really are a crack shot."

"Time to go," Montez said. "They're almost here." He disappeared from the window, gathering his things, and Magdalys had to remind herself he was still that goofy kid who loved reading and looked out for everyone at the orphanage. Kind of.

JUH!! the huge toad beneath her boomed. It was a

guttural, raspy chirp that only Magdalys could hear, or feel really, as it seemed to rise like a tiny marvelous earthquake from within her. And she understood it, this ancient creature's strange one-sound language — he was ready to go too, and he wouldn't wait long. Behind her, two of the dactyls they'd flown into the swamplands, Beans and Dizz, huddled protectively over the third, Grappler, who'd been wounded just before they found the toads.

Come! Magdalys sent her thought arcing to the lake behind them, felt it reach the other two toads, felt their attention turn suddenly toward her. *Come!*

"Brace yourself," she said to Mapper, and then the whole planet seemed to rock with the sudden explosive landing of a toad on one side of them, and then again as the second one landed on the other side.

"Yeeesh!" Mapper yelled, steadying himself.

Magdalys wiggled her eyebrows at him. "I warned ya!"

He shook his head. "What happens now?" Mapper had been with her all the way from New York — in fact, he was the only one left of the tight-knit squad they'd formed back in Brooklyn. Two Step and Sabeen had been swept up in the Battle of Chickamauga and were probably holed up in Chattanooga with their new friend Hannibal and the rest of the Army of the Cumberland, surrounded by Confederates and anxiously awaiting General Grant to help them escape. Cymbeline Crunk, one of the greatest Shakespearean actresses ever (as far as Magdalys was concerned, anyway) and a Union spy, had flown to Tennessee with General Grant on the back of Stella, the giant pteranodon that Magdalys had saved from a silo back in Dactyl Hill. And Amaya was headed west to find her father, an eccentric general in the US Army, and figure out the riddle of her Apache mother.

Kwa-THOOM!! A mortar shell hurtled through the top tower of the mansion, obliterating it and showering Magdalys and Mapper with debris and broken glass. She glanced at the window Montez had been in just as he poked his big toothy grin out of it and waved. "I'm alright!"

"Let's move out!" Corporal Hands yelled.

Magdalys exhaled. Just like that, after all that . . . her brother could've been killed. Could still be killed.

She narrowed her eyes at the approaching sinornithosaurs as the corporal barked orders. "Summers and Bijoux, take the toad on the left! Toussaint and Briggs, the right!"

At some point along the way, the journey had stopped being just about saving Montez, and become something much bigger inside Magdalys. *The Union needed her*, generals kept saying. With her abilities, she could crush the Confederacy. And she knew it was true.

"Aye, aye, sir!" The men called as the magnificent toads lowered themselves toward the windows.

She'd seen firsthand how being able to get inside the minds of dinosaurs could sway the tide of battle. And she'd seen what could happen when agents of the Knights of the Golden Circle, a secret society trying to build a slavery-driven empire all throughout the Americas, had used it to their own ends. In fact, she'd seen it less than an hour ago, when Earl Shamus Dawson Drek, a Bog Marauder who had the same power she did, had bombarded her with swarms of dinos. She'd bested him, breaking through the lock he had on those reptilian minds to divert the attacks away from her and Mapper, but it took everything she had. And Drek was still out there.

She knew they had to be stopped. She knew she was one of the few who might be able to do it. So she'd agreed to join the US Army.

But it wasn't the Union she cared about, not really.

"Roca," Corporal Hands called, "you and I will hop on with your sister here."

Montez nodded and, as bullets whistled through the air around them, climbed out the window and leapt onto the snout of the toad.

Her brother. She watched him make his way up toward her. Yes, it was still for him that she'd done this, but now it was for all her brothers, and her sisters too. She thought about the plantations they'd flown over as they approached the Atchafalaya, the scars etched across her friend Big Jack Jackson's back. No one she loved would be safe until the Confederacy fell and the Knights of the Golden Circle were defeated forever.

Montez slipped and let out a grunt as he scrambled for purchase — that hide was slippery with slime and swamp water, but the warts and folds allowed for easy footholds. A few more shots rang out but whizzed harmlessly past. Montez pulled himself to his feet, and then made it to the top and wrapped Magdalys in a quick hug as Corporal Hands grumbled and stumbled his way out the window and toward them.

She had an army at her back now. And General Grant had given her the command of her own special elite unit of dinowarriors, had even put it in writing. She could hunt down the Knights and take apart their organization piece by piece.

"Thanks for rescuing me," Montez whispered.

She punched his shoulder. "Anytime, big bro."

And taking apart the Knights was exactly what she planned to do.

She turned to the lake behind them, and the toad waddled from one side to the other, turning too.

"Whoa! Whoa!" Wolfgang yelled, his hands stretched out to either side for balance as he made his way up to them. "Gotta warn us when he gonna do that, young lady!" He scurried to the spot between the toad's eyes where Magdalys, Mapper, and Montez stood prepping their weapons. Out over the lake, the sinornith riders yelped and let off a volley of musket fire.

But before Magdalys could take apart any evil organizations, she'd have to get out of this mess.

"Get ready," she yelled. The three soldiers around her raised their weapons. Off to either side, Toussaint, Briggs, Summers, and Bijoux did the same.

JUH!!! the toad burped urgently, lowering itself. Then it hurtled out over the lake amidst the crackle of gunfire.

"ATTACK!!"

LAKESIDE SKIRMISH

THEY CAME CRASHING down at the far edge of the lake with a tremendous *fwa-SHOOOOOM!!* And a wall of water blasted up on either side of them. Magdalys was pretty sure they'd taken out a few sinorniths on their way down, but a bunch of others were cascading toward them from nearby treetops, their riders howling with glee.

Montez and Mapper were on their feet first, and they'd each taken two shots when a shadow covered the approaching Bog Marauders. The Confederates looked up and their howls turned to screeches and then were cut off entirely when the gigantic toad blitzed out of the sky on top of them and landed with a *kaFOOOM!!*

JuhJuhJuhJUH! the toad chortled beneath Magdalys.

SHASHOOM!!! came the splash announcing that the third toad had landed on their other side.

More sinornith riders were coming though, and they seemed to be closing in from all around.

"How many of these guys are there?" Mapper grunted. He let off shot after shot at the approaching swarm with his carbine, but Magdalys couldn't tell if he was hitting any of them. A few bullets zinged past, none too close.

"They've been pestering us since we holed up about a week ago," Wolfgang explained. "First it was just a few, but they musta sent word out and more and more started gathering." *BLAM!!* He had a pistol in each hand and shot one and then the other. *BLAM!!*

The sinorniths glided toward the treetops up ahead, probably so their riders could take more accurate potshots.

"Corporal!" Summers called from the toad to their right. "Private Bijoux has been hit!"

"Crikey," Wolfgang muttered.

"Ju-ju-just a flesh wound, sir!" Bijoux yelled. "I'm alright!"

The sinoriders dismounted amidst the canopy of live oaks and cypress trees, and then their steeds immediately launched back into the blue skies. They were ugly creatures, with gray-brown feathers, thick hind legs, and narrow necks leading to those fierce raptor-like jaws, which would deliver a deadly dose of venom to anyone they grasped. And they were swooping toward Magdalys and the others with a clamor of squeaks and caws.

Earl Shamus Dawson Drek. Magdalys narrowed her eyes. It had to be him. He'd survived the toad attacks, had probably been hiding in the underbrush all along, biding his time, and now, wherever he was, he had a whole squad of sinorniths at his command.

"Take aim, lads!" Wolfgang commanded. "But we don't have much ammo to waste, so wait till you have a shot before you fire."

And it was one thing to fend off attacks against her and one other person, but seven other people, spread out over three toads? Maybe one day, but she wasn't there yet.

But Drek . . . if she could get to Drek . . .

"Can you and your men hold them off for a few minutes, Corporal Hands?" Magdalys asked, trying to get the sharp, clipped military tone right.

"Fire, boys! Give 'em everything you got!" He looked down at her as gunfire erupted around them, gave a kind of sideways tilt with the top of his head. "I think we can handle 'em for a bit. Don't be long though. I already have a wounded soldier and we're all in desperate need of a bath."

"Yes, sir!" Magdalys said, snapping off a salute as best she could. "Can I also borrow my brother for this mission?" She was already backing toward where the dactyls were huddled.

"Alright, but make it quick!" Wolfgang nodded at Montez, who let off two more shots, then stood and followed Magdalys.

"Great," she said. "Just try not to hit us while you're at it."

"Hit you? But . . ."

"Dizz!" Magdalys yelled, breaking into a run, and the tall purple pterodactyl perked his head up and blinked. "Let's go." Dizz nuzzled Grappler once more and then hopped twice toward Magdalys. She wrapped her arms around his neck and heaved herself onto his saddle; Montez leapt up behind her and with two powerful flaps, they soared out into the sky.

"How did you, ah, get a handle on dinos so fast?" Montez asked over the whipping wind and gunfire. "Our guy Toussaint is the best wrangler in the 9th and he's been training his whole life."

"It's . . . it's hard to explain," Magdalys said. She had promised her friend Redd that she wouldn't half step anymore in talking about her powers, and she'd been pretty good at it so far, but somehow . . . telling her brother that she could communicate with dinos using her mind just seemed impossible. "But I will! Once we're out of this mess. Can you handle yourself with a dactyl?"

She veered them in a wide circle and then sent Dizz careening toward the attacking sinorniths.

Fubbafubbafubba fooooooo came Dizz's jubilant war cry.

"I'm pretty decent," Montez said.

"Good," Magdalys said. She pulled Dizz into a sharp climb over the sinorniths, then leveled out and carefully stood up in the saddle.

"Why?" Montez asked. "What're you — AAAH!!"

Magdalys leapt.